ONE KIND TOUCH

One Kind Deed Series

Book Three

by Christine DePetrillo

A kind touch can heal a heart!

Christine DePetrillo

Author Contact:

Website and Newsletter Sign-up:
www.christinedepetrillo.weebly.com

Facebook:
www.facebook.com/christinedepetrilloauthor

Find our cozy Reader Group, SMALL TOWN HEARTS, on Facebook and join!

Dedication

To those of you I'll actually hug...
your numbers are few.

ONE KIND TOUCH

Chapter One

The scent of cigarette smoke made Dena Brenton all the more eager to get away from her tablemate at the Managing Money Conference in Providence, Rhode Island. Hours away from the beloved smell of wood at her family's sawmill back in Maplehaven, Vermont, she hoped she'd make it through the final workshop of the day. Dena's throat had grown scratchy and her hazel eyes were getting drier the longer she sat beside Mr. Nicotine. Unfortunately, the dude had followed her through the last three workshops and she couldn't shake him. That was what she got for venturing out into the world, for making eye contact with strangers. She should have known by now that everything she needed was in Maplehaven.

"The secret to a truly successful business plan is…"

Dena tapped on her tablet, capturing every kernel of information the presenter offered. She'd attended the conference in hopes of improving things at the sawmill, thereby improving things for the town that relied on the sawmill and for her family. Brenton Sawmill had been in her family since 1798 when her father's descendents had founded the cozy little town which was guarded by Birch Peak, Mount Woodrich, and Brenton Mountain. Everything was still going

5

well—extremely well—at the sawmill, but Dena was a firm believer in the idea that there was always room for improvement. As the sawmill's chief financial officer, she took her duties seriously and hoped to pass a successful legacy to the next generation of Brentons.

That generation would most likely be produced by her older brother, Dakota, who was marrying his fiancée, Leah Greenstead, next week. He'd no doubt have adorable kids whereas Dena hadn't had a serious boyfriend in ages. Currently she was playing around with Leah's best friend from New York, Carter Bennett, who had made Maplehaven his home a few months ago, but she wasn't all that sure where it was headed.

Probably nowhere.

Carter was a cool guy. No question about that. He made video games, and though Dena wasn't super interested in video games, the way Dakota, his best friend Noah Williams, and Noah's soon-to-be stepson, Luke Davidson, reacted to the games told her Carter was damn good at his job.

He's good at other things too.

Kissing, for example. The man knew what he was doing every time they locked lips. She had no complaints there. She absolutely enjoyed everything about kissing his full lips and feeling the slight scratch of the dark scruff he let grow around his mouth and jaw. That was as far as they'd gotten, however, in the two months or so they'd been hanging out. Dena couldn't decide if she was totally okay with that slow pace or if she was completely frustrated. All she knew was that whenever they were together, they laughed, made out a little, and always orchestrated plans to see each other again. She didn't need to know if it was leading to something more. She could be content with whatever this was.

For now.

Dena nearly laughed aloud at herself as she typed a final note on her tablet while the presenter wrapped up his lecture. It was one thing to *say* she could be content with the aimlessness of her relationship with Carter. It was quite another to actually believe it.

If she were truly content, why was she missing Carter right now? Why had she been missing him since she'd set foot in Rhode Island four nights ago? Why had she wanted to call him each night as she'd nestled in her hotel room bed alone, surfing the limited television channels and watching reruns of shows she'd seen a million times?

Why had she dreamed about him?

Erotically.

"That was a great talk," Mr. Nicotine said, the cigarette smoke odor intensifying as he moved to pack his tablet in his bag.

"They've all been great." Dena stood, hoping she could pack up before him and scoot out. All that thinking about Carter had her considering checking out of the hotel tonight instead of in the morning and making the four-hour drive back to Vermont to see him.

"Yeah, this conference was worth the price." Mr. Nicotine, whose nametag actually said *Gary Warner*, got up from his seat and shouldered his bag. He was taller than Dena's five feet eight inches and probably twice as wide with short blond hair and tired blue eyes. During the first workshop where they'd been seated next to each other, he'd told Dena he worked for a restaurant supply company. He'd gone on and on about how lucrative the business was, but she'd suspected some of his figures had been inflated to impress her.

She wasn't impressed.

Anyone who smelled that heavily of smoke consumed packs of cigarettes too numerous to count. She could forgive a good many things, but intentionally tempting the Grim Reaper by smoking wasn't one of them. Besides, he stunk. He didn't even have a lit cigarette, but the secondhand smoke was killing her.

"Listen, I have a dinner scheduled with this presenter." Gary motioned to the man at the front of the room still chatting with conference attendees. "Hoping to bend his ear a bit and pick up a few more tidbits. Would you like to join us?"

Dena squinted an eye at Gary who held up his hands.

"Not a come-on. I swear." He offered her a smile with yellowed teeth as he smoothed the wrinkles out of his dingy, once-white dress shirt. "I thought maybe you'd like a few more tidbits yourself. You know, make the most of your money on this conference."

She chewed on her bottom lip a bit and cast another glance at the presenter. The man had been a dynamic speaker with a wealth of knowledge. It would be nice to tap directly into that, and she was already here. She could wait another night to see Carter.

To get home. Yeah. That was what she meant. To get home.

"Sure. Thanks." If she'd endured the cigarette smell for this long, she could take a few more hours.

"Cool," Gary said. "You have to eat anyway, right?"

She nodded and threw him a smile. Being cordial wouldn't hurt. Gary might smell like a factory smokestack, but he'd been nice to invite her to dinner. She could be nice too. Her mother didn't raise a jerk after all, and she was here to network, as much as she hated doing that.

"We planned to meet at five o'clock in the hotel's restaurant," Gary said. "Does that work for you?"

Dena checked her phone. Forty-five minutes from now. "Sure, that's perfect. Are you sure it's okay if I join you?"

"Absolutely." He gave her a lingering look. "Trust me, no one would object to your company."

She shouldered her bag, letting it rest in front of her to block Gary's view of her... her goods. Maybe this dinner wasn't a good idea. Perhaps he *was* coming on to her.

In the next moment, however, Gary gave her a casual wave. "See you at five." He navigated away from the table—taking his scent with him—and soon Dena could no longer see him in the crowd.

As she made her way out of the conference room, her phone buzzed in her hand. Looking down at the screen, she smiled at Carter's name. She grinned—he'd caved first and called before she did.

"Miss me?" she asked.

"Not even a little bit." Carter's low voice made something warm unfurl inside her.

"Ass."

"Yes, I have an extremely nice one. Thanks for remembering."

"You'd only know you had a nice ass if you'd spent time admiring it in the mirror, you narcissist."

"Oh, no. I know from the hordes of women who have written poetry about my perfect ass. It's quite the Muse." Quick and clever comebacks were another area in which Carter excelled. Considering all he'd gone through—losing his younger brother, Chase, to a shooting incident at an airport in New York several years ago—he still had the ability to be silly. Once in a while though, Dena caught the eternal sadness in his deep brown eyes behind his black-framed glasses. When she saw that, she did her best to ease it with a snarky comment.

"If I get bored later, I'll see what words I can toss together to describe your ass," she said as she made her way to the escalator. "Roses are red, violets are blue… your ass might be nice, but it still smells like poo."

Carter's raspy laugh filled her ear, making that warmth inside her spread a little farther. She did enjoy making him laugh.

"Real classy, Dena."

"Hey, I keep it upscale *and* truthful." She stepped off the escalator and took a left to head toward her hotel room so she could freshen up before dinner. A dinner she no longer wanted to attend now that she'd heard Carter's voice.

"In the interest of being truthful," Carter began, his voice lowering to a husky whisper Dena rather enjoyed, "it's possible that perhaps I miss you. Just a little. Maybe. Nothing too wild. I'm not huddled in a corner, blubbering your name or anything, but let's say your absence has been noticed."

Dena couldn't stop the smile from stretching across her face. "I knew it."

"You could just say, 'I miss you too, Carter,' you know?"

"I could, but it doesn't change the fact that you admitted to missing me first."

"So damn competitive."

"Says the man who does a victory dance every time he beheads a Grimaldi in *Zombie Wars 8*."

"It's not Grim*a*ldi," Carter said, an eye roll nearly audible. "It's Grim*o*ldi."

"Whatever, nerd."

"I make a living from being a nerd. I'm not ashamed."

He had no reason to be. While Dena wasn't well-versed in all things video game, she was quite aware of the popularity of the games Carter designed. Before they'd had their first date—a blind date set up by Dakota—she'd searched Carter online at the urging of her twin sister, Jacy. Nano-seconds after hitting the search button, a whole slew of award-winning games had filled her screen. She'd read a handful of reviews and soon realized they all said basically the same thing.

Carter Bennett was a video game god.

"Do nerds have asses as fine as yours?" Dena pushed her keycard into the lock mechanism and opened her room door. "Maybe you're not a nerd."

"You take that back right now, Brenton!" Carter said. "If shit like that gets out into the video game world, I'll be ruined. I. Am. A. Nerd." He cleared his throat. "A hot one."

She barked out a laugh as she set her bag down on a desk in the room. "If you do say so yourself."

"I do. And you know what? You're a hot nerd too. The way you crunch numbers at the sawmill is so…"

"Ridiculously Type A?"

"Adorably Type A. Sexy Type A."

Dena liked this flirty Carter. Perhaps her little trip to Rhode Island had made him realize a few things about how he felt about her. Maybe it had made her do the same.

"I miss you too, Carter," she said before she chickened out.

"What's that? You what?"

"Carter…"

"I'm sorry. I didn't catch what you said." His chuckle made her smile. "Could you repeat it? Louder. I'll pay attention this time."

"I said I miss you, Carter." She flopped back on the hotel bed where she was instantly reminded of the dream she'd had of him last night. One in which they did much more than hang out and kiss. One where she'd gotten a good look at what was hiding under the silly T-shirts Carter always wore.

"Dena Brenton misses me." He sighed, a rush of air sounding in her ear. "My life is now complete."

"You are such a goof."

"You like that about me."

"I do."

"Do you like it enough to hop in that SUV of yours and get yourself home tonight? Tomorrow seems too far away." The slight whine wrapping around the words tugged at her. This conversation made her feel as if they were on the edge of something more.

"I was invited to a dinner where I can pick the brain of one of the presenters," she said. "I think it could be a good idea to go to this."

"Boo," Carter said, and she pictured him giving her a thumbs down.

"But… I suppose I could fit all my questions into an hour's worth of time, only eat a salad, and be on the road after that."

"Hurray!" Carter cheered. "Come directly to my house and I'll… I'll properly welcome you back to Vermont."

What? Was he saying what she thought he was saying? Did she want him to be saying that? *Hell, yeah.* Her mind wandered back to the dream. If he was half as good as he'd been in that fantasy, her toes would be curling in no time.

"Okay. That sounds great," she said.

"It does?"

She pictured him hooking his chin-length black hair behind his ear and pushing his glasses up his nose. "It really does, Carter."

"Yes!" He was quiet for a minute then he said, "I wasn't sure if you wanted to level up with me."

She grinned over his video game speak. "This time away from you has made me realize you've earned the codes to defeat the game."

"Oh, I don't intend to merely defeat, my lady," Carter said. "I plan to completely conquer."

Suddenly an hour-long dinner was too big of a barrier to scale. "I'm leaving right now."

"What? Are you sure?" Anticipation was clear in his voice.

"I've never been surer."

It was high time she was completely conquered.

****

Carter stared at his phone, amazed Dena was actually coming home tonight on his request. He'd debated calling her all day as he'd worked on his current project—designing the prequel game to his *Andromeda Rebellion* series. Gamers had begged for an experience that allowed them to play in the world that had led to the Andromeda Rebellion. Of course he'd had no idea what that world looked like until this week when he'd filled his home office walls with rough sketches of characters and settings and weapons and ships. Neon sticky notes with character names and challenges for gamers to meet littered the walls too. He had an almost complete storyboard going as well.

All of this would have to wait now. Dena was heading back to Vermont and he wanted to make good on his promise to properly welcome her home. He'd surprised himself when he'd issued that statement, but their entire conversation had been more flirty than most of the ones they'd had before. Something had felt right about saying what he'd said and he had no regrets. He only hoped she wouldn't either once they *leveled up* as he'd put it.

God, I really am a nerd. Who asked a woman if she wanted to level up? Only a dork too caught up in the gaming world to remember how to function in the real world.

But it had worked. Dena was coming home, and tonight they'd do more than kiss. Not that he minded all the kissing. From that first date—one he hadn't been sure about, but Leah had coaxed him to go on—being with Dena was easy. She was the first woman he'd ever told about Chase, his younger brother. His younger brother who had gotten a shit deal in this life when some fucked-up asshole thought shooting up an airport was a brilliant idea.

Poor Chase and Leah's parents and her sister. They were all in a car together, aiming to pick up Leah at the airport and take her to a party to celebrate her engagement to Chase. Carter was supposed to meet up with everyone, but when he'd been about to leave his house, he'd caught the news on TV about the shooter. Unfortunately, Chase and Leah's family had been a casualty when a stray bullet had hit Chase, who had been driving at the time. His vehicle had reached unheard of speeds and crashed, killing all four of them.

Actually killing all six of them because Carter and Leah had died inside that day too. Sure, they'd still walked around, still drew oxygen into their lungs, but they'd only been shells.

Until Leah moved to Maplehaven and met Dena's brother, Dakota, whom Carter really liked. He'd thought he'd wanted a shot with Leah upon first coming to Vermont to visit, but soon realized Dakota was the guy for his best friend. He wouldn't do anything to screw up Leah's second chance with a good man.

So he'd been playing around with Dena since that blind date where he'd spilled his entire sob story and she hadn't run for cover after hearing how damaged he was. In fact, she may have been part of the reason he'd made the decision to move to Maplehaven as Leah had. He could create video games anywhere, and a fresh start had sounded wonderful. So far, he'd been feeling better about life in general. He still missed his brother like hell—still felt that why-him-and-not-me thing—but he didn't feel as guilty about each breath he took anymore.

Hadn't wanted to drink either.

Giving his storyboard a final glance, Carter got up from his seat and turned out the light in the office as he left. He made his way into the small kitchen and opened the fridge.

Step #1: Hit the grocery store.

When he was working on a game, he tended to forget food and basic living necessities. That wouldn't do if he were going to have Dena over. She was a sophisticated chick. Way more cultured and fancy than he was, but she didn't seem to mind his perpetual college student looks or way of life. She'd tolerated him and his antics for the past two months, so she must have seen something redeemable in him.

16

And what would she tolerate tonight? Kissing was definitely on the menu. They were good at that. Maybe he'd follow up with a massage. Chicks liked massages, didn't they? And flowers. His cottage needed some flowers.

What else?

Clearly it was time to get some help on Operation: Proper Welcome Home. He tapped his phone screen a few times.

"Hey, Carter," Leah said when she answered.

"I need you."

"For?"

He quickly told her about his phone conversation with Dena. "And now I'm freaking out a little. I need to get this right."

Leah laughed. "If you just be you, Carter, you'll get it right. I've seen you two together. Dena is definitely into you. I don't think you can get this wrong."

"I'm a guy, Leah. Guys fuck things up all the time."

"That might be true, but you got this. Come pick me up and I'll help you at the grocery store. Dena's a good baker so you'll need to wow her with the meal. She won't be impressed by dessert."

"I basically live on sandwiches and potato chips. You know this."

"Then you're going to do an indoor picnic, but you'll romance it up a bit."

"A picnic? I can do a picnic." Some of his nerves settled down. *Some.*

"Of course you can. Come get me. We'll make this happen."

17

"Okay." Carter searched for his shoes and his car keys. "And Leah?"

"Yeah?"

"Thanks. For everything. I wouldn't be about to move on to something serious with Dena if it hadn't been for you."

"Sure you would ha—"

"No. I wouldn't have," he interrupted. "I was stuck. In New York, I couldn't climb out of the misery, Leah. That visit to you changed everything. Seeing how you had rebuilt your life here in Vermont changed everything. You inspired me."

"And look at you now." Leah's voice sounded a little scratchy as if she were trying not to cry. "It's time for the world to have Carter Bennett back."

"I think you're right."

"Good. Now let's get this romantic picnic organized so you can rock Dena's world."

Thirty minutes later, Carter stood next to Leah in the market. She'd filled his cart with multiple kinds of deli meat and cheese, fresh baked rolls, fancy pickles and olives, a selection of fruits, and two giant cannolis which she assured him Dena would like because she never made them herself. A bottle of wine, a bouquet of roses, and a few white candles topped off their supplies.

Carter eyed the cart as they got into the checkout line. "Are you sure Dena will be satisfied with sandwiches? She's fancier than sandwiches."

Leah rested her hand on his forearm. "It's not about the food, Carter. It's about the atmosphere and you. She's coming back tonight to see *you*."

"So my next question is are you sure Dena will be satisfied with me? She's fancier than me." Carter tugged at the T-shirt under his flannel shirt— one with a giant game system controller on it and the words *If you don't know what this is, we can't be friends* emblazoned around it.

"She's been satisfied with you so far," Leah said as she unloaded the cart onto the conveyer belt. "Why do you think she won't be tonight? You're a successful, attractive, funny, nice guy, Carter. Dena is smart enough to see that and make the decision to come home tonight to be with you. Think about it." She paused and gripped the edge of the cart's basket. "She's choosing to drive four hours *tonight* to get back to you. No woman wants to drive four hours at the end of what was probably a long day unless she really, *really* wants something. In this case, that *something* is you." She reached across the cart and poked him in the chest. "Now relax and have fun."

"Relax and have fun. Got it." He gave her a thumbs-up.

Leah squinted at him. "And change that T-shirt. You're not eleven years old." She chuckled when his mouth dropped open. "What? I said a bunch of nice things about you. I'm allowed to give one piece of constructive criticism."

"And my shirt is the target?"

"Yup."

He paid for the supplies and they piled everything into his car. "Is everything ready for the big wedding next week?"

Leah fastened her seatbelt, her face instantly brightening with a beamer of a smile. "Yes. I can't wait!"

"You deserve this happiness, Leah. I'm so glad you found Dakota."

She rubbed his forearm on the console between them. "Thanks, Carter. After Chase..." She shook her head. "I didn't think I'd ever get to a place where I'd want someone else, where I felt I had the right to *have* someone else, but Dakota is so amazing and he was so patient with me."

"You guys are a perfect match and your children will call me Uncle Carter. I'm not wavering on that one."

"Deal." Her expression turned serious for a moment, her blue eyes focused on his face as he prepared to pull out of the market's parking lot. "You deserve happiness too, Carter. Chase would want that for you."

"I think I finally understand that."

"Good. For you and for Dena."

After dropping off Leah and repeating her directions for setting everything up, Carter headed back to his cottage to follow his best friend's instructions. He set the flowers in small bunches in mason jars around the living room. After moving the coffee table out of the way, he placed the candles on the fireplace mantle and hearth, the end tables, and along a skinny table behind the couch. He unfolded a big quilt in the center of the room and put it down like a rug on the floor.

The temperature was still cold enough for a fire so he got one burning brightly, making the entire room cozy. At least he hoped. Dena had spent the past several nights in a hotel geared for businesspeople so he figured she'd welcome a dose of cozy tonight. Plus, cozy was good for snuggling and snuggling led to other things he desperately wanted to explore with her.

In the kitchen he assembled sandwiches, taking care to make them neatly and not all sloppy the way he usually did. He didn't much care for presentation when it was all going to mix in his stomach anyway, but chicks—especially chicks like Dena—liked order and aesthetics and attention to detail. He was certainly capable of all three as evidenced by his video games. Without them, his games would be crap.

He remembered the first game he'd coded. A simple game he'd made for Chase because his younger brother was having trouble mastering his multiplication tables. Carter had programmed a game requiring Chase to solve multiplication problems correctly to receive a virtual puzzle piece and build a complete image. All the images were of things related to firefighting because Chase had been obsessed with firefighters when he was a kid. Actually that obsession had stuck because Chase had chosen that as his career too.

The game had worked its magic right away. Chase wouldn't stop playing it, and in about a month he knew his multiplication tables better than anyone in his class. Chase's teacher wanted to know what had changed and when she found out it was Carter's game, she'd asked him to sell it to her. His parents had worked out all the legal and financial details and his gaming career had begun.

What he treasured most about that memory, however, was the way Chase had looked at him as if Carter were a wizard who had used magic to banish his little brother's multiplication problems. Carter only wished he could have helped his brother when he'd needed it at that damn airport.

Sighing, he tidied up the kitchen, removed his comic book action figures from the bookcases in the living room—just for tonight—and took a quick shower. Taking Leah's advice, he put on a pair of dark blue jeans and a black, long-sleeved, thermal T-shirt. It was a plain one with no silly sayings or crazy graphics. One of the few he owned. Working from home developing video games didn't require an extensive wardrobe, but if he were to level up with Dena, he probably should invest in a few more mature pieces of clothing. Just a few. He wasn't ready for a complete makeover for some chick.

But Dena isn't just some chick.

He'd known she was something more the moment he'd seen her. The way she'd listened to his story of Chase while sitting on the tailgate of her brother's truck that first night told him Dena Brenton was a woman of the highest caliber. Not only was she beautiful with her hazel eyes, long brown hair, and amazing body, she also had the brains to match. She handled all the finances at her family's sawmill—a super successful business and hub of Maplehaven.

She was too good for this tiny town. A woman like Dena could dominate in any of the world's biggest cities, but then he'd watch her with her parents, her twin sister Jacy, and her brother and he understood why she stayed. He'd had close family like that once. After his parents had passed, it had been just him and Chase, but they were tight. You didn't often see one of them without the other nearby.

Then it was just Carter. The only Bennett left standing.

Barely.

But that was changing. Being here in Maplehaven was healing him. Being with Dena was helping. Tonight might cure him completely.

Carter glanced at the clock on the microwave as he walked into the kitchen. If Dena had left when she'd said she would, it would be about another hour before she arrived. He hoped to God she followed his orders and came directly to his cottage. He didn't want to wait another minute to see her. Stopping at her house first would delay getting his lips and hands on her. That wouldn't do. Not when he'd finally made up his mind that he was all in. No more dabbling. No more watching other people live their lives. No more keeping Dena in the Kissing Only Zone. He was ready to feel something for her. Something real. Something risky.

Something he wouldn't want to lose once he had it.

He took a glass of water into the living room and lowered to the couch, a clock on the mantle ticking off the minutes until Dena arrived. He'd waited this long. He could wait a little more. Dena was worth taking a chance, though it was scary.

Because if he loved her and lost her as he'd lost his parents and his brother... well, there'd be no recovering from that.

Chapter Two

Dena tapped her foot as she waited at the hotel's front desk. She felt bad about skipping the dinner after Gary had been nice enough to invite her, but Carter's voice had caressed her ears in a way it never had before. They'd done a ton of talking with their kissing, but never had the mere sound of his voice gotten to her like it had tonight. Spending a few days away from him had awakened this need, a need she wanted to fill.

Immediately.

Of course the person manning the front desk wasn't a believer in haste. She'd used one finger to navigate across the keyboard of her computer, hunting and pecking, until Dena almost catapulted over the desk between them and checked herself out. It was nearly 5:00 now and it would be 9:00 before she arrived in Maplehaven with another five minutes to drive to Carter's cottage. Unless she ignored the speed limit. It might be worth risking a ticket to get Carter's welcome home sooner.

What was he planning? From what she'd seen so far, he wasn't exactly a romantic guy. While he was intense when it came to his video games, he didn't appear to have the focus required to tune into a woman and figure out what would make her swoon.

Although… a mere phone call had made her swoon, so maybe she had no idea what Carter was capable of when he was really trying. She'd find out tonight.

If she ever left the damn front desk.

"So that was four nights at the special conference rate, Miss Brenton?" the woman asked for the third time.

"Yes." Dena nudged the credit card she'd put on the desk. "Put it on this card."

The woman looked up through thick lenses, but didn't grab the card. "Do you want to join our rewards program? You get free stays in some of our more exotic locations."

The only exotic location Dena wanted to see right now was Carter's bed. "No thank you. I'd like to settle this bill and be on my way." *Quickly.*

"One of our locations is in Bermuda," the woman said. "I remember spending my thirtieth wedding anniversary at that one. Tom had surprised me, the old romantic that he was. We had such a lovely time. He died three months after that trip."

The pained look on the woman's face stabbed at Dena's heart. "I'm sorry to hear that,"—she squinted at the name tag on her sweater—"Marjorie. It sounds as if you made some beautiful memories to hold on to." Which was what she planned to do tonight. If she ever got out of that hotel. "Sign me up for the rewards program."

Marjorie's face brightened. "Oh, wonderful. You won't be sorry. Do you have someone special you can travel with?" She went back to hunting and pecking on the keyboard.

"I do." Surely after tonight, she and Carter could call what they had an official relationship. People who had relationships went away on trips together, didn't they? Although Carter wasn't fond of airports for obvious reasons, they could see plenty of other destinations within driving distance. Maybe she could convince him to drive down to Disney World. The Brentons had done that once when she and Jacy were in middle school and they'd had an absolute blast. Her father had closed the sawmill—something he'd never done before—and given all his employees a paid vacation while they were in Florida. She'd never forget that trip. She looked forward to having some never-forget times with Carter.

Starting tonight.

When she was done at this front desk.

At some point soon, for the love of God.

"You're thinking about your someone special right now, aren't you?"

Dena met Marjorie's magnified eyes. "How did you know?"

"That blush on your cheeks, missy." Marjorie chuckled. "That says it all." The woman tapped a slip on the desk between them and wiggled a pen. "I asked you to sign this. Twice."

"Oh." Dena cheeks heated, no doubt deepening the blush Marjorie had mentioned. "Sorry."

"Thinking good thoughts about a good man is nothing to be sorry about." Marjorie took back the signed slip and pen. "He is a good man, right?"

"Very."

"Thatta girl. Don't settle for anything less than the best." Marjorie gave her a warm smile and perhaps her slow speed hadn't been all that bad. Dena probably needed to tamp down her eagerness to see Carter anyway or she'd make a fool of herself. "Thank you for staying with us and enjoy your night, dear."

"Thanks."

Dena grabbed the handle of her rolling suitcase and quickly backed away from the front desk… right into Gary.

"Whoa." Hands gripped her biceps, keeping her from falling.

"Sorry, Gary," she said, taking a step back so he wasn't touching her anymore.

"No problem." He glanced down at her suitcase then to her purse on her arm. "You bringing all that to dinner?"

"Umm. No. Gary, something came up and I need to head back home now." *To have some long-overdue sex.* She bit her lip on that thought.

"Oh, is everything okay? Did something happen to a family member?"

His concern was appreciated, but this conversation was also delaying that sex she wanted to get to some time in this century.

"Yes, everything's fine. Thanks for your concern. And thanks for the invite to dinner. I hope you get all the tidbits you want. Good luck." Smiling at him, she made a move to roll her suitcase around him, but he stepped back into her path.

"Are you sure you can't join us? We'd love to talk shop with you."

"I'm sure, but you have a good time, okay?" She waited for him to move, which he did reluctantly. "Nice meeting you, Gary."

"You too, Dena," he said slowly.

She felt like a jerk, but dinner hadn't been in her original plans anyway. She'd come to Rhode Island for the conference. She'd attended that conference. She had a ton of new ideas to implement at the sawmill. Mission accomplished. Time to get back to Vermont and accomplish another mission.

A sexy mission.

Once she made it to the parking garage, she hoisted her suitcase into the back of her SUV. As she was closing the door, her phone sounded from her purse. Thinking it was probably Carter—hoping it was—she turned her attention to rooting around in her cavernous handbag to find her phone.

Something big slammed her into the back of the SUV. Her purse dropped to the ground, the contents spilling out and scattering at her feet. Her phone hit her left foot and she had a second to see Carter's name on the screen before something sharp poked her under her ribs.

"When a man invites you to dinner," a gravelly voice said into her ear, "and you accept that invitation, you go to dinner, bitch."

Dena wiggled to gain some space, but Gary was using his entire body—his entire *aroused* body—to press her against the vehicle. "I'm sorry, Gary. I explained that something came up. I didn't intend to go back on my acceptance of your invitation."

"You're all the same. Never intending to treat me like shit, but doing it anyway. Over and over again." He reeked of fresh smoke, making Dena's eyes tear.

Yeah, that's why they are tearing. She wasn't going to cry. No fucking way. She wouldn't give this asshole the satisfaction. She squirmed against Gary's hold again, aiming to give him an elbow or fist to something important, but that sharpness against her ribs came again and she realized he had a knife. In her haste to leave the hotel, she hadn't put on her winter jacket. She only had a blouse and a suit jacket between her flesh and that blade.

But he wouldn't cut her. Right? This wasn't actually happening, was it?

I've always hated parking garages.

"Look, Gary. I'll have dinner with you if you back up."

"Here come the lies now." Gary pushed the knife more firmly against her. "Typical."

Dena gritted her teeth against the prick of the blade. "Not lying. I have time for dinner."

"Really?"

"Sure. Back up so I can gather my things. You made me drop my purse."

Gary stepped back as Dena's heart raced. If she were going to do something, now was her chance.

"I'm sorry," Gary said, pressing the back of his hand still holding the knife to his forehead. "My wife left me last month and I'm not doing well with that. She was cheating on me."

Imagine. "Sounds as if it's been a difficult time for you," Dena said as she slowly lowered and shoved her things into her purse. As she went for her phone, however, Gary stepped on her hand and the phone. "I'll take that."

When he bent to pick it up, Dena launched the heel of her hand into his jaw. She'd been aiming for his nose as Dakota and Noah had once shown her for a quick self-defense move, but she couldn't reach from her current position. This hit was enough, however, to make Gary stumble back in surprise. Enough to allow Dena to grab her phone and purse and take off at a run.

Gary was fast. Faster than he looked. Faster than she'd anticipated. He was on her heels in no time.

She spotted a security car the next row over from her location and headed for it, but Gary got to her first. He grabbed her around the waist, turned her around, and pinned her to a concrete support beam, her phone clattering to the parking garage floor somewhere in the process. Sweat dotted Gary's forehead and a vein in his temple pulsed.

Pure fury blazed in his eyes.

"You spent the last three workshops flirting with me and now you act like this?" He was winded, but the arm that held her in place was like steel.

"Flirting? I never flirted with you, Gary. I was nice because that's how people are supposed to be upon first meeting. I never gave you any indication I was interested in more."

"You accepted my dinner invitation." He had the knife back at her ribs so she didn't dare scream for the security guard.

"To talk more shop with you and that presenter. Nothing else." She swallowed around a throat gone completely dry. Why hadn't Marjorie been a bit faster at that front desk? If Dena had left a few minutes sooner, she never would have crossed Gary's path. Never would have been in her current situation.

Never would have been scared to death.

"This is what women like you—like my wife—do. You think we men don't have feelings. That we're here for you to play with, to make fools of." His voice had risen and over his shoulder, Dena noticed the security guard getting out of his vehicle.

Yes, come this way.

"I'm sorry if you got the wrong idea. I really am." *Keep him talking.* "As I said before, I'll go have dinner with you."

"You ran away from me."

"I panicked, Gary. Try to see things from my perspective right now." *Yes, security dude, you do see something sketchy over here. Investigate. Hurry up!*

Gary shook his head as he slid his hand up her blouse, his sweaty fingers groping. "No, you have to be taught a lesson."

"A lesson? About what?" She backed up, but there was nowhere for her to go. God, she wished Carter was here right now. He had big muscles for a nerd and he'd use them to get this prick off her.

"Lessons about manners. About following through. About at least having the guts to cancel plans instead of just leaving, just walking out." Gary's jaw was clenched, his words barely escaping past his teeth.

"As your wife did."

His eyes immediately filled with tears. "Why did she have to go?"

Because you're a psycho?

"Have you talked to her about what happened?" Dena glanced at the security guard and gave a nod at his raised eyebrows.

"Everything okay over here?" the guard asked.

Gary stilled, his gaze boring into hers. "Yes, officer. Just didn't want to get into the car without giving my lovely lady a kiss first."

The guard angled his head. "I'd like to hear the lovely lady say everything's okay, sir."

Dena hesitated and the knife blade pressed against her side. Before she could say anything though, the officer put his hand on Gary's shoulder in an attempt to turn him around.

An instant later, the hot sting of the knife blade ripped into Dena's flesh. She screamed in pain as the officer yanked Gary back, taking the knife with him. She put her hand to the slice, warm blood seeping through her fingers.

Her warm blood.

She was vaguely aware of the officer wrestling Gary to the ground. Another officer had joined him, and Gary was soon handcuffed and escorted away. The first security guard came to her side. Somehow she'd slid to the ground and blood now pooled in her lap.

"Miss? Miss, can you hear me?" the guard asked as he removed her suit jacket, balled it up, and instructed her to press it to her wound. "I've called 911 and they're on their way. Hang tight, okay?"

She managed a nod.

"Can I call someone for you?" He had a phone in his hand, ready to dial any number she gave him.

But all her loved ones were hours away. No sense in calling any of them. They couldn't get here quickly.

Besides she didn't want any of them to see her like this. Covered in blood. Shaking like a frightened little girl. Dena Brenton didn't look like this. Ever.

The officer made a move to touch her shoulder and she jolted back, causing a spurt of blood to leak from her side.

Dena Brenton didn't want anyone to touch her cither.

Ever.

****

At precisely 10:49, Carter became officially concerned about Dena's whereabouts. If she left when she'd said she was going to, she should have been in his arms right now. An hour delay he could rationalize away. Perhaps she'd gone to that dinner after all. Maybe there'd been traffic on the way home. Possibly she'd blown past a state trooper doing over a hundred miles per hour to get back to Vermont and had gotten a ticket.

But why hadn't she called him if it had been any of those potential scenarios? And why hadn't she answered her phone when he'd called her?

The only conclusion Carter could come to was that something much, much worse had happened to Dena. He'd tried calling her a few more times, but she hadn't picked up. Texted, but she didn't text back. Voicemailed, but still no reply.

Did she change her mind? Maybe he'd come on too strong with his welcome home proposition. She'd seemed into what he'd suggested though. Dena wasn't the type to play along for the hell of it. She was far too goal oriented to merely talk the talk. If she had said she was leaving Rhode Island tonight to come to his cottage that was exactly what she'd planned to do.

So what had stopped her?

Carter picked up his phone from the arm of the couch and texted the only person he could at nearly 11:00 at night.

Have you heard from Dena?

He lowered to the couch to keep himself from pacing the length of the living room as he'd been doing for the past hour and a half. By now, the candles he'd lit were melted globs of white wax. The fire in the fireplace had died down, embers still glowing red, but the sexy roar of it had long since silenced. He glanced down when his phone vibrated on his thigh.

No. Isn't she with you? Leah texted.

That had been the plan. *She hasn't shown up. I'm worried.*

Did you call/text her?

Yes. She's not answering anything. Did Dakota hear anything?

Hang on.

Carter drummed his fingers on his knee as he pictured his best friend waking her fiancé to ask questions. Maybe he should get in his car and search for Dena himself. This sitting in his cottage and waiting was making him insane. Dena was the most punctual person he'd ever met. She was never late for anything. In fact, most of the time, she was early.

Dakota hasn't heard anything, but he's calling his parents right now, Leah texted.

Carter stood and began pacing again. *Didn't mean to upset anyone.*

Of course not, but we have to locate her. I'll call you after Dakota talks to his parents.

Okay.

Carter felt like an ass for waking up Leah and Dakota and now Dakota's poor parents, but it was probably better to do that than wait a second longer for Dena. He said a quick prayer she'd show up. He wanted nothing more than for a soft knock to sound at his door and to find beautiful Dena on the other side of it.

Where can she be?

His slightly warped video-game-world mind easily conjured up gruesome situations that could have befallen Dena. Shaking his head, he attempted to clear those images from his brain, but they were stuck there. Shit, when had he turned into such a worrier? He'd no doubt have Dena laughing her gorgeous ass off when he explained how he'd imagined fifty ways she could be hanging on for dear life. He needed to simmer down and think logically.

As Dena would. She wouldn't get all dramatic and carried away. She'd look for the most logical explanation and then problem solve from there.

So what was the most logical explanation? That she'd chickened out. That she was afraid of *leveling up* with him. That she didn't think he was actual boyfriend material. Carter guessed he had that coming. He'd been keeping things light and easy for the past two months. No wonder she hadn't truly believed he was capable of more, that he *wanted* more. She'd probably seen this conference trip as a way to gain some distance from him and his suggestion she come back tonight was too little, too late.

It was his own fault. He'd told Dena everything about his brother and how he was afraid to depend on people too much. Any woman in her right mind would run in the other direction from a commitment-phobic video game developer who lived—and sometimes behaved—like a college student.

He was an idiot for contacting Leah and bugging Dakota. When it all came out that Dena was avoiding Carter, embarrassment would get a chokehold on him.

His phone rang and he nearly dropped it, the ringtone loud in the quiet of his cottage. His cottage that was supposed to have one Dena Brenton in it by now. He should be worshipping every inch of her stunning body at this very moment.

"Hey, Leah," he said after swiping his screen. "What's the word?"

"Stay calm," Leah said.

Not the words he'd expected her to say.

"Come over and I'll fill you in," his best friend said.

"No. Tell me now. Is Dena okay? What happened?" His heart was pounding, and suddenly he was back in his apartment in New York watching the news of the airport shooter where his little brother was picking up his fiancée with Leah's parents and sister. Carter's breath came in rapid spurts and spots danced before his eyes.

"Carter." Leah's voice was stern. "Carter, don't time travel back to losing Chase. We haven't lost Dena."

"So you found out where she is?" He wiped his sweat-soaked palm on the thigh of his jeans.

"Yes. She was attacked in the parking garage of the hotel, but—"

His legs wobbled and he lowered to the couch. "Attacked? What do you mean *attacked*?"

"Dakota's father talked to a Providence police officer who explained that another conference attendee had invited her to dinner. She'd checked out of the hotel instead, intending to head home, but she ran into the attendee. He got upset that she was scooting out, so he came at her when she was at her vehicle in the parking garage. A security guard saw them, thought something was suspicious, and investigated. A slight scuffle followed and…"

"And what, Leah? Oh, God, and what?" Carter squeezed his eyes closed.

"Dena is being treated at a Providence hospital for a minor stab wound."

Carter shot to his feet. "Stab wound! Jesus."

"She's okay, Carter. Nothing fatal. Some stitches. Dakota's father and Jacy are headed to Rhode Island right now. They'll probably stay overnight and head back to Vermont tomorrow."

"Why didn't she call any of us?" He would have hopped into his car and driven at warp speed to Rhode Island if he'd known what was going on.

"Her phone was dropped in the parking garage. The security guard picked it up, but it was broken. Priority one was getting Dena to the hospital."

Did that mean the wound was worse than Leah was saying?

"I'm going to Rhode Island," Carter said. Screw more waiting for Dena. He had to see for himself that she was all right.

"Carter." Leah's voice had taken on that teacher tone she used with her students. "There's nothing you can do right now, and I can tell you're upset. Not a good idea to drive for four hours when your head isn't clear. Come over here instead, buddy, and we'll wait together."

"No. I didn't go to the airport when Chase was…" His throat completely seized up and the words wouldn't come out.

"I know, Carter. I know, but this is different. Dena is going to be fine. She'll be home by tomorrow. The hospital said they're keeping her overnight for observation. She really is okay. This isn't like Chase. Not at all."

But wasn't it? With Chase he hadn't been able to go to his brother's side. He hadn't been there when Chase needed him. He'd been waiting… for his brother to die apparently. Carter was sick of waiting.

"There's nothing you can do by going to Rhode Island tonight, Carter," Leah said.

He hated that Leah was right. "Can you at least give me a phone number? I'd like to call her. I need to call her."

"I have the number for the hospital right here." Leah rattled off the numbers and Carter jotted them down, hoping he'd be able to read what he'd written. "Are you sure I can't convince you to come over here, Carter?"

"I'm sure. I'm okay. I'm worried about Dena though. I knew something wasn't right." Maybe if he'd called Leah sooner, there would have been time for him to drive to Rhode Island to be with Dena.

"If you change your mind," Leah said, "stop by. We don't mind."

"Thanks, Leah."

"Carter?"

"Yeah?"

"What you were planning tonight should definitely still happen," Leah said. "I haven't seen you that excited in a long, long time. Dena excites you. She brings you joy, and you deserve every ounce of that joy. When she gets back, you hit her with that romance and charm. You tell her what you're feeling. We both know how quickly life can change."

Carter's eyes stung. He managed another soft *thanks* and hung up. After downing a glass of water at the kitchen sink—and wishing it were whiskey instead—he dialed the hospital number, asked for Dena Brenton's room, and held his breath as each ring sounded.

"Hello?" A scratchy, weak voice filled his ears. A voice not at all like the powerful, successful, take-no-shit Dena's voice he'd become accustomed to over the past two months.

"Dena, it's me. Are you okay?" Of course she wasn't. Even if the physical wound wasn't bad, the

40

emotional one caused by the horrific situation would fester for quite some time. Here he was, years after his brother's unexpected death, and the emotional bruises were still black and blue, still tender. Sudden rage filled him. "What's this bastard's name?"

A puff of air resonated from Dena's end. "His name doesn't matter."

"It matters if I'm going to hunt him down and—"

"You're not a violent man, Carter Bennett," Dena interrupted. "Besides, the police already have the asshole, and I'm fine."

"I'm coming down to Rhode Island," he said. "I'll leave right now."

"No. I'm so tired. I'm just going to sleep. My dad and sister are coming. I'll be home tomorrow." It sounded as if every word she said took a mammoth effort to utter. What shape was she in?

Carter wasn't sure he could wait until tomorrow to make sure she was truly all right. He raked his hand through his hair as he slouched onto one of the stools at his kitchen island. "I'm sorry, Dena."

"Sorry? You have no reason to be sorry, Carter."

"It was selfish of me to ask you to come home tonight. You would have gone to the dinner that assclown invited you to and all this bullshit could have been avoided."

"For all we know, I could have gone to that dinner and said assclown could have gone psycho at any point during the evening. It's not your fault. It's *his* fault."

A few heartbeats of silence stretched between them and Carter thought Dena had fallen asleep. The hospital had no doubt given her something to make her more comfortable.

"Dena?"

"Yeah?"

"Are you in pain?"

"Everything's... numb right now." She yawned. "Listen, my eyelids weigh about two tons each so I'm going to catch some sleep before my father and sister get here."

"Right. Okay." He wasn't nearly done hearing her voice, nor nearly convinced she was all right. "I'll check on you tomorrow."

"Sure." And then she hung up.

Carter sat at the kitchen island, staring at his phone, wishing he could rewind time and change the course of this night. Only hours ago, he'd had a light, fun, playful conversation with Dena. A conversation in which he'd solidified plans to have sex with her tonight. To sail past the safe kissing phase directly into the exciting waters of making love.

Because that was what it would be with Dena. *Making love.* That was the kind of woman she was. The kind of woman a man made love to.

The kind of woman Carter *wanted* to make love to.

The conversation he'd just had with her, however, was not light, not fun, not playful. This conversation had been a simple exchange of information, a confirmation she was alive and breathing. A hey-we-had-plans-but-shit-happened chat.

42

Carter didn't want to have any more of those conversations.

Sighing, he stood and made his way to the bathroom to grab a shower and collapse into bed. Of course, as he stared at the ceiling in his bedroom, eyes wide open, he kept reviewing the description Leah had given him of what had happened to Dena. His fists curled and uncurled at his sides. If he'd gotten the idea into his head sooner that he and Dena should move things to the next level, maybe he would have gone to Rhode Island with her. Perhaps they would have made a little vacation out of it. A little romantic vacation. He would have been there. She never would have met that bastard.

Never had him close enough to fucking stab her.

A growl vibrated deep in his chest and he threw off the blankets. Carter got out of bed and stomped into his office. If he wasn't going to sleep—wasn't going to get over what had happened to Dena, *his* Dena—he'd dive into work until he was too tired to continue. A fleeting thought of alcohol scurried across his brain, but he hadn't indulged since moving to Maplehaven. He liked to think he'd learned a lesson about using alcohol to deal with his problems. Hopefully the sun would rise quickly and tomorrow he would do as Leah had recommended.

Tell—no, *show*—Dena exactly how he felt about her.

Chapter Three

"I could heat up soup, lasagna, the roasted chicken for dinner," Chennie Brenton said as she stood in the doorway between Dena's living room and kitchen.

"Because you cooked all that, Mom?" Dena shifted her position on the couch, wincing when her stitches pulled at her skin. Moving around would have to be done in slow motion for a little while as the gash under her ribs healed. She still couldn't believe she had been stabbed.

Stabbed!

A simple trip to a financial conference should not have ended with a trip to the hospital. How could Gary have been so far off his rocker? Why couldn't she stop picturing his face up close to hers as he cut into her? She hadn't slept a wink last night in the hospital and something told her being at home in her own bed wouldn't guarantee a peaceful slumber either. Even her beloved cow statue collection, proudly displayed on the shelves in her living room, wasn't a comfort right now.

And she swore she still smelled cigarette smoke.

"Of course she cooked all that. Have you met our mother?" Dakota leaned forward, his elbows resting on his knees as he sat in the cushiony chair

44

across from the couch. "But if you don't like any of that, there are probably six other options."

"Zip it, son!" Chennie called from the refrigerator. "There are only *five* other options."

Dena laughed, but she quickly stopped when pain shot through her mid-section.

"Easy there, sweetheart," her father, William, said. "I know you are my doesn't-sit-still-for-long daughter, but this injury calls for slowing down so you can heal."

Her father knew her so well. Of course he would. They'd spent so much time together, both as a family and as business associates. When her brother hadn't wanted to take over the sawmill, Dena and her sister had been happy to. A part of Dena had felt as if she'd been preparing her entire life to run that place. Sawdust was in her blood. She loved handling payroll, invoices, budgets, everything. If it had to do with the sawmill's money, she was all over it. She prided herself on being meticulous in her recordkeeping, and William had told her repeatedly how pleased he was with her work.

"What would we do without you at the sawmill?" her father had asked her last week when she'd found a more cost effective method of tracking delivery expenses.

She shivered over how close the sawmill had come to finding the answer to that question last night. If Gary had stabbed her a few inches higher, he could have buried that blade in her lungs or something else important. Thank God he'd slashed her in a non-critical area and it hadn't been that deep either. Dena didn't necessarily fear death, but to go out of this world at the hands of a nutjob in a parking garage in Rhode Island didn't seem fitting for a Brenton.

Or anyone really.

She waved at Jacy as her sister walked by the couch. "Can you send me the—"

"Nope." Jacy held up her hand. "I will not send you anything from the office. You will be too busy recuperating."

"I can recuperate and get a few work things done at the same time." She desperately needed something to keep her mind busy. Otherwise the replay of her time in the parking garage with Scary Gary would make her insane.

"No," her father, mother, sister, and brother all said at the same time.

"Well, that was unanimous," Leah said. "Guess you can't fight that."

"Oh, she'll try," Dakota said, pulling Leah down onto his lap and pressing a kiss to her neck.

Dena looked away quickly, the physical contact between her brother and his fiancée making her anxious. "If I don't work," she said, "what am I supposed to do?"

"Take some time for you," William said. "While I love your work ethic at the sawmill, you're allowed to take care of yourself, you know."

"I feel fine." Dena motioned to her stomach area. "It doesn't hurt."

"Good," Chennie said, carrying a plate piled high with lasagna that Dena definitely didn't want. "But we're still going to insist you take it easy, honey. You don't want to do anything that will delay getting back to one hundred percent."

Dena flopped her head to rest on the back of the couch. She was going to go stir crazy if she couldn't work. Maybe once her family left she'd at least review her conference notes and figure out what new ideas she'd try to implement at the sawmill. Surely reading and thinking about finances wouldn't endanger her healing process.

"I could teach you to knit," her mother said. "You never let me teach you before, but now that you have some time, it could be fun."

When did I sign up for the senior-citizen-in-training course?

"I don't plan to be on this couch for long, Mom, but thanks."

"We should all go anyway," Jacy said. "Carter is on his way over." She gave Dena a wink and a smile bloomed on Leah's face.

"What?" Dena straightened in her seat, but again the skin around the wound throbbed as it stretched and moved with her. *Dammit.* That asshole Gary had reduced her to invalid level.

Jacy wiggled her phone. "He texted me after we got you home. That man is *dying* to see you, Dena."

"I don't want to see anyone." The thought of Carter coming over made a literal sweat break out on her body. Everywhere. And not an anticipatory sweat. More like a panicked sweat. An I'm-not-ready-to-see-him sweat.

Their plans had been to be intimate last night, to take their relationship to the next level. After what happened in Rhode Island, being physical with anyone was the last thing Dena wanted. The mere notion of a hug made her skin itch. She'd never been an overly touchy person, but now...

Now I want a permanent bubble around me.

"Carter had a special night planned for you guys last night." Leah's eyes were sympathetic. "He was so excited for you to come home."

Dena cleared her throat, the corners of her eyes pricking with potential tears. She'd been excited to see Carter too. So excited, in fact, she'd attempted a premature exit from the hotel. Everything would have worked out better if she hadn't been so clumsy in turning around from the front desk with her luggage. If she'd never run into Gary, she and Carter would have become an official *thing* last night.

The only official thing she wanted now was a *Do Not Touch* sign around her neck.

"You owe him the chance to see you're in one piece, don't you think, Dena?" Dakota asked. "I mean, I didn't believe you were okay until I saw you with my own eyes."

Normally she'd have some sassy comeback for her brother, but she didn't have the energy for that sort of wit today. Instead she shook her head. "I really want to sleep this whole thing off."

Jacy peeked out the front window. "Too bad. Carter is here." She turned to face Dena and, as always, it was like looking in a mirror. Same long, straight, brown hair. Same hazel eyes. Same lean build. The only difference was fashion sense. Dena liked sophisticated clothes. Sure, the sawmill could be a dirty, dusty place, but she always looked neat and put together with a hint of preppy style. Pressed dress pants with blouses in pastel colors were the norm for her, while Jacy took on a trendier, more creative air with her long floral skirts and bold colors.

Today, though she looked like her sister physically, Dena felt disconnected from the twin thing. Actually from her entire family sitting around her now. Her experience in Providence had separated her from the nice little Maplehaven cocoon where you could basically leave your front door unlocked without fear or worry.

I'll be locking everything tonight. And checking those locks twice. And maybe sleeping with a baseball bat.

Another shiver rattled through her as an image of Gary up in her face flashed behind her eyelids. Would she ever feel truly safe again? Were people like Gary lurking around every corner? Were they in plain sight too? How could she trust anyone beyond her family?

The doorbell rang and Dena cringed. She did not want to see Carter right now. In fact, she wanted everyone to leave. She needed some time alone. Some time to clear her head.

If that's even possible…

"What do you want me to do, Dena?" Jacy asked.

Send him away. But it was probably better to face Carter with her family there as a buffer.

"Let him in."

Jacy nodded once and went to the front door. Conversation in low voices wafted into the living room though Dena couldn't see her sister and Carter in the foyer. When Carter did appear in the living room, the anguish on his handsome face made her sorry she'd caused him so much worry.

She started to get up, but Carter was in front of her in two long strides.

"Don't move," he said as he held out a bunch of roses. "These were from last night." He stared down at her, his brown eyes intense behind his black-framed glasses. His black hair was hooked behind his left ear, and though Dena's hands had been tangled in those soft strands plenty of times over the last two months when they'd kissed, the thought of having him that close to her now made her chest tight.

"Why don't we... be somewhere else?" Leah rose from Dakota's lap and tugged him to his feet.

"You don't have to go." Dena's chest tightened another notch. What was that weight pressing down on her? Was she about to have a heart attack? Pass out? Be reduced to a sniveling ball of nerves? She gave herself a mental shake and searched within for the confident woman she'd been yesterday.

Where had that chick run off to? More importantly, how did Dena get that woman to come back?

"I told Noah's grandmother I'd size up her cats for those knitted collars I make," her mother said. "I should get over there before it gets too late." She looked at her husband. "Come on, old man. I could use your help in wrangling cats."

William saluted his wife. "Professional Cat Wrangler reporting for duty, my lady."

"I'm not sure which is crazier," Jacy said, shaking her head. "The fact that my mother knits cat collars or that my father thinks he's a cat wrangler."

Christine DePetrillo

"Probably a tie on that one." Dakota clapped his father on the back. "But I have to say, Leah's cat, Fey, looks pretty damn cute in her handmade collar."

A smile bloomed on Leah's face. "She really does."

"I need to make bigger ones for dogs," Chennie said as she slipped into her coat William held out for her.

"Ginger would love one," Dakota said, herding everyone—except Carter—toward the front door. He paused by Carter who was still standing in front of the couch. "We leave Dena in your hands. A word of caution though, she can be cranky when she's not running on all engines."

"Dakota," Dena bit out, glaring at him.

"Okay, okay." He shot Carter a grin. "She's cranky all the time."

Leah yanked Dakota to the front door. "Sorry, Dena. Give us a call if you need anything. I promise to leave Dakota at home."

And in the next minute, the house was quiet. Uncomfortably quiet as Carter studied her.

"I'm not a science experiment," she said with more bitchiness than she intended—or he deserved.

"I know," Carter said softly. "I'm just looking my fill now. Just in case."

"Just in case?"

"Yeah. Just in case it's the last time. You'd think I would have learned that lesson already. With Chase. You never can tell when someone might be taken from you." He lowered to sit on the coffee table across from her, his long legs bending so his knees were level with the couch.

Shit. Dena had been so wrapped up in her own thoughts about her situation she hadn't stopped to consider how hard this probably was for Carter. He knew better than anyone how a simple trip could cause life-changing catastrophe.

"I'm fine, Carter. Honestly." She gestured to her stomach beneath her flannel shirt. "A small wound. It'll heal up in no time." Not a lie. That physical wound would be scabbed over and gone in a few weeks. She had no idea, however, how long the wounds on her psyche would take to heal.

Carter reached out and when his long fingers made contact with her knee, she flinched. He took his hand back so fast it was as if he'd been burned by her quick movement.

"I'm sorry," he said quietly, his hand resting on his own thigh now. "I wanted to comfort you. You know I would never, *never* hurt you, Dena, right?"

She managed a nod. Of course he wouldn't hurt her. She knew that. Dena had never witnessed Carter even raise his voice in anger. Most of the time he was making her laugh.

It was hard to remember that right now though.

"I think…" she began, but she had to clear her throat. "I think I need some time, some distance."

Carter looked to his feet while his fingers tapped on his knee. "Please don't, Dena." He raised his head to meet her gaze, his eyes filled with so many things. Compassion. Need. Hurt. "Don't push me away."

Dena pulled her legs up under her on the couch, the movement sending an ache through her midsection. "I have to," she whispered.

Carter shook his head. "No, you don't. I'm here for you. I want to be here for you. With you. What about what we discussed last night? What about taking this," he motioned between them with his hand, "to the next level? I still want that. Don't you?"

"I don't know what I want right now, Carter."

"That's why I'm not going to leave you alone." He slid to the edge of the coffee table.

She held up her hand to stop him. "But that's the one thing I am sure of. That I want to be alone."

Carter's shoulders rose and fell as he took in a deep breath. He didn't say anything more. He simply got up from the table, leaving the roses behind, and left quietly through the front door.

Dena listened as his car started then the engine noise faded away. The quiet she was left in was overwhelming, but entirely what she had wanted. It was better this way.

It was.

****

Carter walked down the makeshift aisle in William and Chennie's barn as he practiced his groomsman duties at Leah's wedding rehearsal. A beautiful brunette was supposed to be by his side, but Jacy had told him Dena wasn't coming tonight. Something about a headache. He knew for a fact, however, that she'd gone to work today. Spent almost a full day in the sawmill's office catching up.

She didn't have a headache. He knew what was going on. She didn't want to see him or be near him.

All week he'd replayed the conversation they'd had in her living room. The conversation where she'd basically told him to buzz off. All week he'd waffled between giving her the space she'd requested and calling to beg her to let him come over. A part of him understood why she wanted to have some distance. When he'd first lost Chase, the trauma of the incident had turned a portion of him to stone. He'd felt nothing. He hadn't wanted to leave his house. He hadn't wanted to pretend to be okay in front of anyone.

Another part of him, however, had yearned for someone to reach out and pull him from the abyss. He'd wanted a beacon of light, of hope, to shine on him.

He'd wanted rescuing.

Alcohol had done that for him, but in the end, he'd realized the only thing that could truly rescue him from his depression was him. Moving to Vermont had given him the fresh start he'd needed, as it had for Leah. It'd allowed him to turn the corner and not see darkness.

What if Dena decides to move?

He shook his head as he neared the gorgeous, wooden archway William had made for Leah and Dakota to exchange their vows. Dena wouldn't move. As much as she'd been hiding this week, Carter was certain her ties to her family were much too strong for her to live anywhere besides Maplehaven. Now that she'd seen how scary areas outside of Vermont were, she'd probably not want to visit other places, let alone live in them.

Carter couldn't blame her. Something about Maplehaven was… soothing. Its cozy small town vibe, its stunning natural landscapes, and its kind people all contributed to creating a place like none other. He'd done quite a bit of traveling. Before losing Chase. His career had sent him to comic cons across the globe, meeting rabid fans of his games and speaking on panels. He'd never visited a town quite like Maplehaven.

The fact that he'd convinced himself Dena wouldn't move settled him some. The fact that she was outright avoiding being in the same room—or barn—with him undid all that settling. He'd thought the two of them were on to something deep. Something mature. Something where he did things to Dena that made her pant in pleasure. He knew he could do it. He had it in him. He was up for the challenge.

But she isn't.

Would she ever be? Once her physical wound healed, would she be able to put the parking garage incident behind her? Would she be able to dive back into her life? Or would she want to travel that path alone forever?

Grumbling to himself, Carter reached the archway and made a right as he'd been instructed to do. Tomorrow at the actual wedding in this barn, Dena would be releasing his arm and making a left to stand with the other bridesmaids. He'd get to touch her for a few moments and steal glances at her at least. How pathetic was it that he looked forward to peeking at her?

He took his position next to Kyle Lennings, owner of Mountain View Pizza and husband to Heidi, Leah's close friend at Maplehaven Elementary school where they both taught fourth grade. Kyle was a cool guy who Carter had hung with on several occasions during his time living in Maplehaven. The dude could dominate in *Kings of the Court*, a virtual tennis game Carter had developed a few years ago. The crazy thing was Kyle had never picked up an actual racket in his life.

Noah Williams stood on Carter's other side. He'd been Dakota's best friend since they were kids and was currently engaged to Krista Davidson, Dakota's *other* best friend who worked for Dakota at Birch Peak Adventures. It appeared everywhere Carter looked in that barn he found people madly in love. He'd never been madly in love, but Dena made him want to explore such a notion.

Jacy walked up the aisle next with one of her cousins on her mother's side. Shit, she looked so much like Dena that it freaked Carter out a little bit. At first the only way he could tell them apart was by their style of dress, but as he'd gotten to know Dena better, he'd picked up on the... aura of each sister. Different women definitely lived inside those identical exteriors.

When Jacy took her spot next to Krista, leaving an empty space for where Dena would have been standing if she'd made an appearance tonight, her hazel gaze connected with Carter's for a minute.

She offered him a sad smile as if to say, *Sorry my sister has shunned you.*

He returned her smile with one of his own, adding in a slight shrug. Everything was out of his hands until Dena agreed to see him or shut down their budding relationship for good. How he hated when his fate was in another's hands.

"Okay," Dakota's cousin, Michaela, said. She'd become a minister online for the wedding ceremony. "Next the music for the bride will play and William will escort Leah down the aisle." Since Leah's own parents had passed, she'd asked Dakota's father to stand in. He'd been delighted and the way he paraded her along the wide-planked flooring in the barn—smile bright, eyes shining—was proof.

William joined Leah and Dakota's hands when they reached the archway. He gave them both a kiss then took a seat with Chennie in the first row of the audience. "I still think we need some dance music when we walk down the aisle, Leah," he said, a chuckle following his words.

"There will be plenty of dancing after the ceremony," Leah said. "And you better save me a dance, William." She wagged a finger at him and he winked back at her.

Carter was thrilled Leah had found the Brentons. They'd assimilated her into their family and he'd never seen his best friend happier. While he would have loved to see her marry his brother, she definitely belonged with Dakota. Like on a soul mate level. She'd been in love with Chase. Carter had no doubts about that. The way she'd grieved over his loss was all the evidence a person needed to see how deep her feelings had gone for his little brother. However, she hadn't glowed as she was right now, standing across from Dakota, smiling up into his face. That kind of love was pure magic.

Magic that appeared to look at Carter and wave as it sailed right past him.

The rest of the rehearsal went smoothly and soon the entire wedding party was crowded around several tables pushed together in the function room at Mountain View Pizza. Kyle had insisted on cooking for everyone as his wedding gift to Leah and Dakota and no one was going to argue with him on that. He was a master when it came to pizza, rivaling anything Carter had tasted in New York.

Only one thing ruined the evening. The empty chair beside him. If parallel universes existed, maybe Dena sat next to him in one of them. Perhaps in that universe, they'd gotten serious about their relationship right away and were now deeply in love with each other. Possibly they were on their way down the aisle.

Unfortunately, he was stuck in *this* universe, and his hands were tied. If he went after what he wanted—Dena—he wouldn't be respecting her clear wishes. If he didn't go after what he wanted—still Dena—he would be having many more evenings where the seat next to him was empty. Neither of these paths stood out as the right choice. He wasn't sure what to do.

"No contemplative expressions at my rehearsal dinner." Leah nudged his shoulder then lowered onto the seat next to him.

Carter blinked the room back into focus to see people out of their seats and mingling. In his ponderings, he'd been left alone at the table. "Sorry, Leah." He covered her hand with his on the table. "I'll try to smile more."

Leah shook her head. "You don't have to do that. Not unless you truly feel like smiling."

Not likely.

"I'll bet you can't wait until tomorrow." He at least owed his best friend some small talk, didn't he?

Leah's face brightened as a smile turned up her lips. "We've only been engaged since December, but I feel as if I've been waiting for so long to marry Dakota." She slid her gaze to her fiancé currently standing with his parents, deep in conversation about something. A moment later, however, he turned his head and grinned at Leah.

"Now that's in tune," Carter said.

"Huh?" Leah blew Dakota a kiss then turned her attention back to Carter. "What do you mean?"

"I mean he totally knew you were looking at him. Did you see his face? It was as if he'd forgotten what he'd been saying to his parents the moment your gaze landed on him. That's some connection you guys have."

Leah rested her hand on Carter's shoulder. "You'll have that too. You just need to give her some time."

"I don't think Dena wants to be with me at all, Leah." He patted her hand on his shoulder.

She shook her head. "I think you're taking this too personally. It's not like she just doesn't want to see you, Carter. Jacy and I had to march into her

59

house yesterday and talk her into coming to the wedding tomorrow."

Carter's eyes widened. "You mean she might stay home?"

"I sure hope not. For Dakota's sake. It'll put a damper on things if she doesn't come, but what I want you to know is that she doesn't want to be around *anyone*. She's not singling you out. I don't think it's about you at all, honey. She's putting up a wall to keep everyone away."

"We can't let her do that. She needs to see that what happened in Rhode Island was the result of one douchebag. No one here would treat her like that. No one."

"I think she knows that, but let's consider us for a moment," Leah said. "You and I lost people who were extremely important to us and we lost them tragically. We didn't bounce right back into life, did we?"

Carter shook his head.

"No. That trauma… well, it fucked us up, Carter. It made me scared to do anything. It made you drink and get into fights. It locked us both up. We were prisoners of that grief." Leah cleared her throat and Carter hated to see her getting upset when she should be nothing but overjoyed tonight. She was getting married tomorrow for Christ's sake. "It took coming here to Vermont and meeting Dakota to free me. I think you moving here and meeting Dena did the same for you. I mean, you told Dena about losing Chase on your first date. Had you ever been with anyone else who you felt you could share that story with?"

"No."

"Right. So, my expert advice"—she elbowed him when he smirked—"is to be patient. If Dakota hadn't been patient with me, I wouldn't be becoming Mrs. Leah Brenton tomorrow. I'd be missing out on all this." She arced her arm out to encompass all the people in the room. All the people who now loved her. "Don't cheat yourself—or Dena—out of something awesome. You guys are good together. I can see it."

"Patient. Got it." He didn't have the chance to say more because Kyle wheeled out a huge sheet cake.

"Leah is going to kill you," Dakota said as uproarious laughter filled the room when people circled around the cake.

Leah popped out of her seat. "Why? Why am I going to kill Kyle?" She took a step to go see the cake, but her hand came back and wiggled at Carter. "C'mon, buddy."

Carter took her hand and allowed her to pull him to standing. He followed her to the cake and couldn't resist joining in on the laughter.

"Kyle!" Leah shouted, but she was laughing at the picture on top of the cake too.

Back in February, the weather had been unseasonably warm for a week. A great deal of snow had melted and the dirt roads had been reduced to total mud. Dakota had invited a bunch of them to go ATVing in a field near Birch Peak Adventures. It had basically been the guys tooling around in the mud getting filthy and loving every minute of it while the women refused to get that close.

Except for Leah. When Dakota had offered his ATV to her, she'd accepted the challenge. The only problem was she never made it to the ATV. One of her boots got stuck in the mud and she'd ended up flat on her face, wet, brown slop completely covering her. Carter had never seen a person so entirely encased in mud quite like that.

Dakota had rushed to her side and scooped her up, but there hadn't been anything he could do to immediately clean her off. In stepped Kyle with his phone to capture an epic picture of Dakota holding a filthy Leah in his arms. A picture that now graced this very large cake in front of all of them.

Leah's hair was a wild mess, the golden tresses caked with globs of mud. Her face was streaked with brown splatter and her purple jacket looked like an entry in some weird, earthy art show. Mud dripped from her body as Dakota held her. He, of course, was only dirty where she'd rubbed against him. Otherwise, he looked like the male model he always appeared to be.

Dakota slid his arm around Leah's shoulders as he regarded the cake now. "You looked like a swamp monster that day and I still wanted to marry you."

She shot her elbow into his side. "Gee, thanks." Her gaze went to Kyle whose eyes were full of humor. "And *you*... you better watch your back, sir. Payback will be forthcoming."

Kyle arched an eyebrow. "Bring it on."

"I want to say, for the record, I had nothing to do with this," Heidi said, holding her hands up. "I mean, I thought it was hysterical when he proposed the idea, but I never officially approved of my husband's choice here."

"I think the mud brings out your..." Carter angled his head at the cake, but Leah gave him a shove.

"Mud doesn't bring out anything," she said. "And let's hope there isn't any mud tomorrow. My white dress won't survive."

Cake was passed around to everyone and the party atmosphere continued until Dakota picked Leah up in a fireman's carry and announced he was kidnapping his fiancée. Applause and well wishes were showered upon the couple and little by little the guests filtered out.

Carter drove home to his cottage, passing Dena's house on the way and fighting the urge to pull into her driveway. To stomp up her front steps. To demand she not give up on them.

Patient. Leah had advised him to be patient and that made total sense. He'd be patient. Maybe Dena would see him at the wedding tomorrow, however, and realize she had to be with him.

Hey, a guy could dream.

Chapter Four

The fabric of Dena's purple bridesmaid dress rubbed against the bandage covering the still healing slice in her gut. When all the bridesmaids had tried on dresses two months ago, Dena had fallen in love with this particular dress. She'd been the one to convince the others to choose it. Now, she wished they'd gone with something less fitted, less form revealing.

Less sexy.

She didn't feel sexy. Hadn't since coming back from Rhode Island. She'd spent the week in baggy sweats and old T-shirts at home. When she'd gone into work yesterday, she'd worn jeans. *Jeans.* She never wore jeans to work. Getting up in the morning had always been an occasion to dress up to Dena. Sure, she worked in a sawmill where few actual customers came in because most of their business was lumber deliveries to various locations. Hardly anyone saw her during the course of a day. She spent most of her time hunkered down in her office, crunching numbers, entering data, and preparing reports. Still, she'd always taken pride in her appearance.

Until now.

Drawing attention to herself by presenting a put-together style was the last thing she wanted. In fact, if she could go about her daily business and be invisible, she'd love that.

No chance for invisibility today though. She had to make an appearance at the wedding. She owed her big brother and his fantastic bride that much.

But she wouldn't stay long.

And she positively wouldn't spend too much time with one tall, dark, and handsome video game developer.

Jacy had come over this morning so they could help each other get ready and she'd mentioned how Carter had looked a little lost at the rehearsal dinner. Dena pushed the guilt aside. She couldn't be responsible for how Carter felt. She had her own feelings in which to drown.

"I knew I shouldn't have eaten that second piece of cake last night," Jacy said, busting into Dena's bedroom and motioning for help with the zipper on the back of the bridesmaid dress. "I had to butter up my hips to get this dress on."

"Bullshit." Dena zipped up her sister. "You and I both know your ass is smaller than mine."

Jacy shook her head. "Look." She turned around and spun Dena so their backsides were visible in the mirror above Dena's dresser. "I'm pretty sure there's an extra inch or two on either side of my rump that you don't have, dear sister." Jacy faced Dena. "But of course, I ate three solid meals every day this week. You did not."

"I ate."

"No, you didn't. I looked in your refrigerator and everything Mom made you is still in there. Unless you ate nothing but cereal, you haven't eaten at all since you came back from Rhode Island."

Busted.

"I haven't been hungry. Must be the medicine I'm on to keep away any infection." She gestured to her midsection, not able to add *after being stabbed* to her sentence. Four times this week she'd awakened in a total sweat, certain Gary was leaning over her and preparing to carve out her intestines. Waking up like that sucked ass.

"I recommend having Carter as a snack after the wedding tonight." Jacy sat on Dena's bed to put on her shoes. "The man is clearly missing you, D, and he looks as if he could be delicious."

Dena put pearl studs in her earlobes and added the string of pearls around her neck. As she put on the pearl cuff bracelet, she turned to face Jacy. "Honestly, I miss him too."

"Then what's the situation?" Jacy got up from the bed and took a step toward Dena, causing Dena to back up. "It's not getting any better, is it?"

Dena shook her head. "I can't seem to stop myself from recoiling from anyone who reaches toward me. I keep seeing Gary and I feel as if I'm going to pass out. Yesterday, Noah went to give me a hug to welcome me back to the sawmill and I literally ran to the other side of my desk. I pretended that I remembered something I had to write down, but he knew I was avoiding the hug. I've known Noah my entire life. He wouldn't hurt me." She thrust her hand out to Jacy. "You're my twin, my best friend, and I can't even let you in my personal space."

Christine DePetrillo

"Oh, sweetie." The look on Jacy's face—one that looked like her own—made her heart ache.

But not enough to take those few steps and embrace her sister.

Instead she waved a hand. "Things will go back to normal after some time."

"Of course. You're a badass Brenton woman," Jacy said. "We don't let anyone get the best of us."

That had been true for the past thirty-one years, but did that kind of strength have an expiration date? Could it all be erased by one jackhole with a knife?

"Maybe..." Jacy began. "Maybe you should talk to someone. Like professionally. To help with the trauma of what you went through."

She'd considered this herself as she failed to get any sleep night after night. "I don't know. The thought of talking to some stranger..."

"A *Doctor* Stranger though," Jacy said. "Someone who could give you some tips."

Dena shrugged then glanced at the clock on her bedside table. "C'mon. We're going to be late if we don't get a move on." She wasn't looking forward to encountering Carter, but she wouldn't let Dakota and Leah down. Not on their wedding day. And she didn't want to talk about speaking to a therapist. The notion made her palms sweaty.

Twenty minutes later, Jacy pulled into their parents' driveway where glittering white heart ornaments dangled from all the trees lining the shoveled path to the barn. A significant amount of snow still blanketed Maplehaven, but something about the way the sun made it all glisten created a magical ambiance perfect for a winter wedding.

"I thought Leah was nuts for wanting to get married in March," Jacy said as she pulled the key out of the ignition, "but this actually looks beautiful."

"Yeah. It's not too cold out today. She got lucky."

"Of course she did. Leah is marrying our brother, one of the best guys in Maplehaven." Jacy pointed a stern finger at Dena. "And if you *ever* tell Dakota I said that, I'll smack you."

Dena managed a laugh. Leave it to Jacy to pull a chuckle out of her. "He is pretty great."

When Jacy and their father had brought Dena home from Rhode Island, Dakota was waiting for her at her house. Her front walkway had been shoveled, her driveway plowed, and a fire crackled in the fireplace, making a cozy welcome home. Dakota was always taking care of them even if they all teased each other mercilessly.

"Okay, enough of this nice talk. We don't want to slip and actually say something sweet to his face. It's our duty as annoying younger sisters to make his life miserable." Jacy grabbed her purse and opened the driver side door. "We can ease up today. He is getting married after all, but tomorrow, it's all insults, all the time."

Dena followed Jacy to the barn, careful in her heels on the few patches of snow still sticking to the bricked path. Immediately their parents came over to them.

"You haven't been sleeping," Chennie said to Dena.

"Well, nice to see you too, Mom." Dena looked at Jacy, wanting some backup.

"She's not eating either," her sister added instead.

"Rat." Dena stuck her tongue out at Jacy.

"Do you want to stay with us for a little while, Dena?" William asked. "Until things settle down for you."

She loved her parents for their concern, but she wasn't going to stay with them. "I'm okay, guys. Went to work yesterday. Things will be back on track next week. Don't worry." That sounded like a good plan even if she had her doubts about it.

From the look in her father's eyes, he had doubts too, but he didn't press her.

Bless him.

"Is Leah in the back?" Jacy asked, pointing to the little room her father had sectioned off in the barn with a removable wall.

"Yes," William said. "Head on back. I'm going to check on the guys." He dropped a kiss on Chennie's cheek, stopped to talk to a few guests who had come in and taken seats, then continued out of the barn to the house where the men were supposedly gathered.

Where Carter was no doubt hanging out, looking all gorgeous in his suit and tie and glasses. Dena hadn't been lying when she'd told Jacy she missed Carter. She did. Miss him. Quite a bit. He'd become important to her. The man was also a seriously good listener. When she thought about talking to someone about what had happened to her in Rhode Island, his name always popped up in her

69

head. He'd, of course, shared his secrets about losing his brother with her. If anyone would understand the ordeal she'd been through, he'd be the one.

Perhaps pushing him away had been stupid.

"There you are!" Leah made a beeline for Dena and threw her arms around her.

Instantly, Dena couldn't breathe. She yanked out of the embrace and winced when she saw the surprise—the hurt—on Leah's face.

Taking a few steps away from the bride, Dena held up her hands. "Sorry. It's not you. It's me. I just…"

"Oh my God, Dena…" Leah shook her head and clasped her hands in front of her. "No, I'm sorry. I shouldn't have rushed up to you like that. What was I thinking?"

"You weren't thinking," Jacy said. "You're only focused on one thing. Getting married."

"As you should be," Dena added. "Today is your day, my friend. My sister-in-law. You shouldn't be worried about anything else but saying *I do.*"

"Yes, but—"

Dena held up her hand. "I'm okay. We're all okay. We're going to enjoy watching you marry our brother."

"Despite our cautions that you don't know what you're taking on," Jacy added, earning a laugh out of everyone.

"Right. Dakota is officially your problem now. Good luck." Dena made the sign of the cross in the air in front of Leah.

"Dakota is a problem I want to have." Leah's blue eyes took on a dreamy quality that made Dena think of Disney princesses.

"I still think he slipped her a love potion or something." Jacy shook her head. "There's no other explanation for why she loves him."

"Be nice," Chennie chided. "Leah knows what she's getting into."

Leah did a little twirl in her wedding dress—a form-fitting stunner with lace sleeves, a heart-shaped bodice, and a swell of silk down the rest of her body. "I'm getting into a happily ever after."

Jacy and Dena both made a gagging gesture at the same time. Dena winked at her sister. Good to know her twin powers had been reactivated. Perhaps there was hope for more.

"Okay, let's get you all in line and ready to move," Chennie said as she organized everyone.

Dena did a quick check of her armpits because she felt as if her sweating had grown to an alarming level. In a few short moments she would see Carter. Have to loop her arm around his. Have to feel him next to her. So close. Every one of the guests' gazes would be on her. She hoped she could keep her shit together.

The music started and Leah let out a little squeal. "This is it!"

Dena had to admit seeing Leah's excitement lightened her own mood. Today was about love. The real deal. Love that would last a lifetime. Her brother had found that with Leah and Dena had to be happy for him. For both of them. She had to put her own issues aside and celebrate the treasure the two of them had uncovered.

And perhaps... someday... she'd be ready to let someone close enough to find that treasure for herself.

Heidi left first. Then Jacy. Then it was Dena's turn. Her heart hammered in her chest. She shouldn't be this nervous. This day was not about her.

She turned the corner and Carter was there. Waiting for her. A smile on his beautiful face. His elbow angled toward her. Ready to accept her arm.

I can do this.

She forced herself on wooden legs to step up next to Carter and loop her arm through his.

"You look like a movie star," he whispered to her, but he didn't give her a chance to reply. Instead, he took a step onto the aisle and she had to step with him.

While she focused on not freaking out over touching Carter, being that close to him, and having everyone in the audience look at her, Dena put one foot in front of the other. A warmth seeped from Carter's arm into hers. The brush of his suit jacket against her bare arm was... oddly comforting. His scent—something sandalwoodish—soothed her. She risked a glance up at him. His beard was neatly trimmed. His hair tamed with an elastic at the nape of his neck. The suit he wore fit him... well.

Very well.

He must have felt her gaze on him because he turned his head to look down at her when they were about to part ways before the archway where Dakota waited for his bride. One dark eyebrow rose over the rim of Carter's glasses.

"You totally miss me," he whispered as he released her to go to the groomsmen's side.

She proceeded to the bridesmaid's side, but once she'd gotten into position beside Heidi, she couldn't help but give Carter a smile.

****

Dena had been as stiff as a mannequin beside Carter as they walked along the aisle toward the archway. When he first saw her face, she'd looked so pale, her hazel eyes wide open, her blinking too rapid. He hadn't been sure whether to nudge her along into the procession or quickly escort her out of the barn altogether so she could have the panic attack brewing under her skin. The fact that she'd taken his arm had caused him to follow the scheduled wedding activity and lead her to their places on either side of the archway where Dakota waited for Leah.

When he'd caught her studying him as they'd walked, his heart had swelled. She may have pushed him away at her house a week ago, but obviously his absence had affected her. Maybe, just maybe, she regretted asking for distance. Or perhaps she'd had enough distance. Possibly his banishment was over now and she'd welcome him back into the fold. It was crazy how much he wanted that.

This past week had been the longest in history. Carter wasn't sure he could make it through another week away from Dena. Last night at the rehearsal dinner Leah had told him to be patient, but he was eager for the next phase of his life to begin. He'd been depressed about Chase for too long. He'd let too many years of unhappiness plague him. The time to finally move on was now, and he wanted Dena to play a major role in that moving on. He also wanted to keep away from the call of alcohol that was growing louder the longer he was alone, the longer he waited for Dena.

He was greatly encouraged by the smile she'd sent him upon taking her place near the other bridesmaids. A smile like that could fuel a man for days. As could the vision of her in that purple dress. It hugged every curve Dena owned and made Carter's fingers itch to get underneath it.

Her legs were toned and went on for miles. And the heels she wore… oh, God, the heels made a slideshow of sexual fantasies scroll through his vivid imagination.

Dena's long brown hair had been curled into large waves that rested on her shoulder, and though Jacy's hair had been styled in exactly the same fashion, Carter didn't have the urge to bury his hands in hers as he did Dena's. That hair would look amazing fanned out on his pillow as he trapped Dena below him and… and…

Shit. He had to stop this line of thinking or everyone seated in that audience would know exactly what kind of racy thoughts were running through his head. God, he hadn't had sex since moving to Vermont from New York. Too long. Carter shifted his weight from one foot to the other and thought of something other than how much he desired Dena.

Paper cuts. Sour milk. Cat vomit. Thinking of these things killed the mood a little, but he was sure if he glanced back at Dena, a new loop of arousal would begin. *Get it together.* His best friend was getting married for Christ's sake. Today was about celebrating Leah and Dakota and the life they'd start together. It wasn't about plotting how he could get Dena to pop the bubble she'd placed around herself.

But shit, he longed for a pointy stick.

Resigning himself to the fact there was nothing he could do about Dena at this particular moment, he paid attention to the ceremony. He kept a pleasant expression on his face. He clapped at the right times. He surveyed the crowd in their seats.

And then the groom kissed the bride and it was time to loop arms with Dena again. Carter reminded himself not to do a giddy dance, but to just get them safely down the aisle and over to the tables that had been set up beyond the ceremony area where the food would be served. Where he would be allowed the pleasure of sitting beside Dena for a meal. One she couldn't avoid. Carter wasn't above using the situation to his advantage.

"Beautiful ceremony," he said as they neared the head table.

"Very." Dena hadn't let go of his arm yet and he took that as a win.

"It's wonderful to see you."

She nodded. "Nice to see you too."

A few heartbeats of silence passed between them as Carter led them to the place cards with their names emblazoned on them. Dena slid her arm from his and picked up her place card.

"Wow." She whistled softly. "This calligraphy is amazing."

Carter rocked back on his heels. "Thanks."

Dena shot her gaze up to meet his. "You... you wrote these?"

"Every last one." He rubbed his left hand. "And Leah didn't let me take a break." She had, however, kept him supplied with chocolate chip cookies and fresh markers in exchange for his calligraphy skills.

"I didn't think men had talent like this in them." Dena picked up his place card and studied it. Something about seeing his name in her hands made a zing of pure joy shoot through him.

"Most don't." He lowered his head so his mouth was nearer to her ear. "I'm kinda exceptional."

A slow smirk turned up the right side of her mouth. "Humble too."

He gave her a slight shrug. "I learned to do calligraphy in art school. It relaxes me."

"Hmm. Maybe I should take some lessons." She rolled her shoulders, tension coming off her in waves.

Carter instantly wanted to fold her into a hug, but he knew that would be too much too soon. He had to go about this the right way or he'd send her running. "I'd be happy to teach you. I've seen your handwriting. You'd be a natural at calligraphy."

She put his place card down at his spot and looked up at him as if she were about to say something, but Jacy called her over for a family photo. "I'll be right back."

"I'll be right here."

Another smile came at him and if he were keeping score, the points would definitely be in his favor. This was going better than he'd hoped. He hadn't even turned on the charm yet. He did have the sense, however, that he had to be careful. He had to ease into earning a spot in Dena Brenton's life. He'd do whatever it took.

A hand clamped onto his shoulder and Carter looked to his right to see Noah Williams. They shook hands, forcing Carter to tear his attention from Dena-watching.

"You have a science geek T-shirt under that suit, right?" Noah teased.

"Went with my Superman T-shirt." Carter tapped his glasses. "I often get mistaken for Clark Kent anyway."

"And you've got your eye on a Lois Lane, don't you?" Noah motioned with his chin toward Dena, who was currently talking to her mother.

"I do, but I have to play it cool. I don't want to scare her away."

Noah nodded. "Smart man. Good things come to those who wait."

"I've always hated that saying."

"Yeah, me too, but it's true."

"And you would know, Noah," Krista Davidson, Noah's fiancée and the woman he'd been in love with since the third grade, said. They'd only started dating a few months ago though they'd known each other for decades.

"Hey, timing is everything." Noah slid his arm around Krista's shoulders and the way she snuggled in against him made Carter's desire for Dena nearly overwhelm him.

He grabbed the back of the chair in front of him for support. "Where's Luke?" Krista's son was the greatest kid Carter had ever met. He'd had the opportunity to spend a good amount of time with the boy as they'd bonded over their love of video games. Luke had turned out to be a superb tester. He also had lots of ideas for games that Carter had scribbled down in his idea notebook. One idea—a virtual Birch Peak Adventures game—had Carter seriously interested. As soon as he finished his current project, that was next in line.

Krista pointed to the far end of the barn. "Luke and two of Dakota's cousin's kids have discovered a mutual interest in card games." She shrugged. "As long as they aren't running around this barn I'm happy."

"And if you're happy,"—Noah pressed a kiss to her temple—"I'm happy."

Krista grabbed Noah's face and smooshed his cheeks a bit. "You'll want to remember that for the rest of your life, sir."

Noah gave her a salute then captured Krista's mouth in a kiss Carter didn't feel the need to witness. Fortunately, when he looked away, he saw Dena coming toward him. He liked everything about that scene.

"All pictured out?" he asked.

"Just about." Dena rolled her eyes. "I hate taking pictures."

"I love it," Jacy said as she sidled up to both of them and angled her phone so they could see a picture of Jacy and Chennie together. "I mean, when you look this good…"

"Another humble one." Dena shook her head.

"Hey, if you got it, flaunt it." Jacy did a little dance then scooted off to another table.

Dena let out a soft chuckle that sounded promising to Carter. "Sometimes I wonder how we could be related."

"Yeah, despite looking alike and ruthlessly teasing your brother, the two of you are opposites." It was interesting to Carter that though the Brenton sisters were identical twins and both gorgeous, he was only attracted to Dena. Something about her personality hooked him.

"Adds a good dose of variety to the Brenton family I suppose. It would be weird if Jacy and I were truly identical."

"A bad sci-fi movie idea for sure."

Another chuckle encouraged Carter as he pulled out Dena's chair.

"Thanks." She sat and he quickly took the seat next to her.

"Is it okay if I ask you how you're doing?" He reminded himself to keep a certain distance between them though all he wanted to do was pull Dena into his lap and make everyone else in the barn vanish.

Dena gave him a solemn look. "I'm okay, Carter." She blew out a breath. "And I probably owe you a massive apology."

He held up his hand. "Not necessary."

"No. It's totally necessary." She angled in her seat to face him, her knees nearly touching his thigh. *So close.* "You deserved better treatment than what I gave you when I came home. I just… I just…"

"You just experienced a traumatic event, Dena. I get it. Boy, do I get it."

"Which makes it even more awful that I treated you the way I did." Dena waved her hand at the guests milling about. "Out of everyone here, you and Leah are the ones who understand what I'm feeling. You're the ones I should be talking to most."

"So talk." Carter reached for her hand, but she quickly pulled it away, her eyes squeezing closed.

"I might be ready to talk," she said as she wrung her hands in her lap, "but touching is another thing."

Carter held up both of his hands. "No problem. Whatever you feel comfortable with is fine with me. I want to be here for you, Dena. I want to be whatever you need."

When she lifted her head to meet his gaze, her hazel eyes had tears in them. Nothing overflowing. Nothing hysterical. Just a glossiness that told him of her struggle. He'd never wanted to hold anyone so much, but he restrained himself. He could easily picture her fleeing from the table if he made any little move toward her.

"I need a friend." She took a drink of water then looked him in the eye. "Right now I need a friend, Carter."

Had he hoped she'd say she needed a night of untamed sex? Sure. Would he take being her friend? Absolutely.

For now. He wouldn't give up hope they would someday—someday soon—be more than friends.

"We are friends. Always." He gave her a reassuring smile. "You can even come over to play video games and I'll let you win."

80

A true laugh bubbled out of her, and he pumped his fist in victory.

"You totally have an unfair advantage seeing as how you *made* the games. You know all their secrets."

"We could play a game I didn't make."

"It won't matter. I suck at video games. There's too much on the screen for me to keep track of. I always end up getting ambushed by something I didn't see coming." The laugh she let out now didn't have any humor in it. "I guess that might be true of more than video games."

"It'll get better, Dena."

"Promise?"

"I'm living proof." He toyed with the silverware at his place setting. "I know I told you about Chase, but I didn't tell you about the drinking I did to try to cope. The drinking that led to the fighting. The fighting that led to a few trips to the police station." He stared at the table, replaying the various scuffles he'd gotten involved in purely because he was so torn up inside. "I couldn't get myself out of the loop, you know?" He looked up at her. "Only two things helped me dig out of that hole." He held up two fingers.

"What were they?"

"Moving here." He angled those two fingers at her. "And meeting you."

"Me? What did I do?"

"You gave me a reason to think beyond myself and my misery. You were the first person I told about Chase. You were the first person I *wanted*

81

to tell. Saying the story out loud… I don't know… it freed me. You freed me, Dena."

And he wanted to be the one to free her.

Chapter Five

Dena tidied the stack of informational handouts on her table at the Maplehaven High School Internship Fair. The event was held every year and usually Jacy handled this sort of thing. The sawmill needed to replace one of its delivery trucks, however, and William had put Jacy in charge of that today. Dena had fought. Nothing about sitting behind a table at her old high school for hours sounded attractive to her, but every community business was represented at this fair. Furthermore, Brenton Sawmill was *the* community business in Maplehaven, the first company in the town. Without the sawmill there would have been no Maplehaven.

So when William had instructed Dena to set up the sawmill's booth at the fair and, in her father's words *wrangle a good one*, she'd had no choice but to scope out the high school students looking for internships.

And she'd been doing that for three hours now without anyone showing any interest. Actually, that wasn't true. A few students had slowed down a few feet in front of her table, but then they'd scurried along. Dena went to the other side of the table now and checked her display. Was something off about the setup? Was something spelled incorrectly? Was her table uninviting?

No. Everything on the table looked wonderful. Neat. Colorful. Grammatically superior. So what was keeping everyone away?

Dena went back on the other side of the table and sat in the chair, her arms folded across her chest. In the absence of potential interns, her mind turned to the wedding.

And Carter.

He'd been an absolute sweetheart through the entire event. Staying close by, but not too close. He didn't keep reaching out to her. He didn't keep asking her if she was all right. He didn't smother or hover or make demands. And yet, he subtly checked in with her through smiles that said, *You're doing fine* or winks that said, *I know what you're going through* or raised eyebrows that said, *Do you need me to rescue you?*

She was tempted to nod to those raised eyebrows a few times, but managed to make it through the night without nodding. She did, however, keep her eye on him as he talked to other guests and her family members. Everyone who interacted with him ended up laughing, and she definitely didn't miss her cousin, Shelley, drooling over him. She couldn't blame Shelley. Carter Bennett was drool-worthy... especially in that black suit, purple dress shirt meant to match the bridesmaid dresses, and black tie. While she didn't mind his ultra-casual everyday look of T-shirts, flannels, and jeans, something about a dressed-up Carter got a little fire going in her belly.

Okay, maybe not her belly. Perhaps a bit lower. And maybe that fire wasn't so little either.

The fact that she could be turned on merely by looking at Carter was encouraging. Since the attack, she was worried she'd never be attracted to anyone, never want anyone in her space ever again. Being in Carter's orbit, however, had proven that to *not* be the case. In fact, several times last night her mind had wandered to what would have happened if she'd made it home on the night Carter had offered to properly welcome her back to Maplehaven. She was curious about that welcome home and that had to be a good sign she wasn't permanently broken.

Right?

Puffing out a breath now, she scanned the sea of high schoolers wandering from table to table. Except for her table of course. Teenagers were an odd breed. Old enough to think about what they might want out of life, but still unsure about how to get there. That was one of the main purposes of the internship fair—so the students could try on different jobs in the town for two-month periods and see if something led to their passion.

Dena hadn't attended the fair when she was a high school student. She'd had no reason to. Working at the sawmill had always been her goal even though she'd thought Dakota would be the one to take over running it. When he hadn't wanted it, her every career dream had come true. Since then, she'd never thought she'd made a mistake in taking on the responsibilities of the sawmill's finances. The job was a perfect fit for her mathematical, analytical mind. She was busy every day, and being able to see her father—though he was semi-retired—made the deal sweeter. She couldn't imagine her life without the sawmill.

So where are the interested interns? Surely three hours was enough time to get a bite.

She looked up, but it was still a ghost town in front of her table. Meanwhile *Sarah's Scents* across from her had a bunch of girls crowded around it, sniffing the samples Sarah had on display.

Should have brought a handful of sawdust with me. Sawdust was one of those irresistible fragrances. A manly scent. Better than any cologne.

Her thoughts turned back to Carter, who didn't appear to wear any cologne aside from whatever that sandalwood scent was she'd sniffed at the wedding. He often smelled like scented markers though, which made Dena grin. When she'd asked about the fragrance, he'd told her the "smelly markers" helped him think through his video game artwork designs better than "just some ordinary markers." She'd laughed at him, but had quickly stopped when he didn't laugh along. He hadn't been kidding. Smelly markers were a bona fide part of his creative process.

And that had made him sort of adorable.

He'd kept to his promise of being a friend last night also. After the music had kicked up and the dance floor had become the hot spot, Carter had asked her to dance to the first slow song that came on. She'd declined and he'd given her one of his smiles.

"I had to ask," he'd said, a sheepish expression on his face. One that had almost convinced her to leap into his arms.

He hadn't asked her to dance again, but he also hadn't taken anyone else into his arms when more slow songs played. Sure, he'd gotten it on when the fast, bass-heavy tunes pumped, but the moment the tempo wound down, he'd slipped off the dance floor. He'd busied himself with talking to a few guests also not dancing, but mostly he'd found her and did that witty, small-talk thing he did so well. She'd ended up laughing every time, and before she'd realized it, the night was over.

When he'd come to her side, his coat hung over his right arm, she'd gotten a little nervous he'd try to kiss her goodnight. After all, kissing had been their thing so far.

"I'm glad we got to spend time together tonight," he'd said to her.

"Me too."

"Yeah?" The surprise in his big brown eyes brought back her regret over telling him she wanted distance. She'd obviously hurt him even if he'd told her not to worry about it.

"Of course." Her hand had almost risen to touch him, but she hadn't been able to quite make the contact. Instead she'd said, "Never doubt that I enjoy your company, Carter."

He'd flashed another stunning smile. "And I yours." With a regal bow, he'd given her a wave. "Call me when you feel like hanging out. Ball's in your court, beautiful."

She'd nodded and watched him exit the barn, loving the respect he'd shown her. Nice to know not all men were like that douche Gary. Some were genuine gentlemen.

Carter Bennett was a genuine gentleman.

"Hey."

Dena flinched in her seat as the man currently consuming her thoughts appeared in front of her table. God, he looked sexy in his vintage Pac-Man T-shirt with an unbuttoned, black-and-white checkered flannel shirt over it and a pair of dark blue jeans. His "fancy" jeans as he'd told her once. The red classic Converse sneakers on his feet gave him an 80s vibe that made an automatic smile spread across Dena's face.

"Hey." She got to her feet and leaned against the table between them. "How's it going at your booth?"

Carter raked his hand through his hair, the longish strands pulling away from his face then falling back into place. He hooked the left side behind his ear and rubbed his slight beard. "I can't keep up. I must have twenty-five students interested in interning with me."

"Twenty-five!" Dena cast an embarrassed look around the immediate area after realizing her voice had been way too loud. Lowering her volume, she said, "Are you pulling my leg?"

Carter shook his head then adjusted his glasses on his nose. "I wish I were. Now I have to read all their applications and try to decide which one to choose." A semi-pained expression tightened his features. "I'll feel bad for the ones I don't choose. How do people do this every year? This is my first time, and while it's an awesome idea and wonderful opportunity for the students, there will be some disappointed kids."

"All part of growing up, I suppose," Dena said. "Competition out in the real world is tough."

"True." Carter shoved his hands in his pockets and rocked back on his heels. "I also have to remember that some of these geeks might make me obsolete at some point."

Dena waved a hand and puffed out a breath. "I'm sure Carter Bennett is always relevant."

His smile was instant, and hell, it drew her in. He had the capacity to make the rest of the world melt away with that smile. Someone ought to video it and prescribe watching it as a treatment for depression or something. Dena didn't see how anyone could be in a bad mood in the presence of that smile.

"So how many intern potentials do you have?" he asked.

"Ah... well..." She gathered her hair onto one shoulder and toyed with the curled ends. "It's been what I'd call a slow day." She shrugged. "I don't understand why though. When Jacy mans this booth, she always gets a bunch of signups. Then she, Dad, and I comb over the applications to choose one. I'm doing something wrong."

"Can I offer a suggestion?" Carter asked.

"Sure."

"I've been watching you... not in a stalker way." He held up his hands. "But in a she's-so-gorgeous-how-can-I-not-look-at-her way. The problem is, however, you're sitting and standing here like this." He folded his arms across his chest, furrowed his brows, and frowned.

She would have laughed if he hadn't been impersonating her. "I don't look like that."

He dug out his phone, tapped the screen a few times, then held it out. "I beg to differ, Miss Brenton."

Dena snatched the phone, convinced he was bullshitting her. No such luck. There in the palm of her hand was a picture of herself in the exact pose Carter had displayed. "Good God."

"Now don't get upset. I only showed you to prove my point." He took the phone back when she set it on the table between them. "And maybe to look at it later and imagine some fantasies where you get bossy with me." Giving the picture a final glance, he licked his lips then shoved the phone back into his pocket. "Maybe try smiling a bit and not looking so… intense."

He was right, of course. She was letting her non-interest in being at the fair keep students away. Her new personal policy of *Stay Away* wasn't right for this event… or for the sawmill. Her father was counting on her and she'd be letting him down if she didn't score at least *one* interested applicant. She'd also be wasting her time, and Dena hated wasting time.

"I'll consider your advice." That was better than telling him he was right.

Carter gave her a quick nod then glanced back at Sarah and her teenage groupies. Shaking his head, he looked back at Dena. "Why anyone would want to overload their sniffers on those candles and creams and whatever else she's got over there is beyond me?"

"Don't fancy the scents, Mr. Bennett?" Why did that please her?

"Ugh." He waved a hand under his nose. "Too many mixed together."

"Not at all like your smelly markers, huh?"

He pointed a finger at her. "Hey, don't make fun of my smelly markers. They are not to be mocked."

"Of course. You are, after all, a professional."

"Yes, I am."

"In a Pac-Man shirt."

"Now you're trying to pick a fight with me, beautiful." He narrowed his eyes at her. "I'm going back to my table to fight off the hordes of interested interns."

She stuck out her tongue, surprised at her sudden playfulness. Was Carter aware of his skill for relaxing her, in helping her fight off the demons?

"Don't tease me with that tongue," he said in a low voice that rubbed her in all the right ways. "You do understand it's taking all my willpower to stay on this side of the table, right? To respect your wishes?"

Her feet decided at that moment to take her around the table to stand in front of him. Her brain hadn't approved the move, but her brain wasn't in control at the moment it seemed. "Thank you, Carter." She looked up at him. "My wishes... well, they might be changing."

"Is that right?" One of his dark eyebrows rose over the top of his glasses. "Tell me more." He took a tiny step closer.

Dena's heartbeat kicked up several notches, but she squeezed her hands into fists at her sides, released them, squeezed again, released. "I don't know. The more I see you, the more what happened in Rhode Island fades away."

"Clearly you should spend more time with me then." Another step closer, but he slid his hands in his pockets. "I told you the ball's in your court and I meant it. We can take this as slow or as fast as you want." He settled that deep brown gaze on her. "I will play by your rules. I want to be with you, Dena. That simple truth hasn't changed."

Her throat was too tight to reply so she simply nodded.

It was time for her to face the truth as well.

****

Forcing one's body to do something it did not want to do was a weird thing. Carter had done that twice in the last two minutes. He'd kept his hands to himself when all he wanted to do was pull Dena up against him and kiss her until they had to come up for air. He'd also turned away from her table—away from her—and walked back to his table. His body wanted to fight him on both counts, but he'd promised her he'd let her take charge. He was pretty convinced the only way to start something back up with Dena was to let her set the pace, let her define the next step, let her only do what she was comfortable doing.

The waiting might kill me though. Telling Dena they could go slowly was easier than actually going slowly. Every time he saw her, he wanted to do everything he'd had planned for her welcome home from Rhode Island. His feelings for her hadn't waned. In fact, this time away from her had only made his desire grow. She was like forbidden fruit and he was dying for a taste.

Who was he kidding? A taste wouldn't satisfy him. He wouldn't be happy until he'd completely dined on her.

Her playful flirting at her table was a good sign. His patience and understanding was paying off. He had to stay the course.

"I thought computer geeks weren't supposed to be so hot."

Carter blinked at the two female students in front of him. "Excuse me?"

Giggling assaulted his eardrums. It reminded him of yipping small dogs. He'd never been a fan of small dogs.

"You don't look like a nerd," Giggler One said.

Giggler Two nodded. "The computer science club members at our school do not look like you."

"They'll *never* look like you," Giggler One added.

Carter shook his head. "Are either of you interested in video game development?" They certainly didn't look like his typical gaming brethren. Both were sporting short, tight dresses with more jewelry than was necessary. If they fell over the side of a boat, they would both hit bottom pretty quickly. He didn't want to unfairly judge though, so he gave them a moment to answer his question.

"No," Giggler Two said, looping her arm with Giggler One's. "We're hoping to intern with *Sarah's Scents*. We can't wait to test all of Sarah's products and learn how she makes them."

"It's going to be so much fun!" Giggler One did a little dance, turning Giggler Two in a circle. "We love smelling pretty."

"You sure you don't want to intern at the sawmill? I hear sawdust is a lovely fragrance as well." He could at least see them enjoying dressing up for a job with Dena.

"No way," Giggler Two said, shaking her head.

"We don't want to work in that dusty old place," Giggler One said as both girls scrunched up their noses.

Well, at least he'd tried to send some business Dena's way. It was probably best neither of these chicks were interested in the sawmill though. Somehow Carter could envision several catastrophes they could cause.

"Well, good luck with *Sarah's Scents*," Carter said, hoping that statement would send them along.

"Thank you," the girls said at the same time as they sashayed away.

Carter picked up the stack of business cards he had on the end of the table and put them in the plastic storage box. He grabbed the simple figurine he used for character movement design. He'd put it on display on his table to draw in the artsy types. Hopefully he'd find an intern in his stack of applications that was interested in both the tech and the art involved in video game design.

"Cleaning up already?"

"Already? C'mon, man. Tell me this thing is over," Carter said as he shook Dakota's hand. "I've been here for hours."

Christine DePetrillo

"Tell me about it. I'm not used to standing in one place for so long." Dakota pointed to the Birch Peak Adventures logo on his sweatshirt. "My business is all about *not* standing in one place."

"True. And you have a honeymoon to go on, don't you?"

Dakota's face lit up with a smile. "I do. Leah's packing the rest of our necessities and then we're on the next flight to Fiji. I can't believe she's willing to go that far."

"Dude, you've cured her of her travel fears."

"Love is some powerful shit."

"And you're such a philosopher too."

Dakota chucked him a subtle middle finger and they both laughed.

"Did you get any good intern potentials?" Carter asked.

Dakota nodded. "Yeah, we have a nice collection of candidates, but I think Krista and I have already agreed on one. I mean, we'll be fair and read all the applications, but you know when you just have a feeling about someone."

I sure do. But Dakota wasn't talking about Carter's feelings for Dena.

"What happens if a business doesn't get an intern?"

Dakota raised an eyebrow. "Traffic slow at your table today? Don't half these kids want to make video games?"

Carter tapped the stack of applications under his laptop. "No. *I'm* good."

Dakota swiveled and scanned the immediate area. He leaned toward Carter. "Was one of your neighbors unpopular over here?"

"Not so much unpopular as sending out a..." Carter searched his mind for the right words. "A *keep walking* vibe I guess you'd say."

Dakota pinched the bridge of his nose. "I know who you mean now. I told Dad not to let Dena man the table." He sifted out a breath.

"It's not her fault. She probably wasn't ready for this sort of thing." Carter swept his arms out, gesturing to the room around them. "Also, she's used to being the numbers person, not the human relations person."

"You're right," Dakota said, "but Dad's still going to kill her."

"Not if we help her."

Dakota snapped his fingers. "Brilliant." He surveyed the few groups of teens still wandering. "What about them over there?" He pointed to a pack of boisterous boys.

Carter joined Dakota on the other side of the table. "Too loud." He did his own scan and found a trio of girls who looked as if they were the type to discuss saving endangered species and two boys who resembled lumberjacks. "Them."

Dakota followed Carter's gaze. "Perfect. How do we get them to go over to the sawmill's booth?"

"You go over there, be all adventurous Dakota Brenton, and work your magic." Carter gave him a little shove toward the group.

"Magic? What magic?"

Carter shrugged. "I don't know. I'm not Maplehaven's Golden Boy, now am I?"

Dakota let out a grumble, but he started walking when Carter nudged him again. Within a few minutes of Dakota talking, all the teens were nodding then following him toward Dena's table.

Carter went back behind his table, content that Dena would soon have a few intern applications. He packed up the rest of his display items, but as he secured the lid on his storage box, he became aware of a presence on the other side of the table.

"Hi," he said to the lanky kid standing there.

"You're the video game guy?"

"I am." He extended his hand to the boy. "Carter Bennett."

"Rohen Sears." The kid had a firm handshake that immediately got Carter's attention. You could tell a lot about a person from the type of handshake they gave you.

"Rohen... very Middle Earth," Carter said. "I like it."

The boy gave him a half smile. "If only Middle Earth were a real place."

"I've often said that exact sentence." Carter pulled out one of his handouts and a business card. "That's why I make video games. I try to build a world I'd want to explore."

Slowly, Rohen raised his arm and took the handout and card. "That's why I like playing video games. They let me escape."

Carter wanted to ask what the boy wished to escape, but he'd just met the kid. "Ever try your hand at making them?"

Rohen nodded. "Simple stuff. Nothing like what you make."

"You're familiar with my work?"

The kid rolled his eyes. "C'mon, Mr. Bennett. Everyone who is into gaming knows your work."

"Well, I don't go around assuming that. I'd be a jerk if I did. And call me Carter." He slid an application out of the file folder he'd put into his storage box. "You want to fill one of these out?" He had more than enough intern candidates, but something about this kid compelled him to make room for one more.

Rohen took the application and as he scanned it, Carter couldn't help but notice an undercurrent of sadness in the boy's blue eyes. This kid was hurting over something. Something that didn't leave physical scars, but internal ones. Carter knew a thing or two about those kinds of scars.

"I'm not real good with words," Rohen said, wiggling the application, "but I can draw. Could I submit artwork with this?"

"Do you have some with you?" Carter asked.

Rohen nodded then opened the backpack he had slung over one arm. He rummaged around inside and pulled out a paper that had been folded into fourths. Without unfolding it, he dropped it on the table between them.

Carter picked it up and carefully unfolded the sheet. The picture that stared back at him made his mouth drop open. A fierce dragon with intense yellow eyes and sharp spiky scales nearly leaped off the page. The colors and shadows and details were unlike anything Carter had ever seen.

"This is like looking at an actual photograph of a dragon," he said. "You drew this yourself?"

Rohen gave him a small shrug. "I live in the group home down the street. There's not much else to do there and I'm not what you'd call *social*. I have a lot of time to draw."

Group home. So the sadness in Rohen's eyes had not been imagined.

"How long have you been in Maplehaven?" The skinny jeans the kid wore did not scream Vermont teenager.

"I've been here for about a month. I'm from L.A." He frowned. "I miss California."

"Don't give up. This place has a way of growing on you. I'm from New York myself, and although Vermont is quieter, slower, and greener than NYC, I've come to enjoy it here."

"I don't have a choice anyway. My parents are dead and the aunt I came to stay with in Maplehaven just died too. I'm told there's no more family to ship me off to so group home in Vermont it is. Until I'm eighteen next year. Then I'm out of here. Back to California."

This kid's tale is as sad as mine. Possibly sadder because Rohen wasn't old enough to make his own decisions about living arrangements. At least Carter had that option.

He also had the option to decide to give this kid a chance.

"Fill in your name and contact info on this form," he said. "I'll accept this artwork for the rest of the application." He looked at the dragon again. "It really is exceptional."

"Thanks." Rohen took the pen Carter held out to him and bent his blond head over the application as he wrote his name, address, and phone number in the blanks.

"Have you filled out any other applications today?" Carter asked.

"No. Art is the only thing I'm interested in." He waved a hand toward a table down one of the aisles. "The only other art-related booth is the art gallery. I'm not so much about having my work on display for people to view and walk on to the next piece. I'd rather have them... I don't know..."

"Live inside your art?"

Rohen's eyes widened as he looked at Carter. "Yeah. Live inside it. Exactly that."

Carter held out his hand again. "A pleasure meeting you, Rohen. I'm glad you stopped by my booth."

"Me too." Another firm handshake. Rohen hiked his backpack up onto his shoulder again, gave Carter a wave, and shuffled off toward the exit. His shoulders were low, his back slightly hunched as he disappeared out the auditorium doors.

Carter studied the dragon picture again. This was raw talent he could definitely mold and shape. He'd look at the other applications, but he was fairly certain he'd just met his future intern.

Still thinking about Rohen, Carter gave his table space another glance then picked up his bag and his storage box. Time to go home and find something else to do. His choices were slim. He could either work on his game or... work on his game. He couldn't bother Dakota and Leah as they'd be heading out on their honeymoon. Kyle and Heidi were both working at Mountain View Pizza tonight so they were busy. Noah and Krista were probably doing something with Luke on a Sunday night.

Bottom line? There was only one person he wanted to hang out with tonight. She was no doubt available too, but was she ready? Why did he have to be such a damn gentleman and respect her wishes?

Because that was the way his parents had raised him and Chase.

Sighing, he headed for the doors. He smiled when he saw several teens at Dena's booth, happy that she'd gotten some applications thanks to Dakota. He would have hated for her to have gone back to the sawmill empty-handed and feeling as if she'd disappointed her father. William wasn't the type of guy you wanted to disappoint. He was too nice.

"Carter, wait!"

He immediately stopped walking, but couldn't be sure he'd actually heard Dena call his name. He did have a vivid imagination after all. Perhaps he wanted her to talk to him so badly, he'd only thought he heard her.

Slowly, he turned toward her table and sure enough she was rounding it to come to him.

"Hey," she said, slightly winded after jogging over to him.

"Hey." He motioned back to her table with his chin. "Got some interested peeps after all?"

"Yeah. Enough to shut up my dad." She studied her hands for a minute then turned those gorgeous hazel eyes up to him. "Umm, listen, I've been thinking about what you said about the ball being in my court."

"Oh, yeah?"

She nodded. "And well… I'd like to get back into the game. With you. I'd like to get back into the game with you, Carter." The words all came out in one big rush as if she'd had to psych herself up to say them.

"What did you have in mind?" he asked, desperately trying not to jump around the auditorium in victory. She wanted to see him. It had been worth every hour he'd sat behind that table at his booth today if the end result was picking things back up with Dena.

"I was planning to do a little baking when I get home. Want to meet me there and help?"

"If by *help* you mean taste test, then yes, I'm in." If she'd asked him to help her clean her bathrooms, he would have been in for that too. He didn't care what the activity was. He just wanted to be in her company as much as possible.

"There will be taste testing." She gave him a small smile and he hoped to God more than baked goods were on the menu. "Go home and put your stuff away." She tapped the storage bin he held between them. "Then come on over."

"You're sure about this?" There was that damn gentleman again. He'd kill that guy if Dena said she wasn't sure.

"I'm sure." She gestured back to her table. "I was sitting there thinking that going home to my empty house tonight wasn't going to cut it. I don't know how much I can let you touch me, Carter. I'm still a little messed up here." She tapped her temple. "But I know I want to move past all this and I trust you to help me."

He felt as if he'd been given a prestigious award. "I'm honored you feel that way. You can trust me… to eat all your cookies, pies, cakes…" He grinned when she laughed. "I'll see you in a few, beautiful."

And just like that, his night had turned from pathetically lonely to potentially amazing.

Chapter Six

Dena had dropped the intern applications off at her father's house, happy to not have to tell him she'd failed at the task he'd asked her to do. Those teens that had come over in a little group at the end of the fair had saved her day.

Two of them had been super adorable. Their hand holding and the way they leaned toward one another as they'd stood at her table had told Dena they were dating. While the girl was interested in the actual lumber production portion of the sawmill's business, the boy had a bunch of finance questions Dena had loved answering for him. They were a cute pair. She'd starred both of those applications, thinking they deserved an opportunity to experience what they were interested in.

And speaking of things to be interested in… when was Carter going to arrive? She'd surprised herself yet again by asking him to come over. Something about seeing those two teens who obviously had a good thing going between them had her wanting the same. She could have that.

If she'd let herself.

When Carter had walked by her table, ready to leave the fair, she'd made the snap decision to spend time with him tonight. She hadn't planned on baking, but it'd seemed like the perfect guise for getting him to come over. Besides it would give them something to do and make things less awkward. Focusing on a task would allow them to ease back into things.

And what things *do I want to ease into exactly?*

She couldn't deny that being near Carter today, even briefly, had stirred something inside her. It'd been like that since she'd first met him on their blind date months ago. His casual charm instantly relaxed her. The fact that he wasn't pressuring her gave him a ton of points too. Most guys wouldn't be as patient as he was. She appreciated that about Carter, and despite how the incident with Gary had fucked with her, if anyone was going to help her get back on track, it was Carter.

She wanted it to be Carter.

Dena changed out of her business attire and slipped on purple leggings and a gray fleece sweatshirt. That was another thing about Carter. He didn't seem to mind comfortable clothes. She'd never dated anyone who she'd felt comfortable enough around to let him see her chilling clothes, but she didn't have to think about it with Carter. He didn't appear to associate his attraction to her with the garments she wore. The same could be said of her, regarding his style. Normally she wouldn't tolerate the scruffy, T-shirt-and-jeans look Carter regularly sported. He'd be a guy she'd dismiss on lack of fashion sense alone. Somehow, though, he'd wiggled his way onto her radar despite his unpolished approach to clothing. She possibly *liked* his style.

Shaking her head, she padded out to the kitchen in a pair of fuzzy sleep socks in a black-and-white cowhide pattern and began pulling out her mixer, bowls, wooden spoons, and all the ingredients to make her famous chocolate cake. Did she remember that particular cake was Carter's favorite?

Maybe.

Did she enjoy hearing the yummy noises he made whenever he ate it?

Definitely.

Chocolate cake was the perfect bridge to mending their budding relationship. The relationship she'd put the brakes on. The relationship she hoped could be revived.

As she pulled a new bag of dark chocolate chips from her hall closet, the doorbell rang. Dena smoothed her sweatshirt, her hand brushing over the bandage on her healing wound. She could do this. She could put the Rhode Island attack in the past and move forward tonight.

Move forward with Carter.

She opened the front door to a huge bunch of red balloons. All she could see of Carter was his legs sticking out from the bottom of the balloon bundle.

"You are a true clown, Carter." She reached out her hands and parted the balloons to expose his smiling face.

He shrugged, causing the balloons to shift up and down. "I've been called far worse. Trust me."

"By whom? Don't you charm everyone you meet?" She stepped aside and he wrestled the balloons into the foyer, following behind the bunch.

"Everyone? No." He shook his head. "Only a select few people appreciate my uniqueness."

"Well, count me among those people."

He beamed a smile at her. "I will gladly do so." He released the balloons so they floated to the ceiling, their curled ribbons dancing like springs. "My natural inclination is to kiss you hello. Would that be okay?"

The hopeful gleam in his brown eyes made her nod.

"I'd like a kiss hello."

He looked right then left. "From me, right?"

She swatted his chest and he grabbed her hand.

"Hey, just making sure. I don't want to do the wrong thing."

Dena leaned her forehead against his chest, the contact feeling completely natural and not at all Gary-esque. "Oh, Carter. I'm sorry." She craned her head back to look up at him. "Let's assume that you can do no wrong tonight."

"Oh, I'm sure I can do wrong." He gave her a heart-stopping grin, the corners of his eyes crinkling behind his glasses. "Especially if you let me anywhere near the dessert baking."

She cupped his cheek. "Kiss me, you clown."

Slowly, he lowered his head and dropped a soft, chaste peck on her lips. He pulled back slightly, his gaze meeting hers as if assessing the effect of his kiss.

"I'm okay. I promise," she said.

With the green light given, he rested his hands on her waist and nudged her closer. When their fronts touched, Dena held her breath for a second, expecting anxiety to well up inside her as he held her in place.

No anxiety came.

What came instead was a surge of arousal. Carter's hands were warm and strong on her hips. His scent wrapped around her. Something fruity. He must have been working on one of his games before he came.

Smelly markers should not be a sexy scent.

But it was tonight. Faint notes of ~~strawberry,~~ watermelon, and citrus filled her nose as she pressed closer to him.

"I've missed you, beautiful," he whispered.

His mouth captured hers and she was instantly swept into the kiss. Quick nibbles turned into a deeper melding of lips. When Carter ran his tongue along the seam of her lips, Dena opened to him as she skated her hands up his arms and clamped them onto his shoulders.

A low rumble sounded in Carter's throat, ratcheting up Dena's own desire. The sound was so primal, so male, so sexy. She wanted to hear it again and again. Wanted to feel the vibration of his chest against hers as he growled his pleasure. Relish the grip he had on her hips as he took possession.

How had she thought she could stay away from him?

Before she could have another thought about how wonderful Carter tasted, how amazing it felt to be in his arms, he ripped his mouth free of hers and blinked rapidly down at her.

She instantly missed his kiss. "What happened?" Things were about to get good and now he was easing back on the throttle.

Hell, no.

Running one hand through his hair, he puffed out a breath and took a step back. "I'm sorry, Dena. I promised to go slow, let you set the pace, and the moment I get my mouth on you, I go wild. My apologies."

Dena grabbed a fistful of his T-shirt. "There is only one thing you have to apologize for." She pulled him down a little so his face was level with hers. "Breaking that kiss. I want more, Carter. A great deal more."

He cupped her cheeks, the expression on his face so sweet, so tender. "I'm happy to hear you say that. I want the same, but we don't have to rush." He angled his head to peek into the kitchen. "And are those ingredients for your famous chocolate cake?"

"How can you think about cake right now?" Her entire body vibrated with a need for him. The cake was the farthest thing from her mind.

"Dena, I'm a man. I'm always thinking about food." He focused on her face. "Even after a gorgeous woman throws herself at me."

Her mouth dropped open and her hands went to her hips. "I did *not* throw myself at you, Carter."

"I don't know about that. Let's roll the video."

"It's a good thing there isn't any video," she said, laughing, "because I'm about to strangle you."

"Now, now." He tapped her on the nose as he squeezed by her to head to the kitchen. "There will be plenty of time to strangle me, tie me up, whips, chains, whatever... later."

"You're impossible." She followed him and squeaked when he turned around suddenly in the hallway.

"Yeah, impossible to resist." He grabbed her hand and tugged her into the kitchen. "Now let's bake some cake. Or more precisely, you bake some cake while I watch."

She shook her head. "If you want to eat some, you have to help." She'd missed this banter with Carter over the week she'd banished him. The teasing, the flirting, the jokes. He knew how to loosen her up and push her buttons in all the right ways. If ever a man existed who wouldn't hurt her, Carter Bennett was that man.

"Okay, okay," he said, stepping up to the sink and washing his hands. "I'll help, but don't blame me if the recipe flops."

Dena arced out her arms. "Never has a dessert flopped in this kitchen, sir."

"You've never had me as part of the equation." He sat on a stool at the island. "Did Leah ever tell you about the time I attempted to make a turkey dinner for my family?"

She shook her head as she washed her hands then opened the canister of flour. "What happened?" It was rare for him to share a family story. After they'd first met and he'd told her about losing Chase, she figured he preferred to not talk about his brother and parents so she hadn't asked about them.

"Oh, I thought I'd be super cool and deep fry the bird in the backyard. You know, give Mom the day off from slaving away in the kitchen." He rolled his eyes. "I'll shoot to the punchline. We referred to that Thanksgiving as The Extra Crispy Thanksgiving. I wasn't allowed to say the words *deep fried turkey* again." He chuckled then gestured to the materials on

110

the island between them. "So all this? Don't let me touch any of it."

"Okay." She raised an eyebrow. "I have other stuff you can touch later."

Carter rubbed his hands together. "I'm definitely up for that." He reached across the island and rested his hand atop hers. "As long as you are."

"I'm so up for it I almost can't concentrate on this cake business." She flicked a little flour at him, laughing when he flinched.

"You'd better concentrate. It'll kill the mood if there's no cake."

"We can't have that."

"No, we can't." He pointed to the bowl where she'd dumped the flour. "Now mix."

"Hey, it's my kitchen. You can't boss me around." She pointed to the cocoa powder and handed him a measuring cup. "And I'm sure you're not totally useless in the kitchen. A man who can create entire virtual worlds can surely handle the science of baking."

Carter took the measuring cup and the amount of focus he put into filling it with cocoa powder was ridiculously adorable. He bit his bottom lip as he leveled the amount with his index finger. It'd be a miracle if she got through the whole recipe without jumping over the island and stripping the clothes right off him.

They joked around throughout the assembly process, and about thirty minutes later two round cakes were baking in the oven. Soon the house would smell like cake—one of the world's best air fresheners.

"You want something to drink? Beer? Wine?" she asked.

"Water would be great." Carter studied his hands on the island for a minute. Hadn't he said something about drinking and fighting in New York? Was he still vulnerable to alcohol? Was he afraid to misuse it? She'd seen him drink beer and wine before without any disastrous outcomes.

Perhaps he was a little fragile right now.

Because of her.

After filling two glasses with water, she angled her head toward the living room, intending to make sure he didn't feel fragile anymore. "While we wait for the cake to bake, I believe the couch is a good make out area." She rounded the island to stand in front of him. "We have some catching up to do."

"That we do." Carter stood, took one of the glasses of water, and held it up between them. "To catching up."

They clinked glasses and took a sip. Dena then slid her hand into Carter's and tugged him into the living room. She set her glass on the coffee table, as did he, before they both lowered to the couch, moving throw pillows adorned with cows and barns.

"I'm glad you're here," she whispered.

"Me too." He brushed his lips against hers in the softest of kisses. "Let me show you how glad."

Dena returned his kiss and knew inviting Carter over had been the smartest thing she'd done since coming back from Rhode Island.

****

Carter was relieved he'd made it through the cake-baking segment of the evening. It'd been a struggle. Sure, he'd been the one to slow down their evening, but immediately after doing so a little voice in his head asked, *What the fuck, man?* Dena had been all fired up and willing to jump to the naked portion of the night and he'd actually been the one to stop them. He should turn in his Man Club card.

But we're on the couch now. The couch Dena had deemed a good make out area despite the insane number of cow-themed paraphernalia she used in her decorating. He'd asked her about that collection in the past and she'd asked him if he'd ever visited with a cow.

He hadn't.

"They are such gentle souls. I've never met a cow who wasn't a total sweetheart," she'd said.

He still hadn't visited with any cows in Vermont, but maybe he would.

The house was starting to smell like chocolate cake, an indication that several of Carter's hungers would be satiated soon.

He pulled Dena into his lap and loved how her legs automatically went to either side of his waist. She fit so perfectly there, her lovely ass atop his thighs, heat radiating off her. When she slid her hands up his chest and burrowed them under his flannel shirt, his breath caught in his lungs. She really meant to give him more tonight.

This was it.

Dena eased the flannel shirt off his shoulders and peeled it down his arms. Carter helped by grabbing the cuffs and pulling his arms out of the sleeves. He leaned forward and let the shirt drop behind him on the couch.

"Is it too cold in here?" Dena left his lap for a moment to throw a few more logs on the fire in the living room's wood stove. "There. That'll be better."

"The only thing that will truly heat up this room is if you get naked," Carter said.

"Prepare to boil then." Dena stood in front of him as he remained seated on the couch. Her hands went to the hem of her fleece sweatshirt and in one swift motion that garment sailed over her head and got tossed aside. Her hunter green bra with black lace trim showcased her breasts in such divine fashion. Carter couldn't look away.

There is a God. Only a supreme being could have made Dena Brenton.

The only thing that marred her perfection was the rectangle of white bandage below her rib cage. Seeing that made Carter want to track down Gary Jackass and rip him to shreds. He sincerely hoped that guy got what he deserved.

Carter tugged her closer and ran his fingertips over the bandage. "Does it hurt still?"

Dena shook her head. "No. It appears to be healing well too. Probably a small scar. No big deal."

He encircled her waist with his arms. "But it was a big deal. When I think of how bad things could have been, I... I..." *Want to drink an entire bottle of whiskey.* He shook his head, squeezing his eyes shut. Her soft palm against his cheek made him open his eyes and look at her as she climbed back onto his lap.

She wiggled a little and he lost all sense of coherent speech for a moment.

He took her hand and kissed her knuckles. "I've been looking forward to being with you, beautiful. I'm not sure what took us so long."

She played with his hair and that simple contact increased his desperation to have her. "I think we had some clutter to clear out of the way first. You weren't quite ready when you first told me about Chase, when you moved to Vermont."

Carter puffed out a breath. "You're right. I was still broken. Spending a few months getting to know you—kissing you—mended some things."

"Doctors should prescribe a dose of me."

"You're a miracle drug." A better remedy than any drink he'd had. He hooked his hand on the back of her neck. "Only for me though."

"Don't want me treating half the town?"

He shook his head. "I want you all to myself, Dena."

"You have me." She worked his T-shirt off and let her fingers glide down his chest, sending a shiver through him. Her pupils were huge, black pools as she surveyed him. "You have a lot of muscles for a video game nerd."

Carter chuckled. "Working out helps me when I'm in the design phase of a game."

"Well, your working out helps me get ridiculously turned on." She leaned forward and pressed her lips to his jaw, his collarbone, his shoulder. Her hair tickled his exposed flesh, but he couldn't move. She'd paralyzed him with her soft kisses of exploration.

He ran his hands over her bare back, searching for the clasp on her bra. With a flick of his fingers, her breasts were freed and pressing against his chest. Her taut nipples teased his skin as she moved and he was instantly taken to the edge.

"Looking at you gets me ridiculously turned on." He shifted so he could ease her down onto her back on the couch. "We need to make these pants disappear." He reached up and grabbed the waistband of her leggings. "Ah, no zippers or buttons. Very convenient."

"I didn't want anything to slow you down."

"You could have answered the door naked. That would have allowed us to skip several steps."

"Says the guy who insisted we make cake first."

"Hey,"—he pulled her leggings off all the way, along with her socks—"you can't promise a guy chocolate cake and then not deliver."

"Oh, I plan on delivering." She sat up and went to work on relieving him of his jeans.

He helped by pushing off his sneakers, ripping his socks off, and shimmying out of his pants and boxer shorts.

Something of a purr rumbled out of Dena and the noise only intensified Carter's massive erection.

"I like that you're only wearing your glasses right now," she said as she removed her panties then curled a finger at him.

"All the better to see you, my dear." He crawled up the length of her, hovering on his elbows when he reached her head. "And I like what I see."

"Show me how much."

He didn't need to be asked twice. They'd waited long enough. He captured her mouth, his tongue sliding along hers, each taste leaving him wanting more, needing more. Her lovely breasts beckoned to him and he gave each one the attention it deserved. When he kissed a line between the valley of her breasts, she shivered beneath him.

"Carter…"

He lowered so his body rested atop hers but only halfway. He didn't want to press against her injury and cause her any pain. Tonight was about pleasure only. Pleasure that would take them to that next level Carter wanted so badly. What they were about to do would mean he was finally living again.

Pausing only to grab a condom from the pocket of his jeans and put it on, Carter teased her with the tip of his arousal. Finding her more than ready for him, he slipped into her, losing himself in her heat. She surrounded him and natural instinct took over. He pumped in and out, in and out, and soon they found a synchronous rhythm that brought them both to the peak.

Carter swallowed her moans with passionate kisses, his mouth and tongue mimicking what they were doing with their lower bodies. Everything about being with Dena like this was absolutely amazing. He felt as if he'd been selected to get a glimpse of heaven.

And he wanted to look his fill.

Dena widened her legs, taking more of him into her wet, hot core, and when her muscles pulsed around him, he let out a roar. His pace intensified, but then he slowed down when they were toe-to-toe with the breaking point, drawing out the pleasure, heightening the anticipation, raising them to new summits.

When Dena finally shuddered beneath him, her legs wrapping around his waist and his name slipping from her lips over and over again, he followed right behind her. There wasn't a piece of him that hadn't been brought online by their lovemaking. Never had he experienced something so fully. He swore he lost some of himself, but he didn't give a damn. He'd siphon off everything he had to be with her like this.

Slowly he eased out of her and loved when she repositioned on the couch to make room for him beside her. She snuggled up against him and pressed kisses to his jaw.

"That was—"

An oven timer dinged so loudly they both jumped.

"Shit." Dena raised up to her elbows and glared toward the kitchen.

"That was shit? Nice, Dena. Real nice."

She slugged him in the shoulder. "Don't be a punk." She let her kneecap rub gently against his balls and that massage made a moan rumble in his throat. "That was as far away from shit as anything could be."

"Agreed." He leaned forward and kissed her nose. "And we'd better go rescue that cake before it does turn to shit."

"But I want to cuddle here with you." The pout her lips formed was lethal.

He nipped at her bottom lip then gave her a full kiss in which she enthusiastically participated. "We can cuddle after we finish the cake."

She regarded him for a quiet moment. "Will you stay? Overnight?"

"Are you inviting me to?" His penis liked that idea. Staying overnight might mean junior would see more action.

Dena sat up all the way and reached for his flannel shirt behind him on the couch. "Yes, I am inviting you to spend the night with me." She looked away for a moment as she poked her arms into the sleeves of his shirt. She buttoned two buttons in the middle so her neck and stomach were still exposed as well as those go-on-for-miles legs of hers. All that silky brown hair was cascading over her shoulders and streaming down over her breasts. The image of her in his shirt, looking sexier than any supermodel he'd ever ogled, tattooed itself onto his brain.

"I would love to stay." He stood, rid himself of the condom, and pulled on his boxers. Bringing her closer by tugging on his shirt, he whispered, "Thank you for the invitation."

She waved a hand at the couch behind him. "You earned it." Reaching up on her tiptoes, she dropped a kiss on his lips.

"Maybe I'll get the chance to earn other perks?" He arched an eyebrow, hoping she was game for more shenanigans later.

"What other perks did you have in mind?" She picked up his T-shirt which he shrugged back into as he followed her into the kitchen.

"See, I have this idea of not only frosting a cake, but..." He motioned to her body and licked his lips as he picked up the spatula she'd left on the kitchen island.

"Wasn't I sweet enough for you?" She turned toward the oven. When she bent slightly to open the door and pull out the cake pans, his flannel shirt rose up on her to give him a teasing peek at her superb ass.

"Sweet? You?" He came up behind her and trailed a series of kisses along her neck. "You're too sexy to be sweet."

She set the cake pans on racks to cool. Pulling off a set of oven mitts, she turned to face him. "You're the only one who makes me feel truly sexy, Carter."

"How can that be? Surely, there have been others before me who appreciated all this." He corralled her against the counter with an arm on either side of her body. The way she'd buttoned—or *not* buttoned—his shirt was killing him. He wanted more of his hands and his mouth on those wonderful breasts that kept peeking at him from beyond the flannel.

Dena gave him a small shrug. "I've been with others." She held up her hand. "Not too many. Maplehaven is a tiny town after all, but no one has ever... worshipped me as you just did."

He leaned in to steal another kiss. "Well, from now on it's all worship, all the time."

"I like the sound of that." She ran her hands over his chest and then latched them at the back of his neck. Her body pressed against his and that cake was quickly becoming something he didn't give a damn about. "I promise to worship you back. How's that for a deal?"

"One I cannot refuse."

"Excellent. Let's seal the deal while these cakes cool."

He didn't have to be asked twice. In one swift move, he scooped her up and deposited her on the kitchen island. He swept anything she had on that island out of the way then pulled her by the legs. Her flannel-clad ass slid to the edge of the granite and he opened her legs. He undid the few buttons on his flannel shirt to expose her to him.

"You are exquisite."

"Even if a little damaged." She pointed to the bandage.

Again, the urge to find Gary and pound him to a bloody pulp surged through Carter. "Did you file charges against that scumbucket?"

"I did." She cleared her throat, her face serious. "Turns out Gary has attacked women at conferences before. He gave me some story about his wife leaving him, but I think that was all an act to get some sympathy or something."

Carter clenched his teeth. "Tell me he's going to get some jail time." If not, he wasn't going to *think* about hunting Gary down anymore. He was going to do it.

"I talked to an officer from the Providence Police Department and there will be a trial. None of the other women he's assaulted wanted to press charges."

"But you're going to?"

"Hell, yeah. The only thing that makes me sicker than the fact that he attacked me is that he could do it again to someone else. He has to be stopped." She trembled slightly as she said that.

"You'll have to see him again at the trial."

She nodded, her hands gripping the edge of the countertop.

"If you need someone to go with you, I will. I'll do whatever you want. I'm here for you."

Smiling, she wrapped her arms around his shoulders. "You are a bona fide nice guy, Carter Bennett."

"Uh-oh. Does being a nice guy get me marooned in the friend zone?"

"Shit, no." She shook her head vigorously. "I like making love to you way too much to put you in the friend zone. You're in the lover zone. Right where I want you."

Right where he wanted to be.

Chapter Seven

Dena's dreams had been different last night. Since the attack, nightmares of Gary had plagued the dark hours as she'd stared at the ceiling in her bedroom. Alone. Afraid. Covered in sweat. Pain throbbing at the slice in her gut.

But not last night. Not with Carter's muscled body spooning hers. Not with his strong arms wrapped around her. Not with the steady rhythm of his breathing keeping her company.

They'd frosted that cake after he'd done scandalous things to her with his mouth. She'd never look at that kitchen island the same way again. Even frosting the cake had been erotic with Carter putting frosting... everywhere. And dutifully licking it off. Then he'd taken the decorating bag, filled it with vanilla frosting, and had drawn a moon and stars on the base of chocolate frosting on the cake.

"In honor of our first leveled-up night together," he'd said, licking frosting off his finger and driving Dena absolutely wild. Who knew baking a cake could be such foreplay?

"We should make this cake annually from now on." She'd slid her finger along the frosting bowl and held it up to him, allowing him to take her finger into his mouth and send her a little more over the edge.

"Planning to be with me for at least a year, huh?" He'd rested his hands on her hips, a cocky grin turning up the corners of his mouth.

She'd shrugged one shoulder. "What else am I doing? At least you're entertaining."

His mouth had dropped open. "Is that all I am?"

"You're a gifted artist." She'd pointed to the cake. "Those stars are perfection."

"Any other skills of mine you've recognized this evening?" He'd nosed around in her hair, his mouth finding her earlobe and his teeth clamping on gently.

"It's possible you know how to use that mouth of yours."

He'd pressed his erection against her. "Just my mouth?"

That had been the point where he'd scooped her up into his arms and carried her to her bedroom. They'd made love again, eaten cake, watched a movie, made out, given each other massages, and finally fallen asleep wrapped up in each other.

It'd been the best night of Dena's life.

Lying beside him now, she studied his profile as he slept on his back. She'd never really seen him without his glasses before, but they were on the bedside table now. His eyelashes were super long, fanned against his cheeks, and she wondered if they hit the lenses of his glasses when he blinked. He had two freckles under his left eye she'd never noticed and slight indentations on either side of his nose from where his glasses always rested.

His full lips were surrounded by his slight beard—the beard that had scraped delightfully along her skin when he'd kissed her. The man was thorough. He hadn't missed an inch. No one had ever paid such careful and complete attention to her before and she feared he'd spoiled her for all other men.

Not the worst thing. Maybe he was it for her. Perhaps there would never be any other men.

That thought should have freaked her out a little, but it didn't. In fact, it filled her with such contentment that she hoped it was how things played out. She could see herself with Carter long-term.

"Do you always stare at your bedmates?" Carter's voice was scratchy as he opened his eyes and turned his head to see her.

"How did you know I was staring at you? Your eyes were closed."

"When these don't work so well," he motioned to his beautiful brown eyes, "you hone the other senses."

"Oh, so you *heard* me staring at you?" She pressed a kiss to his bare shoulder, loving that he was the first person she'd interacted with today.

He shook his head. "Don't be ridiculous." He shifted to his side and burrowed his fingers into her hair. The way his fingertips raked along her scalp made her close her eyes. "I smelled you staring at me."

She laughed and opened her eyes to find him smiling back at her. "Must be the pheromones I'm putting into the air because just looking at you has turned me on."

"Yeah?"

"As if you don't realize how hot you are." She rolled her eyes. "When you first moved here, I overheard a bunch of women at Mountain View Pizza gossiping about Leah's sexy New York friend."

"And how did that make you feel, Miss Brenton? Curious? Interested? Jealous?" He tugged on her hair.

"Jealous, for sure. We'd already had our first date. I wanted to pull a chair up to their table and inform them that you were potentially taken."

Carter pressed his mouth to hers in a steamy kiss that ought to become her standard wake up every day. "No *potentially*, Dena. I've wanted to be yours since that date." He frowned, his nose crinkling. "Actually that was the only *real* date we had. You know, one where we got dressed up and went out into the world together. All of our other... encounters have been here, at one of your family members' houses, or at my place. I owe you another real date, beautiful."

"Yes, you do. And big points for coming to that conclusion on your own."

"I'm on it." He sat up and grabbed his glasses. When he turned to look at her with them on, he did this exaggerated flinch. "Oh, hello. When did you get here?"

"Goofball."

"An accurate label." He kissed her on the nose. "Today is Tuesday. Want to go on our real date this Friday night?"

"Yes, please."

126

"Cool." The blankets pooled at his waist and bared his chest to her. She instantly wanted to touch him. "I know exactly where to take you."

"Where?" She sat up too and circled his pecs with her index finger.

He caught her wrist to stop her from continuing her journey along all his delectable muscles. "It's a surprise."

"You are such a tease."

"Says the woman sitting beside me with her perfect breasts on display."

She leaned back on her arm, arching her back slightly, and Carter let out a groan. "If you're not going to play fair, neither am I."

Before she could react, he had launched himself onto her, rolling them both so she was beneath him. "Do we have time for some play right now?"

Dena craned her head to see the alarm clock on her bedside table which announced 6:30 a.m. in neon green numbers. "We have a little time. I am planning to go to work today."

"I can work with a little time." Carter disappeared under the blankets and when his lips pressed against her inner thigh, she let out a moan. "Oh, yeah. I can definitely work with a little time."

He teased her with his mouth and his hands and his very presence. How would she ever wake up alone after this? His teeth grazed her hip, his beard tickling her flesh as he moved to her belly button. He was careful to work around the bandage and travel up to her breasts, giving each one attention until she repeated his name again and again.

She reached down and wrapped her hand around his arousal, eliciting a growl from deep within his chest. The sound did as much to get her ready for him as did his prior ministrations.

"The bedside table," she said, her breathing rate reaching pant level. "In the drawer."

Carter sat up and she got a prime view of his gloriously naked body. His abs bunched as he reached toward the bedside table and pulled open the drawer. He must seriously balance out all that sitting he did while working on his games with an intense exercise regimen. Abs like that didn't sprout on their own. The vision of Carter working out was enough to propel her half into an orgasm.

Fortunately Carter had located the box of condoms and was already sheathing himself. She'd have to keep more of them on hand if they were going to be doing this more often.

And how I want to do this more often.

"Breakfast is served," Carter whispered as he slid into her.

Again, that rhythm, that synchronicity between them was automatic. No fumbling around. No hesitation. Just instant connection. A melding so instinctual there was no denying Carter was made for her.

"You feel so good around me." Carter changed his angle and increased his pace.

Dena ran her hands over his back. "I love having you inside me."

When she'd first come back from Rhode Island, the thought of anyone touching her made her physically sick to her stomach. After a week away from Carter, however, she'd quickly realized it wasn't a matter of touching in general, but a matter of *who* was doing the touching.

Carter had an all-access pass to touch her whenever he wanted. His touch was both gentle and consuming, reverent and hungry. With each caress, Dena felt more cared for, more cherished, more... loved.

Drunk on the sensations Carter caused in her body, Dena exploded with pure bliss as she came apart beneath him. He shattered around her at the same time and they were both left quivering in the afterburn.

"I like a man who can work with a little time."

He laughed into her shoulder as he nuzzled her neck. "Make no mistake, I can work with all night too."

She shivered beneath him. "Good to know, stud."

They caught their breaths as they held each other until Dena finally said, "I'm going to be late."

"I can be okay with that." Carter didn't budge and because his body was half atop hers, she didn't budge either.

"You have to plan our date for Friday."

"I have plenty of time." He lifted his head to look at her. "You're okay with fast food, right?"

"Carter Bennett, fast food is not a *real* date." She sailed a light punch to his bicep.

"I know, I know. It's not a real date unless the napkins are cloth. Leah taught me that way back in the day."

"Remind me to thank her." She kissed him. "Now get off me."

Grumbling, he did as she asked. "So do we have to wait until this real date to see each other again? I'm not going to lie to you. I don't want to wait."

"Friday is a long way away, isn't it?" She went to her closet, but turned to look at him sitting on the edge of her bed. God, she loved having him there. Especially naked.

"We can't have a night like last night or a morning like this morning and then go four days before seeing each other again." He shook his head. "That has bad idea written all over it." He stood and walked over to her, those abs putting on a show again. "Come over after work today."

"Okay." She wasn't going to pretend she didn't want that invitation. "I'll pick up a pizza at Mountain View."

"I'm loving that idea. And bring some of that chocolate cake. I promise to have me waiting for you." He pulled her into a hug, his skin warm against hers.

"I might want you first then the food." She slid her arms around his waist, not wanting to part ways with him.

"That can be arranged." He dropped a kiss on top of her head then nudged her aside to consider her wardrobe. "Let's see..." He selected a pair of black leggings and a green and black checkered flannel dress. "Wear this today with those black boots. The ones with heels." His smile widened. "I love those black boots."

With another quick kiss and a *see you later, beautiful,* he waltzed out of her bedroom, his fine ass giving her something to watch as he retreated. It was a shame he was getting dressed downstairs and preparing to leave. She could easily picture spending the entire day lounging around with him.

I don't lounge. At least she hadn't. Not in eons. Maybe it was time to revisit that particular hobby. Lounging could be fun with the proper partner.

Thirty minutes later, Dena was dressed and on her way to the sawmill. As soon as she pulled into the parking lot behind the main building which housed the offices, her father came out to greet her.

"Hey. I wasn't sure if you were coming in today," he said after kissing her hello.

"Plan on me resuming my regular schedule from now on." She walked into the building with him.

"Only if you're ready to come back full time, Dena. I understand if you need more time." Her father slid his arm around her shoulders and that touch didn't bother her either.

Kind touches. Those were the touches a person could get in Maplehaven. Touches a person could trust.

"I'm ready."

Her father faced her and rested his hands on her shoulders. His blue eyes narrowed as he studied her face. "You look ready."

"Okay," she said slowly, not loving the scrutiny. Could a father tell when his daughter had enjoyed fabulous sex? She cringed, hoping the answer to that question was a big *NO*.

"What's changed?" her father asked. "At the wedding, you still seemed a little…"

"Crazy?" She entered her office, William on her heels.

"No. Quiet. You seemed quiet. As if you wanted to be left alone."

She opened her laptop and waited for it to boot. "I did want to be left alone then. I was working my way through what happened in Rhode Island. I'm past it now." She motioned to her midsection. "This is healing nicely." And hadn't been a turn off to Carter, thank God. "I can't spend my life playing the hermit because I'm afraid of what might happen. I've got to show life who's in charge." She pointed at herself. "Me, I'm in charge."

A smile bloomed on her father's face and he clapped his hands together. "I'm so happy to hear you say that. You're a strong woman, my Dena. I knew you'd bounce back."

"You know us Brentons, Dad. Nothing keeps us down."

Except sexy video game developers who had a free pass to keep her down on her bed whenever he wanted.

****

Carter spent the next few hours sketching like a madman. His office was littered with pictures of an Ergon army—an army he'd invented that predated the Galakot warriors in his *Andromeda Rebellion* games. He still had some work to do on the imposing form of Prime General Tritell, a key new character who would lead the army on its biggest mission yet, but he'd get all the details down in time.

"This game is going to be epic," he said to himself. He'd long ago given himself permission to talk aloud even though he was alone. When you worked from home and didn't have any colleagues present in real life, you had to do something to keep the workplace lively. Talking to himself, acting out battle moves in front of a mirror so he could accurately draw them, and eating lots of red licorice added some interest to his otherwise lonely day.

He wasn't completely alone though. Not technically. His house was filled with his characters, and when he was deep in the development stage, those characters were a genuine presence to him. Their voices were loud and excellent company. Of course, he'd never say that to anyone lest they think he was a little unhinged.

Today's drawings had an added layer of excitement because he couldn't wait to show them to Dena when she came over that night. He rarely shared his work before it was an actual game, but he looked forward to getting her opinion on what he'd accomplished so far. She had a sharp eye—as evidenced by her gorgeous desserts and stylish outfits—and she didn't sugarcoat stuff. She'd offer him solid feedback and not tell him shit to inflate his ego. He could trust her to be honest.

He could also trust her to rock his body. Last night had been amazing. He'd often daydreamed about what it would be like to be with Dena, but his expectations had been far exceeded by the actual lovemaking. When she'd invited him over, he hadn't been sure what to expect or if she'd be truly ready to pick up where they'd left off before her ordeal in

Rhode Island. He'd planned to stick to his promise to let her determine the pace of their relationship. One look at her last night, however, and his body had reacted in the most instinctual of ways. He couldn't have made it through the night without touching her.

Thank God she'd wanted his touch. Had seemed to need it. Fine by him. And her invitation to stay the night had put him over the top. Something magical had begun last night and he was eager to spend more time with Dena.

Right now, however, he needed to work on some setting design. The Ergon army lived deep in the Rydinian Forest, so perhaps it was time to take a walk in the woods behind his cottage to pick up some inspiration. He grabbed his sketchpad and a pencil and walked toward the back door of the small house. As he donned his jacket, he scanned the living room.

"Next order of business after this walk is to make this place presentable." While he wasn't a slob, he did have the tendency to leave his work spread throughout the house. More sketches and notes covered the coffee table along with two half-full cans of soda and a nearly empty bag of tortilla chips. The throw pillows on the couch—which he hated, but Leah insisted he needed—were all collected on one cushion. A blanket his grandmother had knitted him so many years ago was piled on the floor between the couch and the coffee table.

His slippers were under the coffee table and the fact that there were holes in both of them probably earned them a place in the garbage. Then he'd have to replace them though and he hated that idea for many reasons. Those slippers were so comfortable. Not at all like a new, stiff pair. He wasn't a shopper by nature and hated roaming around stores, searching and searching. On top of that, his left foot was a full size smaller than the right one. That little bit of freak in his DNA made shoe shopping the absolute worst. He lived with the fact that either one shoe was too small or too big, or he bought two pairs of the same shoe in different sizes and used one from each pair. That left a mismatched pair that went completely to waste. He needed a buddy who had the same affliction but with the opposite feet.

So yeah. The slippers with the holes were staying. He'd put them away so Dena didn't have to see their rattiness though. She wouldn't approve, especially because she was a fashion queen.

Although... last night, he'd seen a different version of Dena. Leggings and a sweatshirt. He hadn't been sure she owned anything casual until he'd seen her yesterday. A glimpse at her closet this morning told him the ratio of stylish to casual was clearly tipped toward stylish as he'd suspected, but she hadn't fought him when he suggested she wear the flannel dress today. He'd liked picking out her outfit, knowing she'd gone out packaged in his suggestion.

Of course he preferred *un*dressing her to dressing her, but there'd be more of that tonight. Hopefully.

Stepping outside now, he wandered through the snowy woods, deciding that the Rydinian Forest would be a realm of eternal snowfall. He brushed the snow off a boulder and sat with his sketchpad on his lap. March sun beamed brightly, so it wasn't too cold and the sounds of melting snow whispered around him.

With a few strokes of his pencil, he captured some stout, leafless trees, their barks black against the white snow. A cardinal landed while he was drawing, making him turn to a new page and invent a red, dragon-like bird that breathed fire from the branches.

As he added some armored scales, he thought of meeting Rohen yesterday at the fair. He hadn't had time to look at any of the intern applications yet, but he had a feeling about Rohen. The kid had amazing drawing talent and he appeared to need... someone.

Carter pulled out his phone and called Maplehaven High School. He had until the end of the week to announce his intern choice, but he didn't need that long.

"Maplehaven High School," a man with a nasally voice said.

"Hi, this is Carter Bennett. I participated in your internship fair yesterday. I'd like to inform you of my selection."

"Excellent. What is the student's name?"

"Rohen Sears."

"Oh, he actually applied?" The man laughed. "Our principal convinced Rohen to go to the fair. I had the feeling he said he'd go just to get her off his back. I didn't expect him to go *and* apply for an internship. I'm so glad he did."

"People can surprise you," Carter said.

"Thank God for that. Okay, do you want to tell Rohen yourself about the internship? I can call him down to the office. It'll take a minute."

"Yeah, that would be great."

"Please hold."

A click sounded followed by some jazz music that was in opposition to sitting in the middle of the woods, but he tapped his foot anyway. He drew in a few more trees and some crazy looking huts the Ergons would live in.

"Hello? Mr. Bennett?"

"Hey, Rohen. Call me Carter, remember?"

"I do remember, but I'm in the principal's office for this call."

"I see. So you went the formal route. I got it." Good to know the kid had some manners even if he looked a little rough around the edges. "So how would you like to be my intern?"

"Seriously?"

"Definitely. Your artwork was enough for me, man. I did a quick sketch of a dragon-like bird just now and it isn't half as good as the dragon you submitted. I'm thinking maybe we can learn some stuff from each other if we do this internship thing. What do you say?"

"Yes, thank you, Mr. Bennett. I would love the opportunity to intern with you."

"Great. The paperwork I received about internships from the high school said you can spend one day a week working with me for the next two months. Which day is best for you?"

"Best for me?" Rohen asked. "Shouldn't we work around your schedule? You're the one with the actual job. Which day would I be least in your way?"

"Truly any day is fine. I work from my house and you won't be in my way no matter which day you pick."

"Tuesdays," Rohen blurted. "Are Tuesdays okay? I have PE on Tuesdays and if I could work with you and skip that, my life would be complete."

"Ah, yes, the horrors of PE are a part of high school life. I've blocked that time out of my mind. I like to exercise, but not publicly, especially in high school when the other guys were always way more bulked up than I was."

"You're bulked up now," Rohen said.

"Not the case in high school. Not even close."

"So there's hope for me."

"Of course. Working out is part of my creative process, so as intern, you'll be working out too."

"I think I changed my mind."

Carter laughed. "Too late, dude. I've chosen you. And you accepted. I'll see you Tuesday morning."

He gave Rohen his address and finalized everything with the secretary before hanging up. This week was shaping up to be a great one. He'd had fun with Dena, his new game development was going super well, he'd be a Jedi Master to a talented apprentice, and his week would end with a fancy date with Dena. All was right in Carter's world.

Now the trick was to keep it right.

He spent another thirty minutes outside until his fingertips numbed. He took his sketchpad and pencil and headed back toward the cottage. A faint wheezy sound to his left made him stop walking.

What is that?

Carter turned in a circle, searching the immediate area. In the snow at the base of a nearby tree was a rabbit. A rabbit with a trail of blood behind it.

"Shit." He kneeled beside the creature and when it didn't automatically leap away from him, he knew it was definitely injured enough to immobilize it. "Hey there, little guy. What happened to you?"

He stuck his pencil behind his ear and wedged his sketchpad between his arm and ribs. The rabbit's black gaze darted around and its oversized ears twitched, but it didn't make a run for it. When Carter stuck out his hand toward the creature, it extended its neck to sniff his knuckles.

"That's right, buddy. Don't be afraid." He inched closer. "Are you going to let me pick you up?"

He slid his hands into the snow underneath the rabbit and gently lifted it. A small squeak sounded and Carter quickly found the source of the bunny's pain. Its left foot looked as if something had taken a bite out of it. Fresh blood stained Carter's hands, but that didn't stop him from cradling the quivering rabbit to his chest.

"Let's get you inside and check this out." He didn't like taking the critter from its habitat, but if he didn't, the rabbit would surely die. He liked that less. "Not on my watch, friend."

The snow crunched under his boots as he made his way back to the cottage. Inside, he let his sketchpad slide from under his arm to the couch as he passed into the bathroom. He set the bunny in the tub, more blood seeping from the wound and trickling toward the drain.

"You need a vet." He dug out his phone and did a quick search, finding a vet that made house calls

139

because he didn't think a wild bunny would appreciate a car ride and an office visit. While he waited, he stroked the rabbit's soft, white back and searched online to find out what kind of rabbit it was. "So looks as if you're a snowshoe hare. And who was your predator? In the wrong place at the wrong time, huh? Happens to the best of us."

It'd happened to Chase. It'd happened to Dena. It happened to people who didn't ever go looking for trouble. Chase didn't get to survive, but thankfully Dena did. Carter hadn't been able to aid either one of them, but he was going to make sure this rabbit lived.

Fifteen minutes later, his doorbell rang and he left the bathroom to answer it.

"Hi, I'm Carter," he said to the woman standing on his doorstep.

"Dr. Reilly," she said. "You've got an injured rabbit?"

"Yeah. This way."

He led her to the bathroom where she kneeled beside the tub and examined the bunny. She winced when she saw its foot. "Poor baby. Looks as if a dog or something got hold of him."

"Will he be okay? There was a lot of blood where I found him and it still seems to be flowing."

"His toes are all broken. Beyond repair. I suggest amputation to about here." She indicated how much she was talking about on the rabbit's hind paw. "I can stitch everything closed neatly, and he should be able to get around fine. He'll just have one foot smaller than the other."

A rabbit with the same affliction as Carter. "Do it. I'll pay for it."

She nodded and picked up the bunny. "I can perform the surgery in my van then I'll bring him back in." She paused at the front door as Carter held it open. "It's nice of you to see to this animal's care. You know snowshoe hares only live about a year or so in the wild."

"And he's going to get his full year."

About an hour and a half later, during which Carter had tidied up his cottage, Dr. Reilly was back at his door, the rabbit wrapped in a blanket in her arms.

"The patient did wonderfully. He's asleep right now."

Carter took the bundle over to the couch where he tucked it into the corner. He squared away the bill and listened to care instructions.

"Thank you for coming out so quickly," he said as he walked the vet back to the door.

"No problem. I was checking on a pregnant horse down the street."

"You must have some interesting days on the job."

She nodded. "It definitely isn't boring. What do you do for work?"

"Design video games."

"Cool. That must be fun."

"It is, but I don't save anyone's life like you do." He gestured to the couch behind him.

"Tell that to the kid who doesn't quite know how to navigate the real world but feels completely at home in the ones you create in your games. That sounds like a savior's work to me." She gave him a brief salute. "Nice meeting you, Carter. Good luck being a bunny daddy."

He gave her a wave, her words about a savior's work still ringing in his ears. He'd never thought about his video games as something that reached out to misfit kids, but he supposed that might be true. Hadn't he been a bit of a misfit as a teen? Chase had always been the popular one, the one who knew how to charm people. Carter had preferred to hang back and observe, not get involved. People didn't always get him and his imagination.

Dena got him though. Quite possibly she was the first woman to ever have understood him.

He returned to the couch and smoothed back the bunny's ears. "Well, I guess I now have a roommate. What shall we call you?" He studied the sleeping rabbit, its furry white sides contracting as it breathed. "You look like a Theo to me." One whisker twitched. "I'll take that to mean you accept this name. Welcome, Theo."

Carter sat on the other end of the couch and picked up his sketchpad. "But you are no ordinary rabbit, are you, Theo? No, you are a sacred rabbit. Known only through the legends of the Rydinian Forest. Your appearance means great power will be bestowed upon the first Ergon to see you."

He scribbled furiously on a clean sheet of paper, his pencil hardly able to keep up with his brain. The Muse came in many forms.

Today she was a white rabbit.

Chapter Eight

Dena stood on Carter's front porch, holding the remaining chocolate cake and a pizza box. She'd had a busy day at work, but a huge chunk of her brain had been focused on this moment right here. The one where she'd be with Carter again. She'd liked him a great deal before Rhode Island. She'd been a little afraid of him—mostly the intimacy he would want—when she'd returned from Rhode Island... Gary's attack too fresh, too real, too terrifying. She'd missed him more than she'd expected in the week she'd foolishly pushed him away, but now?

Now she craved him.

One night of making love with him and she was totally hooked. She'd pictured what they'd done together all day while at work and just remembering had her body responding. She'd spent half the day turned on.

Which meant she was probably going to launch herself at Carter as soon as he opened the door.

She pressed her fingertip to the doorbell and waited. And waited. And waited. *Come on, Carter. Now is not the time for games.* If she didn't get her hands on him immediately, she'd seriously go a little crazy.

She pounded her fist on the front door and a muffled *coming* sounded from within the cottage. Carter's form became visible through the frosted glass on the front door and Dena had to remind herself not to drop the cake and pizza to embrace him.

The door opened and even in a wrinkled Captain America T-shirt, faded jeans, and bright orange socks, Carter looked like a god. His hair was hooked behind his ears, a pencil perched behind his left one, and a streak of green was on his forearm.

She pointed to the green stripe. "Were you working?"

"What?" Carter pushed his glasses up higher on his nose, caught the pencil that had become dislodged, and glanced at his arm. "Shit." He rubbed at it, but of course it didn't come off. "I totally lost track of time. I was working on my game. I went outside to sketch and found a hurt bunny. A vet came. Things got amputated."

"Amputated!" Dena stepped into the house. "Is the bunny okay?"

"Yeah. Come see him." Carter started for the living room, but then stopped abruptly so Dena crashed into him, the pizza box jolting her in the stomach right where her injury was.

"Ouch!" She sprung back a little.

Carter grabbed the pizza and cake. "Shit, shit, shit. I'm so sorry." He set the box and cake container on the counter in the kitchen and put his hands on her shoulders. "Are you all right?"

"Yeah. I should have been paying attention." She ran a hand over her midsection.

144

Christine DePetrillo

"Nope. That was my fault. I'm all scattered. I should have been more careful. I turned around to properly greet you, remembering that I hadn't at the door." He angled his head at her. "Let's take this from the top." He closed his eyes for a few seconds then opened them, giving her a smile that lit a match inside her. "Hey, beautiful. So happy you're finally here." He lowered his head and captured her mouth in a kiss that made any remaining ache completely fade away. The only thing she felt was the warm press of his full lips against hers, the hard muscles of his chest under her palms, the growing bulk in his jeans.

Dena wanted to say hello back to him, but she couldn't tear her mouth from his. Couldn't put any space between their bodies. Couldn't deny she wished their clothes would magically disintegrate, leaving every naked inch of this gorgeous man exposed to her.

When Carter finally ended the kiss, he licked his lips. "Am I forgiven for my less-than-appropriate first greeting?"

Dena puckered out her lips as if considering his question. "Not quite."

"You just want more kissing." He tugged on the ends of her hair.

She wrapped her arms around his waist and rested her chin on his chest. "Can you blame a girl? You're really good at kissing."

"*We're* really good at kissing." He dropped a peck on the tip of her nose. "And you can have as many as you want. I'm a big fan of spontaneous making out."

145

"Hmm... good to know." She took a step back. "Now that you're not as frazzled as when you first answered the door, what's this about a bunny and an amputation?"

"Oh, right." He took her hand and pulled her into the living room. "So I've been working on my game all day and when I went outside to sketch some setting ideas, I found this guy." He pointed to the corner of the couch where a little white fluffball occupied a blanket nest.

"How cute!" Dena whispered. "But he was hurt?"

"Yeah. The vet thinks something bit his leg. He ended up losing the tip of his hind paw, but the vet said he should be able to get around okay once he's healed."

"You're going to take care of him?"

Carter nodded, and in that moment, Dena fell in love with him. Not only was he sexy and smart and talented and good to her, he was also a friend to nature. He'd rescued this poor rabbit and planned to nurse it back to health. Was there anything more attractive than that?

"Besides this little guy and I have something in common," he said as he pointed down to his feet.

"What am I supposed to be seeing?" Dena asked as she looked at his orange socks.

"My feet aren't the same size and neither are his now."

Dena squinted down at Carter's feet which he'd smooshed together, his heels in line. Sure enough, his left foot was smaller than his right. "Huh? So you're not perfect after all. Bummer."

"Nope. I have freak feet and I can't see for shit without my glasses," Carter said. "Do you want to reconsider this relationship?"

"Hmm..." She tapped her index finger to her chin. "Nah, I guess I'll take my chances."

"Good answer." Carter motioned to the rabbit. "So I named him Theo. He's now a character in my game."

He sat beside the bunny and stroked its back. It didn't move, but Dena assumed it was probably drugged after its surgery—as she'd been. It occurred to her that in the days immediately following getting her stomach stitched closed, Carter would have volunteered to take care of her too. That was the kind of man he was. But she'd pushed him away. She wouldn't be making that mistake again.

"Do you want to pet him? He's so soft." Carter smoothed the bunny's large ears back.

Dena got to her knees in front of man and rabbit. With a hand on Carter's thigh, she leaned closer to Theo and let her fingertips glide along the critter's cheeks.

"When Jacy and I were small," she started, "my dad got us each a bunny for our birthday. Mine was all white like Theo here and I loved that thing so much. It was the first pet that was just mine, you know? We'd had dogs and goats and horses, but that rabbit was all for me. I told it my secrets. I used to let it hop all over my room."

"So you have bunny experience?" Carter pulled her up onto his lap, which was where she'd wanted to be all day. "This is good because all I know about rabbits is what I've seen on *Looney Tunes* cartoons. I'll need your help to make sure this little guy makes it. I promised him he would be okay."

Dena snuggled against Carter. "I'd love to help you."

He ran a hand over her hair, much like he'd pet the rabbit. "We can all take care of each other."

"Deal." She pushed off him so she could see his face. "Shall we start by eating pizza? It's still hot and Kyle said he made this one special for us."

"Yes. I'm hungry." He pressed his lips to hers. "For many things."

"I have the cake too."

"Not the *many things* I meant." He stood, gathering her in his arms and shaking her a bit. "This. This right here is the many things I want."

She let out a squeal when he opened his mouth and gently bit her shoulder. "I'm pretty sure the pizza and cake will taste better."

"Doubtful." He set her down and she took the opportunity to slither her front against his, causing him to shudder and close his eyes. "Very doubtful."

She led him to the kitchen where she paused by the pizza box. Opening it while Carter took out some plates, she chuckled. "Oh, Kyle."

Carter came around to her side of the counter to see the pizza. "A heart outlined with pepperoni. That's the most romantic pizza I've ever seen."

"Gets you in the mood, doesn't it?" She took the plate Carter held out to her.

"Umm… newsflash," he whispered in her ear. "I was already in the mood."

She elbowed him. "Me too. Like all day."

"All day? Really?"

148

"Don't get all overconfident now, Freaky Feet." She plopped a slice of pizza onto his plate then selected one for herself.

"I make you horny even with my freaky feet."

"Oh my God. Eat your pizza."

"What, can't we have a conversation about how horny I make you? Aren't we all adults here?" He gestured as if more people populated the kitchen.

"Talking about being horny makes me less horny," Dena said as she grabbed some napkins.

"Less horny is not good. New topic. How was your day?" He poured them glasses of ginger ale and they took everything to the living room where they both chose to sit on the floor around the coffee table. Dena could count on her hands the number of times she'd been compelled to not eat at a table like a civilized individual. What was it about Carter that made casual feel so comfortable? She didn't even put the napkin on her lap.

"I had a productive day... even if I was distracted thinking about *you*." She motioned to him with her glass. "There's a big project happening in Canville so we have a huge order for Warrior Construction going out at the end of the week. Like multiple truck loads. Noah's been running around like crazy with my dad, overseeing the lumber production and planning out the delivery. Warrior Construction works on some major builds. If we can please them, we'll have a lucrative new customer whose money I can manage." She left out the part where the men of Warrior Construction were all insanely gorgeous with this otherworldly strength and sexiness about them.

She and Jacy had fumbled all over themselves when the guys had come in to the sawmill.

"Awesome. I'll bet your dad is pleased."

"Yup. And when Dad is pleased, it's good for all of us at the sawmill." She pointed to the papers on the other end of the coffee table. "And you had a successful workday too?"

At this, Carter's eyes lit up behind his glasses. "Totally. I drew so many new characters and got the major setting squared away. Tomorrow I'll be able to get working on the actual graphics."

"Can I see your sketches?"

The smile that stretched across his face told her she'd said the right thing. He reached to the end of the table and brought the pile closer. The first drawing he held up had a picture of Theo in the center, but the bunny had piercing blue eyes and an ethereal glow.

"Theo is the sacred rabbit of the Ergons. Players will have to find him on some of the screens to get tips to the next level of the game."

"Cool." She picked up the next sketch. An amazing red creature with scales, wings, and dragon features set a treetop ablaze with its fiery breath. "Wow. Carter, you are amazing."

His cheeks pinked adorably as he focused on his pizza. "Thanks, but you should see the intern I'm taking on." He got to his feet, rummaged around in his bag on the floor by the couch and sat back in his spot. He unfolded a piece of paper and set it on the table between them.

Dena leaned over the drawing, almost afraid to pick it up. "Holy shit, did the intern do this?" The dragon's fierce gaze hypnotized her.

Carter nodded. "Crazy, right? I'm willing to bet he's all self-taught too. Like a natural talent, you know?"

"Well, he'll have a great opportunity working with you."

"I think it's going to be a good match." He folded the dragon drawing back up and set it aside as if he didn't want to chance getting pizza sauce on it. "How about you? Did the sawmill decide on an intern yet?"

"I gave Dad all the applications, but we're going to sit down with Jacy and go through them tomorrow. Today was too crazy."

"It's a cool thing that the high school and town do this internship program," Carter said. "I started in video game development by tinkering around, but a formal chance to study under someone would have been awesome."

"Well, it's a good way to show the students there are great jobs right here in Maplehaven. We're a small town so the more people we can keep here the better."

"It snagged me pretty easily. I had only planned to visit Leah, but once I got here, I didn't want to leave."

"Lucky for me." She squeezed his knee under the coffee table.

He leaned toward her and hooked his hand on the back of her neck. "Lucky for both of us." He kissed her then got up. "You want another slice of pizza?"

"Yes, please. Somehow it tastes better knowing there was a pepperoni heart on it."

His laughter wafted back to her and Dena was struck by how much she enjoyed this. Sitting on the floor, eating pizza, conversing about her day with a wonderful man. She'd always had her family and her job and this cozy town, but having Carter too was an added bonus. *The* added bonus. The sort of thing that made a person's life complete.

A slice of pizza landed on her plate and she looked up at Carter.

"What?" He lowered to his seat again, but kept his gaze focused on her.

"Nothing." She shrugged. "I just... I like being here with you. Like this. Informal and comfy."

"Me too," he said, then his brows furrowed, dipping below the frames of his glasses. "Does that mean you don't want the upscale date I have planned for Friday night?"

"Oh, no. I still want that, but I like this too."

"So you like spending time with me no matter what. Is that what you're saying, Miss Brenton?" He winked as he bit into his pizza.

Dena balled up her napkin and threw it at him. It bounced off his chest and dropped to the floor somewhere between them. "Yeah, you're kind of fun." She looked to the game consoles he had lined up in front of his television. "Speaking of fun, maybe you can show me some of your games?"

Carter stopped mid-chew. "You want to play my games?" he said around a mouthful, his eyes opened wide. "You've never wanted to play them before."

"Not while Dakota, Noah, Kyle, and Luke are here to watch. In my limited experience, I tend to suck at video games, but yeah, I want to see why people line up to buy Carter Bennett creations."

He put his hand over his heart. "You honor me, beautiful. I would love to beat your lovely ass in one of my games."

"You said before you'd let me win. You won't take it easy on me?"

"Maybe for the first few minutes," he said, getting up to pull games off a shelf under the television, "but after that, it's game-on, woman."

Dena was certain she would be an epic failure at video games, however judging by the excitement asking to play had generated in Carter, she'd already won.

****

Carter could hardly load the game disc into the system. He probably should have used the online version, but he preferred the old-school discs. He was so stoked Dena wanted to see his games. Deep down he knew she was just being nice, but asking to play demonstrated her desire to know more about him. He couldn't deny how that made him feel—as if he'd won the lottery or something. When she'd returned from Rhode Island, he'd honestly feared their relationship was over before it had started.

Thank God for second chances.

He didn't intend to waste a minute of his chance either. If she wanted to see his games, he'd show her. If she wanted a fancy date on Friday, he'd do it up right. If she wanted him to strip down naked and take her on the living room floor... oh, wait, that was probably what *he* wanted.

But maybe she wants that too.

Throughout their pizza consumption, she'd found reasons to touch him, and she had admitted to thinking about him all day. Both of those were signs she wanted to make love again. He put that on the night's agenda after he beat her at *DigMasters I.*

"Quick question," he said, sitting on the couch and patting the spot next to him. "You'll still want to get naked with me later even if I completely annihilate you at these games, right?"

She let her head rest on his shoulder and he got a good whiff of the flowery scent of her hair. "Of course. Why punish myself? I want you naked, Carter. In fact, I'm half-considering suggesting we play the games naked."

Carter barked out a laugh. "That would make things interesting." He glanced to Theo. "But we should keep things G-rated for the little guy."

"Why?" She raised an eyebrow. "He's naked."

"He's a sacred bunny, Dena." He rolled his eyes. "Have some respect. Jeez."

"You're right. How irreverent of me."

"You're letting your desire for me cloud your judgment."

"Well, stop looking all delicious and I wouldn't be overcome with arousal."

He handed her a controller. "I can't turn off my attractiveness like a switch."

"Poor you." She nudged his bicep with hers and that simple contact made Carter want to forget playing the game. He had other buttons he wanted to push and they weren't found on the controller in his hand.

"Focus," he said.

"I am focused."

Carter shook his head. "I was talking to me."

Dena nuzzled his neck. "I might actually have a chance of winning this game."

"Because you're not going to play fairly, are you?" He moaned when she ran her tongue along the rim of his ear.

"Nope. I'll use what I have."

"What you have is a lethal tongue." Carter turned his head and busied himself with kissing that mouth of hers until they were both panting for each other. "Maybe this game should wait."

"Not when I have you all good and distracted." She squinted at the television screen. "So how do you play this one?"

His head was too scrambled and his dick too erect to do a good job of explaining *DigMasters I* to her, but he tried his best. A few minutes later, he hit start and the first level unfolded on the screen.

"Wow, these graphics are so realistic, Carter," Dena said as a mummy attempted to wrap up her on-screen character. "Oh, shoot!"

Carter laughed. "Hit the button to bring out your pocketknife. That'll cut through the wrappings."

Dena looked down at the controller for a minute and that was her downfall. The mummy had managed to cover her head and suffocation was imminent. "Crap. Can't look away from the screen, can you?"

"It's ill-advised."

"I knew I would suck at this."

"I'm thrilled you wanted to try though."

"Maybe you can come by my office at the sawmill and I'll let you try your hand at payroll." She stabbed her finger onto the controller, but her character still fell into the dig site hole. "Dammit."

"See, the difference is your failing at this game only affects you and your delicate ego. If I attempt payroll, *real* people won't get paid for their hard work."

She navigated her character right off a cliff and Carter couldn't stop his laughter.

"Don't make fun! I have no spatial ability." She jammed her elbow into his side and he fell over onto the cushion beside him, still laughing. "I think I better focus on things I'm good at." She set the controller down on the coffee table and climbed atop him.

He pretended to ignore her and continued playing the game.

"Carter Bennett, you put that controller down right now."

She didn't give him the chance to obey. Instead she reached over and plucked the controller from his hands. Within a second's time, she'd maneuvered his character into the ditch where hers had disappeared.

"Oh, that's painful." He looked up at her face, loving the playful expression he found there.

"You'll get over it."

And she was right. The moment she unzipped the purple hooded sweatshirt she wore and peeled it off, he didn't give a shit about his character. He could play—and win—*DigMasters I* any time. He couldn't watch Dena's striptease any time because he couldn't be in her presence around the clock.

A shame. And something he needed to problem solve around. Sure, he'd seen her last night and tonight and he'd be seeing her Friday night, but he hated all those hours in between... he wanted her around for those too. What could he do about those hours?

His thinking was seriously interrupted when Dena removed her gray T-shirt, leaving her breasts on display in a black bra that made him want to draw her. He sat up and kissed a line from her chin along her jaw and down her neck. Nipping on her collarbone, he slid his hands behind her back and unclasped the bra so her breasts were unleashed.

She'd already gone to work on his T-shirt, pulling it off and tossing it on the floor. "I could stare at your chest all day." She traced his pecs with her fingertips then ran her index finger along his abs.

"Likewise." He cupped her breasts, one in each hand. "These are works of art." He used his tongue to bring her nipples to taut buds. "I love how you respond to my touch."

"As if I'm desperate?"

"No, as if you trust me to touch you. As if you feel safe in my hands."

She slid her hands up his chest and hooked them on his bare shoulders. When she met his gaze, her hazel depths were watery. "I do trust you. I do feel safe with you. Being with you like this makes me wish you'd been with me in Rhode Island. You wouldn't have let that Gary dude anywhere near me."

Carter ground his teeth. "You got that right." He hugged her close to him. "Say the word, and I'm willing to hunt him down and punch him until he begs for mercy."

"See, I don't usually like that macho crap, but when you say it, it makes me hot for you. Hotter than I already am."

He grabbed at the waistband of her jeans, unbuttoned them, and unzipped them. He peeled away the sides, urged her to her feet, and pulled those jeans all the way off. Then he went back for her panties, which he nearly ripped off her. When she was completely bared to him, he pushed to the edge of the couch, positioning his head so it was level with her hips. He clasped his hands together at her ass and nudged her closer. Dropping soft kisses along her thighs, he cut a path toward that spot between her legs.

"Just how hot are you?" He dipped a finger into her core and grinned when he found her wet and ready.

"Hot enough?"

"Oh, yeah." He stood and unbuttoned his jeans. "Let me get a condom, you know, to protect against getting scorched in there."

"Again, your fault. You caused the temperature to reach roast-a-chicken levels."

As he made his way down the hallway toward his bedroom, he awkwardly pulled off his jeans and boxers, leaving them both on the floor. He grabbed a condom from his bedside table and yanked his socks off as he traveled back to the living room.

"Oh, I like that you came back naked." She reached out her hands to him and immediately pulled him into a hug that pressed her gorgeous breasts to his chest.

He kissed the top of her head. "Trying to save some time."

"I like efficiency. It's sexy." She hooked her left leg around his right thigh, which brought her hot center in line with his erection. The heat coming off her was incredible and he couldn't wait to dive into that volcano.

The music from *DigMasters I*—an ancient-sounding instrumental, heavy on drums—filled the living room and Carter made a move to shut off the game.

"Don't." Dena grabbed his wrist and when he looked at her, she gave him a shy smile. "I like the music. It's mysterious and... I don't know... sensual." Her cheeks flamed and Carter could now name what he felt for Dena Brenton.

Love. He loved her.

Any woman who wanted to make love to a video game soundtrack had been specially made just for him. He looked down at her, wondering if she had any idea how much he wanted her.

"Your pupils are huge," she whispered as she rubbed herself against him like a cat. "See something you like?"

He nodded, not trusting his voice. Desire consumed him. All he could think about was burying himself deep inside her. Hooking his hands under her arms, he picked her up, loving when she automatically wrapped her arms around his neck and linked her legs at his lower back. Her muscles tightened, adding another layer of arousal as she squeezed him like an anaconda.

Their mouths melded with a passion so wild, Carter nearly forgot to breathe. With one arm around her back, he plunged his free hand into her silky hair, palming her scalp, deepening the kiss. She let out a moan that went directly to his dick. If he didn't get inside her right now...

Somehow she knew. Dena shifted so the tip of his erection brushed against her opening. Finding her slick and ready, he eased into her and they both let out a groan as their bodies became one. Their kissing efforts doubled and Carter saw stars as they shared the same space. All his senses were tuned in to Dena. Her flowery scent. Her soft skin. The taste of ginger ale still on her tongue. The sound of her labored breathing as they continued to explore each other's mouths. A pleasured groan vibrating from deep within her luscious body.

No other woman would ever be all that she was to him. He hadn't felt this alive since he'd lost his brother. Dena breathed new life into him and he wanted to live that life.

With her.

Carter's legs weakened as his need to pump in and out of her grew. He stumbled to the couch and slowly lowered them until Dena's back hit the cushions. She didn't ease up her hold on him, but he had enough space to thrust his hips and raise them to the next plateau.

Dena clawed at his back and the little bit of pain that caused set another wave of pure bliss in motion. He released a growl of approval and increased his pace all while their mouths demanded more.

When they both reached the top of the wave, Carter yelled her name at the same time she shouted his. He collapsed on top of her as she raked his hair back and cupped his cheek.

"Holy shit…" The words came out on a breathy whisper. "You sure are good at that. For a video game nerd."

He managed to raise his head to look at her. "For a stuffy number cruncher, you rock my world, beautiful."

She tightened her hold on him and he was content to lay there with her forever.

Until something soft and a little wet rubbed the heel of his left foot. Carter rolled to Dena's side and looked down the length of their naked bodies.

To the corner of the couch.

Where Theo had his black gaze trained on them.

"Oh, we totally disrespected the sacred bunny with what we did on its very throne," Dena said as she looked at Theo.

"He's going to unleash the Ergon army on us. I hope it was worth it." Carter drew a circle around her breast with his index finger. God, her body was perfect. Even with the bandage under her ribs, she was a goddess. He could spend the rest of his life looking at her naked body and still want more.

"Totally worth it." She kissed a line along his jaw. "I never knew playing video games could be such foreplay. I have a new appreciation for them."

Carter pressed his lips against her temple. "You apparently don't even have to be winning."

She poked him in the ribs and he got to his elbows, pulling out of her slowly. Her eyes rolled back, her mouth opening slightly. He'd never seen anything sexier.

"I'm glad you decided to be patient with me, Carter," she said softly, her fingertip rubbing his bottom lip, making him sink back down beside her after he rid himself of the condom. "Thank you. For a lot of things."

"Thanks for choosing to be with me. I know it's difficult thinking about allowing someone this close to you after what happened." He motioned to the almost non-existent space between them as they lay together on the couch. Their bodies were one long line of contact, flesh to flesh, heart to heart.

"I think… I think what happened in Rhode Island changed me though. For the better." She hooked his hair behind his ear then played with the ends of it. The sensation made Carter sleepy, but he focused on what she was saying. "I was pretty strict in my life rules. You know what I mean? Like dressing up for the sawmill every day. It's a sawmill. A dirty, dusty, outdoorsy sawmill. It doesn't require business suits and heels."

"But if you like business suits and heels, there's nothing wrong with that," Carter said. "Especially the heels." He wiggled his eyebrows.

"I do like them, but I also like flannel and T-shirts and jeans. I don't know. I guess I learned to loosen up a bit. Enjoy life." She cupped his cheek. "Enjoy a man like you."

"I second this plan. You have my full support."

And Carter planned to enjoy a woman like her.

Chapter Nine

Dena sat in one of the chairs on the other side of her father's desk in William's office. Her sister sat beside her as the three of them reread two of the intern applications—the ones belonging to the cute couple.

"I'm having a hard time deciding here," William said. "Both students have an impeccable academic record and their applications are equally impressive."

"They're like a power couple at age seventeen," Jacy added as she put the girl's application back on her father's desk.

Dena chewed on her bottom lip.

"What are you thinking, Dena?" William asked.

I'm thinking about seeing Carter tonight. But of course she'd been thinking about that since Wednesday morning when Carter had given her a have-a-nice-day-at-work sendoff not to be forgotten.

"Dena?" Her father waved a hand in her face. "Are you with us?"

Jacy smirked beside her. "She's probably thinking about her geeky, yet hot *boyfriend.*"

Dena swatted her sister's arm. "Don't be a brat."

"As the minute-younger twin, it is my duty to be a brat."

"And you do it so well." Dena focused on her father. "I'm sorry, Dad."

"No problem. I did want to know what you were thinking about these two interns." Her father clasped his hands and leaned his chin on them. "But now I want to know about your boyfriend. Are you and Carter an official couple?"

"Umm… yeah, I guess we are." She got warm all over saying that. Carter was her boyfriend. She was his girlfriend. They were a couple. *Holy shit.* Dena had certainly had boyfriends in the past, but it had always been the sort of situation where if it didn't work out—and it usually didn't—she'd had no problem walking away.

Carter would not be easy to walk away from. It was why she hadn't been able to stay away from him for longer than a week when she'd asked for distance after her trip. Carter was a magnet and the attraction was strong.

"Well, this is wonderful." William beamed at Dena. "I was hoping it would work out for you two."

"Can you hope for something to work out for me?" Jacy asked. "Because everyone is finding someone nice except me."

"Your time will come, my dear," William said.

"How? I've dated almost everyone in my age group in Maplehaven." She nudged Dena. "And this one pounced on the new blood before I had the chance."

"I did not pounce. In fact, as I recall, I tried to get you to go on the blind date with Carter when Dakota suggested it. You were *insert lame excuse here*."

"How was I supposed to know Carter was going to turn out to be hot? You guys wouldn't let me cyberstalk him to find out."

"It'll happen for you when it happens, Jacy," William said.

"That's just one of those things a father says to his daughter to shut her up." Jacy folded her arms across her chest, but she was grinning, as was William.

"True. Page twenty-four of The Dad Manual." William blew Jacy a kiss then turned his attention back to Dena. "Okay, if you could stop thinking about Carter for a moment and help me decide on these interns." He tapped the applications on his desk.

Dena leaned forward with the intention of picking up the applications to read them yet another time, but stopped instead. "Is there anything in the internship program rules that says we can't take *both* of these candidates on as interns? I mean, they're interested in different aspects of the sawmill—one in the actual milling, one in the finances and management. With a business the size of this one, two interns doesn't seem ridiculous, does it?"

William puckered out his lips as he did whenever he was really considering something. "I don't remember there being a limit to the number of interns a business can take on." He held up his hand then picked up his cell phone. "Let me call the high school and find out."

After a brief discussion that was more about town gossip because William was friends with the high school secretary, he hung up his phone. "Nothing says we can't have both. Let's do it. Dena, I'll assign the boy, Nickolas Robbins, to you and the girl, Savannah Weiss, to Noah. You can each make a call to the high school and schedule the internship day that is most convenient for you and the student, okay?"

"Sounds fine to me. I'm sure Noah will agree," Dena said. "I think both of these students will make full use of the opportunity."

"And you said they were dating, right?" Jacy asked.

Dena nodded.

"Now one doesn't have to hate the other one over someone being left behind."

"Ah, Brenton Sawmill," William said with a grin. "Milling lumber and saving young relationships in the process."

"We're real humanitarians," Jacy said.

"Okay, I'm going to call Nickolas and set up our day," Dena said as she got up from her seat. "Then... I think I'm going to leave early."

"What?" Jacy and William asked at the same time.

"My desk is pretty clear at the moment. All the Warrior Construction paperwork is in order. I thought I'd knock off early and... I don't know..." She let the sentence go unfinished.

"Get ready for your big date with Carter tonight?" Jacy asked, her eyebrows raised.

"How did you know I had a date?"

Jacy stood and knocked her knuckles on the wall near the door to William's office. "I heard you on the phone. These walls are super thin."

Dena's mouth dropped open. "You eavesdropped?"

"Oh, sissy, I've been eavesdropping on you ever since we started talking." Jacy reached out and tapped Dena's temple. "Besides, the twin thing also keeps me in tune with you. Your entire aura has been different since Dakota's wedding when you spent most of your time with Carter. You tried to keep him at a distance, but a man like that... well, a man like that is hard to resist."

"And you've realized you shouldn't resist," William added. "We're happy for you. For you both." He stood and shooed Dena toward the door. "I'll text Noah to call Savannah and you go make that call to Nickolas. Then get the heck out of here." He kissed her cheek. "Have fun. I love you."

"Love you too, Dad." Dena looked at Jacy. "Hell, I even love you today."

Jacy hugged herself. "I feel so special."

Laughing, Dena exited her father's office and stepped into hers next door. She picked up her phone and dialed the high school. She waited as the secretary paged Nickolas to the office.

"Hello?" The boy's voice was tentative.

"Hey, Nickolas. This is Dena Brenton from Brenton Sawmill. I'd like to extend an internship to you if you're still interested."

"Oh... yeah... I am." But he didn't sound as if he meant it.

"Did you change your mind?" she asked.

"No. I definitely want the internship," the boy said. "I just feel bad that Savannah will be disappointed."

So cute. Dena didn't remember high school boys being so charming when she was in high school. "I wouldn't feel too bad."

"What do you—" Nickolas stopped speaking for a minute. Then he said, "Savannah, what are you doing down here?" He sounded as if he'd been caught doing something he shouldn't be doing. Poor kid.

Dena waited patiently while she assumed Savannah was taking a phone call from Noah. When a cheer rose up from Nickolas, Dena laughed.

"Thank you for picking both of us, Miss Brenton," he said.

"No problem. You both had wonderful applications. We couldn't decide so we decided not to decide."

"Awesome!"

"I was thinking Thursdays would be convenient for me," Dena said. "Would that work for you?"

Nickolas conversed with Savannah, his voice muffled. Then he came back clearly. "Thursdays would be great."

"Is that the day Savannah picked too?"

"Umm, yeah. Is that okay? We usually ride to school together so it would work out if we had the same internship day too."

When she didn't think they could get more adorable, they did. Riding to school together was so sweet. It made Dena wonder what Carter was like in high school. If she had known him then, would they have been as tight as these two teens? Would he have picked her up for school each day? Carried her books? Most of the boys she went to high school with had been pretty clueless. She'd grown tired of them quickly, but had dated most of them because... well, who else was she going to date? And they were cute after all.

Thank God Carter had come to her from New York.

"Great," she said. "We'll see you both next Thursday then. I'm looking forward to it."

"Me too," Nickolas said. "Thanks, Miss Brenton."

"You're welcome." She hung up, feeling much better about the internship than she had when she'd been rotting behind the display table at the actual fair. Good thing that last group of teens had stopped and filled out applications.

Dena tidied up a few things on her desk then grabbed her coat to leave early. As she waved good-bye to a few employees, her phone buzzed in her pocket. She continued walking out of the office and to her SUV. After sitting in the driver's seat, she pulled out the phone and grinned at a text from Carter.

How's your day going, beautiful?

She loved when he called her *beautiful*. Something about hearing him say it made her actually feel beautiful.

Not quickly enough. Can't wait to see you.
So impatient.
Maybe you could tell me where we're going?
Nope. ☺

So mean! How am I supposed to know what to wear if I don't know what we're doing?

Three little dots wavered on her screen as Carter composed a reply. While she waited, she put her key into the ignition and started the engine, flipping on the heat.

Wear something you can move in.

She frowned. *Are you taking me to a gym?*

LOL. No gym. Exercise bikes and free weights are not for a date.

Good man. You've passed the test. ☺ So fancy or casual?

Fasual... cancy...

Not helping!

OK, OK. Wear that black dress with the cut-out shoulders. The one you bought online the other night. Did it come in yet?

Dena was surprised he'd remembered her ordering that dress. She'd purchased it when she'd been with him after the internship fair. She hadn't thought he was paying attention, but she should have known by now that Carter paid attention to everything when it came to her.

It did come. I'll wear it. Does that mean no T-shirt for you tonight?

No T-shirt. I'll do my best impersonation of a grown-up tonight.

While we_____???

Nice try, Brenton. Pick you up at 5. XOXO

Her heart melted at the hugs and kisses and she sent a few back before pocketing her phone. She would have liked to know where they were going. She was a planner after all, but she trusted Carter.

And if he wanted her to wear that dress, he must have something great planned. Her anticipation ratcheted up another notch.

When she arrived in her driveway, her phone buzzed yet again. Hoping Carter had changed his mind and was going to tell her where they were going, she yanked the phone out as she climbed out of her SUV.

Fiji is amazing! Dakota had texted.

You think anywhere with Leah is amazing, she texted back, loving that her brother had found someone like Leah. If Leah had never come to Maplehaven in search of a new start to her life, Dena never would have met Carter. And that would have been a damn shame.

Because the more she thought about it, the more Dena realized she did, in fact, love Carter. She'd been in love a few times before, but none of those relationships came close to what was going on between her and Carter now. At first when they'd been about kissing and hanging out, she'd thought maybe Carter was like everyone else she'd dated.

Wrong. With a capital W. This thing between them was unlike anything she'd ever had with anyone. It was almost as if pre-Carter time no longer counted. There was only now, only the future. Only Carter.

Leah does have a way of making any place glorious, Dakota texted.

So corny. ☺

Me? Never!

LOL. Glad you guys are having fun.

So much! And I'm told you'll be having fun with Carter tonight. Happy for you.

Thanks. She wondered… *Do you know where he's taking me?*

☺

Jerk! You do! TELL ME!

No can do, little sister. I was sworn to secrecy… but…

But WHAT???

You'll love where he's taking you. Later.

Dena chewed on her bottom lip as she shed her coat and headed upstairs to her bedroom. All she knew was a sexy black dress was required and that she'd love where Carter was taking her. That wasn't nearly enough to satisfy her curiosity, but she was determined to have an awesome time tonight.

Which would be easy with Carter as her date.

****

Carter wanted to personally thank the designers of the dress Dena wore. It had looked pretty wonderful on the online model when she'd been ordering it, but Dena had a way of taking that simple black dress to a whole new level of sexy. The cut-out shoulders offered a peek at her smooth skin and the form-fitting material showcased every lovely curve Dena owned. Her legs were incredibly long and Carter wanted to kiss his way from her thigh down to the chunky-heeled ankle boots adorning her feet.

She was a vision. One Carter would burn into his memory bank so he could pull it out whenever he wanted. Which would be often. *So often.*

When she'd answered the door at her house, he'd nearly swallowed his tongue. "Oh, baby," he'd whispered. "Beautiful isn't a strong enough word for how amazing you look tonight."

Her cheeks had flamed and he'd almost suggested they stay in. All he'd wanted to do was peel that dress from her body, leave it in a heap on the floor, and give her head-to-toe attention all night long.

Dena deserved a real date though. And there would be time for all-night-long activities later.

"You're really not going to tell me where we're going? Even now?" She leaned toward him in the car, her arm pressing against his on the console between them.

He kept his eyes on the road—no small feat considering the view beside him was breathtaking. "No, miss, I am not going to tell you. You've waited this long."

"Exactly," she said, huffing out a breath. "I've waited *this* long. C'mon." The slight whining in her voice almost made him spill the beans, but he pretended to zip his lips closed instead.

"Don't you like the mystery? The anticipation?" He took the exit ramp to Cheshire, a neighboring town to Maplehaven.

She clamped her hand onto his bicep. "No, I don't. I want to know!"

"You'll know in like ten minutes."

"Really? We're that close?"

"We are."

"Hmm…" She peered out the windows, but at this hour it was dark. Nothing much to see.

"Don't try to puzzle it out, Dena." He made a left turn. "Just enjoy the adventure."

"Oh, okay." She folded her arms across her chest, her wool coat bunching up when she did so.

Carter couldn't wait for that coat to come off so he could see more of that killer dress. A tiny part of his brain recognized that other people would see that killer dress too once they got to their destination and she removed her coat. He wasn't wild about that because she would turn heads with her looks. Male heads. Carter didn't feel jealous often, but he was fairly certain it was going to be the natural reaction to other males appreciating her beauty. If they were truly going to do this relationship thing, however, he'd have to get accustomed to his knockout girlfriend drawing attention with her loveliness. He didn't have to like it, but he did have to manage it.

He'd never worried about men looking at his previous girlfriends. Probably because he'd always known those chicks weren't long-term fixtures in his life. He'd had fun with them, maybe had genuine feelings for some of them, but no one had ever wormed her way into his heart quite like Dena had.

He liked having her there. In his heart.

Finally, he made the last turn into a busy parking lot and instantly Dena sat up straighter in her seat, her hands going to the dashboard.

"You did not." She turned to look at him, the whites of her eyes nearly glowing in the dim interior of the car.

"I did."

She let out a squeal. "I've wanted to come here since it opened! How did you know?"

Carter pulled into a parking spot and shut off the engine. "You mentioned it once."

"And you remembered?" She squeezed his forearm, her excitement another entity in the car with them.

He put a finger under her chin, tipping her head up a bit. "I remember everything when it comes to you, beautiful."

"And here I thought you just liked making out with me."

"I'm hoping this entire evening will earn me more make out sessions." He lowered his mouth to hers and took the taste he'd wanted on the entire drive to Cheshire. "Naked make out sessions."

She slid her hand to the back of his neck and scratched her nails up into his hair, which he'd done his best to tame tonight. "Naked make out sessions are pretty much guaranteed when it comes to you, Carter."

He leaned forward so his forehead touched hers. "Why did we wait so long to get to this point?"

"We weren't ready for each other yet."

He could agree with that. He'd needed to get his head clear, settle in Maplehaven after moving, and maybe grow up a bit. When you spent most of your days locked in the world of video games, adulting often took a back seat. He took care of himself and that was pretty much it. Dena made him want to change that though. He wanted to take care of her too.

"We're ready now," he said.

"We'll be especially ready after going in there." She pointed to the building in front of them. "C'mon."

They exited the car and met at the front of the vehicle. Dena immediately looped her arm with his and he tucked her in close, which was where he planned to keep her for the duration of this date. Close.

When they reached the building, Carter opened the door and energetic dance music greeted them. *Beyond* was a restaurant and dance club… in a planetarium.

"Oh my God!" Dena did a little jump beside him. "This place is so cool!"

Carter couldn't argue with her assessment. Just the line to get into the dance area was impressive. Gorgeous pictures of space on high definition screens made to look like portholes on a spacecraft adorned the walls. They were greeted with an array of nebula, planets, asteroids, and other space stuff as they walked deeper into the club. Each image was more stunning than the one before it.

The floor glittered like some foreign mineral mined from an unknown planet in a faraway galaxy. Carter had the urge to get down on his hands and knees to inspect the material, but he refrained, figuring Dena wouldn't approve of her date crawling around on the ground.

"Clearly I need to redecorate my cottage," he said as he stood behind Dena.

She leaned back and rested her head on his shoulder. "Clearly. I'll be disappointed if it doesn't look like this the next time I come over."

He removed her coat to check along with his, unable to resist pressing a light kiss to her exposed shoulder. "This is a convenient dress."

"Easy to rip off in a hurry also."

"Good to know."

He gave his name to the hostess and soon they were led to the dining area which was quieter. The dance music changed to light instrumentals with a space odyssey flavor conducive to conversation and... digestion? Carter wondered what kind of science had been consulted in designing this place.

And are they looking to hire? He would have loved being involved in the designing of such an out-of-the-box setting.

The floor in the restaurant was constructed to look like the surface of the moon, craters and all. High up on the domed, black ceiling, a blue-green-white Earth oversaw everything.

"Didn't think I'd be dining on the moon tonight," Dena said as another hostess seated them at a small table right under Earth.

Carter sat after she did. "Who knows how to do a real date?" He arrowed his thumbs at himself. "This guy. That's who."

"And you managed to keep it a secret too." She applauded. "Most impressive, Mr. Bennett."

"Wait until you see my dance moves." He did a quick series of robot moves, making Dena laugh.

"If you dance like that out there, I'm wandering off."

"I'll find you."

She stuck her tongue out at him and Carter wanted to vault over the table and put that tongue to use. The waitress approaching caused him to stop, but he kept thinking about kissing her. He did his best to focus on ordering drinks then perused the menu.

178

"I love the names of some of these entrées," Dena said. "Valmucian veal, Sinselltia shrimp... I really feel as if we're exploring the galaxy."

"I took you to the stars, beautiful."

"Noted and appreciated." She peered at him over her menu. "I needed a night like this and I'm so happy it's a night with you."

"Aw, gosh." He gave her a bashful expression, but in reality, he ate up her words. Knowing she was happy to be with him filled his heart to overflowing. When he'd watched Leah with Dakota, he'd wished he'd had a fraction of the magic that existed between the two of them.

He no longer had to wish nor did he have to settle for a fraction. He was getting the real deal here. He could feel it and he intended to keep it, grow it, enjoy it. Putting a smile on Dena's face gave him real purpose. Sure, his fans loved his video games and he was making good money doing something he loved, but having Dena in his life—the way they'd had each other this week—added something that had been missing. Losing his parents then losing Chase had carved out a big piece of him. Finding Dena was spackling that hole and turning him into something new. Something better.

When their drinks came, Carter held up his wine glass. "To a real date."

Dena raised her glass. "One with all the trimmings." She gave him a wink then clinked her glass to his.

"Oh, I do love trimmings."

"It's possible I bought something sexy for the trimmings part of the evening." Dena took a sip of her wine.

Carter coughed on his drink. "Something sexy? Details, please."

Dena shook her head. "I seem to recall someone not telling me that we were coming here tonight. You had your surprises. I have mine."

"I suppose that's fair." Carter set down his glass, intent on making it his *only* glass of wine tonight. "I don't like it, but it's fair."

"You really are the most patient man I've ever met."

He stretched his legs out and captured her ankles with his under the table. "Some things are worth waiting for."

"Trust me. This something sexy is totally worth waiting for."

Carter pumped his fist in the air a little. "Yes."

They ordered their food and after totally stuffing themselves, Carter led her to the dance area, which was huge. An enormous domed ceiling hung over the dance floor, flashing images of the night sky. Every once and a while, shooting stars would zip across the blackness above. Music came at them from speakers around the perimeter of the dome, causing a total immersion in the vibrations, the pulsing, the heartbeat of the club. It'd be hard to dance anywhere else after experiencing *Beyond*.

Carter loved every minute of dancing with Dena while the stars looked on overhead. Though other dancers crowded around them, he was able to concentrate on the magnificent woman in his arms.

The way she moved was hypnotic and having his hands on her hips as she swayed and wiggled to the beat made him happy to be alive. He'd often gone dancing in New York and many times it'd been on dates, but this... this was different.

He and Dena were in sync in their steps, as if their bodies had been made for this purpose. She fit against him perfectly and each time her body brushed against his, he became more connected to her. They moved as one entity and it didn't matter if it was a fast song or a slow one. Every tune brought Carter to a new level of desiring Dena.

"Promise we'll come here again," Dena said over the music, her arms looping around Carter's neck as she gyrated against him.

He leaned down, his mouth right at her ear. "You keep dancing like this against me and I'll promise you absolutely anything you want."

She lifted her right leg enough that her knee caressed his balls. "There's only one thing I want." Rising up on her toes, she squeezed him closer and pressed her lips to his.

Carter was rock hard from dancing with Dena, but that kiss made any remaining blood in his body shoot to one area. He actually felt a little lightheaded so when she broke the kiss and tugged him off the dance floor, he didn't protest.

She led him to a quieter corner then turned to face him, her cheeks flushed from dancing. God, she was the most beautiful thing in the world right now with all those brown waves cascading about her shoulders and those hazel eyes gazing up at him.

"I love it here," she said, "and taking me here was the best surprise, but I want the rest of the night to be just me and you. I want the rest of the night to begin now."

"Don't have to ask me twice, beautiful. Let's get out of here." He grabbed her hand and power-walked to the coat room, not wanting to waste a moment of the desire burning in her eyes.

They retrieved their coats, donning them as they walked toward the exit.

"Hope your time was out of this world," an employee said as they passed.

"It was stellar," Carter replied, giving the woman a smile. "Thank you." *Now get out of my way.*

He was a man on a mission—a mission to get his lovely Dena home. And naked.

Chapter Ten

"Mind if I make a quick bathroom stop?" Dena pointed to the restroom sign down a hallway before the exit.

"Not at all."

"Thanks. I'll be quick." She hustled down the hallway and pushed open the door to the women's restroom. She darted into the first stall, not wanting to keep Carter waiting. Eagerness filled her as she thought about what they'd do once they got back to her house. She'd pretty much wanted to engage in some naked activities from the moment Carter had shown up at her door.

Carter. She sighed aloud as she used the toilet. When she'd opened her front door earlier this evening and found Carter there, dressed in black dress pants, a hunter green button-down shirt, and a black and gray sports coat, she'd instantly wanted all those pieces of clothing to vanish. She wanted the man standing before her in nothing but what his maker had given him.

That's next on the night's agenda. She just had to finish up in the bathroom and they'd be on their way to her house where they'd be shouting each other's names in no time.

Dena washed her hands, did a quick finger-comb of her hair, and applied a fresh coat of lip gloss before coming back out to find Carter. The hallway was less crowded than when she'd first come into the restroom, but a few people still littered the area.

She glanced down the hallway to see Carter leaning against a column. He wasn't aware she was watching him and it was a fun game to witness him pulling his glasses off, wiping the lenses on his shirt, and putting them back on the bridge of his nose. He did a breath check by puffing some air into his palm then smelling it and Dena had to contain her laughter. He had nothing to worry about. He had a taste to him that was all vintage Carter Bennett—a taste she'd committed to memory after their first kiss all those months ago.

A kiss she had definitely become addicted to, especially after this week. After making love with him.

She took a step, wanting to be by his side again more than anywhere else in the world. As she made her way down the hallway, however, a tall man coming out of the men's restroom turned toward her instead of toward the exit. In a matter of a second, she found herself being pushed backward by the man.

"Excuse me," she said, thinking the man had made a wrong turn and hadn't seen her.

When he didn't get out of her way but grabbed her wrist instead, real panic surged through her.

"Let go of me!" She pounded her fist against his arm, but his grip didn't loosen. Her heartbeat boomed in her ears and her vision got spotty.

Not again. She had trouble swallowing. An all-over sweat coated her body.

"Tim!" A female's voice cut through Dena's terror. "Tim!"

Suddenly, Tim lurched forward, falling and pulling Dena to the ground. She ended up trapped beneath him and a scream tore out of her.

Tim was lifted off her and Dena's eyes connected with Carter's. He rolled Tim to the ground beside her and ripped open the guy's coat. A woman about her age skidded to a stop beside Carter and fell to her knees.

"Oh, God... he's not... tell me he's not dead..." the woman croaked, tears streaming down her face.

"No," Carter said after feeling Tim's neck. "He's got a pulse. I called 911. Does he have a medical condition?"

The woman nodded as Dena scooched out of the way and leaned against the wall opposite Tim's prone body. She couldn't catch her breath. All she could do was think about Tim's hand gripping her wrist.

About Gary holding that knife to her. Cutting into her. Making her bleed.

Her logical mind registered that Tim had actually had some kind of episode. That he'd been clamping onto her to ask for help, not to harm her. Her emotions, however, were certain Tim had been attacking her, intending on finishing what Gary had started in that parking garage in Rhode Island.

Personnel from the club rushed into the hallway, clearing out onlookers and making way for EMTs that would be on the way, all while Dena sat with her knees up at her chest, her arms wrapped around her legs. She tried her best to stop trembling, but her body had taken over.

"Dena." Carter's voice was tinny, far away. When he put his hand on her knee, she let out a yell and skittered away from him. He held his hands up, a look of pure anguish on his handsome face. "Easy, beautiful. It's just me. Tim wasn't going to hurt you. Neither am I."

This should have been the part where she launched herself into his arms, maybe cried a bit, then allowed him to calm her down so she could get on with their evening.

When he tried to touch her again, however, she shot to her feet. "Take me home. Take me home now."

Carter rose to his feet as well. "Of course." He made a move to put his arm around her, but she shrugged off his hold. She needed to be free to move around, to run, couldn't be tethered, cornered.

Touched.

She pushed open the exit door and took in a solid gulp of crisp night air. It did nothing to help her. Her lungs were only capable of expanding so much right now. Her pulse was a wild animal trapped beneath her skin, her veins barely able to contain the constant, powerful drumming.

"Dena." Carter had caught up and maneuvered in front of her. "Hey, it's okay. He wasn't going to hurt you. That guy just needed help."

"I... I know," she managed to get out around her labored breaths. "But... I... need to go... home."

"I'll take you, but I want you to know you're safe. You're totally safe. I won't let anything happen to you."

She wanted to believe him. She wanted him to take away all this fear, all this anxiety, all this foolishness, but he couldn't.

"Take... take me home. Please," she whispered.

Carter squeezed his eyes shut as he dug out his car keys. She hated seeing that... that disappointment on his face, but she was powerless against how her mind locked her down. It was as if encountering Tim had triggered a security system in her body and walls instantly erected themselves around her.

She walked to the car on shaking legs, and when Carter opened the passenger door for her, she was careful to avoid contact with him.

Which he totally noticed.

Dena locked the passenger door as Carter walked in front of the car and got into the driver's seat. He poked the key into the ignition but didn't start the engine. Instead he angled to face her.

"Dena." His voice was quiet, a note of pleading in it. "Dena, look at me."

Slowly she turned her head and forced her gaze to connect with his. His brown eyes were warm, compassionate, understanding. Somehow that made everything worse.

She held up her hand. "Don't say anything, Carter. I want to go home. I want... I want to be alone. Please."

He nodded, a barely perceptible move of his head. The engine roared to life and without another word, Carter pulled out of the parking spot and headed for the exit. He punched the car radio's power button and alternative rock filled the interior. He gripped the steering wheel with both hands, strict ten and two position. Everything about his rigid posture in the seat and the twitching muscle in his jaw screamed aggravated and frustrated.

She wanted to apologize, but the words wouldn't come out of her mouth. She'd essentially promised him a wild night of sex—complete with sexy underthings—and now she was revoking that guarantee. But he would understand, right? He would realize she couldn't possibly allow him to touch her tonight. Not when everything about Gary's attack had shot to the surface after Tim had grabbed her. It didn't matter that Tim had needed help. It didn't matter that he'd meant her no harm. All that mattered was that another strange man's hand had been on her, making a demand, requiring action. An action she hadn't been prepared for.

Dena was thankful the car's interior was dark. That way Carter couldn't see exactly how spooked she was. He didn't see the trembling, the folding and unfolding of her hands on her lap, the sweat dotting her brow and upper lip. He didn't bother to look over at her either. A barrier had been erected between the two of them as Carter drove them down the barely populated streets.

In the dim light, she was able to close her eyes, a vain attempt to battle the headache currently in charge of her brain. How was it that not ten minutes ago, she'd been ready to make love to Carter and now the mere *thought* of him putting his hands on her made her skin revolt, her stomach pitch and roll?

Logically, she knew what he'd said was true. Tim hadn't meant to hurt her. Carter would never hurt her, but still... she wanted to be alone. She *needed* to be alone. To regroup. To make sure no holes existed in her defense walls. To put everyone at arm's length to preserve her sense of safety.

Safety? That was a joke. Nowhere was safe. She had to come to terms with the fact that every time she set foot in the world, anything could happen. Most likely, it seemed, something bad could—and would—happen.

The music played on as Carter got onto the highway, and when he pulled into her driveway and shut off the engine, she had to find her voice as the sensor light over her garage illuminated inside the car.

"I know we had plans for tonight, Carter, but I... can't." She pressed herself against the passenger door, afraid he'd reach for her.

But he wouldn't do that. Carter Bennett was a gentleman all the way down to his core.

"I understand," he said, his voice raspy in the silence of the car's interior. "Do me a favor though?"

She risked making eye contact. "What favor?"

"Don't suffer in silence, Dena." His eyes were glossy behind his glasses. "I did that and it didn't get me anywhere." He cleared his throat. "I didn't truly start healing until I came to Vermont and saw Leah. She helped me see a new start was possible, that even though sucky things had happened, that didn't mean my entire life—my entire future—had to suck too." He wrapped his fingers around the steering wheel, no doubt keeping himself from touching her. "This may come off as sounding like a crazy stalker,"—he smiled a little—"but I'm not giving up on us. Things were too wonderful this week for me to throw in the towel."

"You shouldn't put your life on hold because I'm fucked up, Carter." She wanted him to be free. "I thought I was okay, but clearly I'm not."

"Maybe you should talk to someone. A professional. Someone who can give you strategies."

It wasn't the first time that particular suggestion had come her way. "Did you see one?"

Slowly he shook his head. "But I'm stubborn. Do as I say, not as I did."

"I have to go." She put her hand on the door handle.

"Will you call me if you change your mind about being alone tonight?" He stared out the windshield.

She didn't answer. Instead she got out of the car, shut the door, and didn't look back as she punched in the code to open her garage door. She ran inside and hit the button to close the door again. As Carter's car disappeared from view, Dena pressed her forehead to the door to the kitchen. She stood there, between in the garage and in the kitchen, an ache throbbing in her chest.

Caught. She was caught in a sticky net that allowed the past to pull her out of the present and destroy her future. Being aware of it didn't help. In fact, it royally pissed her off. She was normally in control, everything organized and calculated down to the precise cent. This fear was a currency she didn't understand.

Letting out a frustrated growl, she jerked open the door and stomped into the kitchen. She shed her coat, hung it on its hook, and kicked off her shoes. Right now she was supposed to be leaving a trail of her and Carter's clothes straight to her bed and the sexy somethings she'd bought to heat things up.

Instead, she was cold. Stone cold, her heart a hardened lump of granite, weighing her down.

She paused by the phone when the blinking answering machine light caught her attention. Pressing the play button, she went to the sink to get a glass of water.

Probably need something stronger than water.

A woman's voice sounded from the answering machine. "Hello, Ms. Bennett. This is Grace Rostella, Attorney Jack Simon's secretary. The trial against Gary Warner is set for Tuesday morning. Jack would like you to come in Monday to review the case. Please call us back."

Dena scribbled down the number Grace had left then slumped into the recliner in the living room. Maybe giving Gary what he deserved would let her build herself back up to the confident person she used to be.

Or perhaps she'd never be whole again.

****

The weekend had gone by without a word from Dena, but Carter hadn't been surprised. Even though she was afraid, she had her pride. She wouldn't ask for help. Not from him. Not from a professional. She'd rather trash what they'd been building together and shut him out. He'd thought she'd learned that the two of them were good together.

More than good. Amazing. Maybe it had only been amazing for him. She'd appeared to enjoy making love last week and spending time together. The way she'd danced with him at *Beyond* had made him feel as if they were completely in tune, moving as one entity around the dance floor. Where had that chemistry gone? The moment she'd gotten afraid, she'd put up her shields, and none of his huffing or puffing would blow them down.

Jacy had texted him on Saturday morning, saying she'd stopped by Dena's and found her sister in grouch mode. He'd explained the encounter with Tim at *Beyond* and Dena's subsequent request to be left alone.

Dude, I'm sorry, Jacy had texted back.

I'm sorry it happened. We were having such a good time.

Hang in there.

He intended to, but he couldn't ignore that his feelings were hurt and they were wasting time. All the days he and Dena had been apart were missed opportunities to grow closer, to make their relationship stronger.

To fall deeper in love.

Carter knew from experiencing the loss of his brother that each day was a miracle. You had no idea how many days you'd be granted. To waste any of them seemed like a sin and he'd wasted too many on his own already. Though time might heal Dena, being

192

around those that loved her would speed up the process.

And Carter loved her.

He'd gone back and forth all weekend, wondering if he should drive to Dena's and say those three little words. Would it make a difference? Would she believe he truly loved her or would she think it was merely a strategy to worm his way into her bed? Would she understand the magnitude of him saying those words to her? He'd never said them to another woman. She'd be the first. He wanted her to be the first, but sitting in his cottage, burying himself in his work, while she avoided interacting with people wasn't going to make that happen. He had to respect her request for alone time, but at what point did he get to march over to her house and make some demands? He had to be the one to take the initiative because she might not. The idea of not being with her was unacceptable so he'd make the first move.

If she doesn't contact me by tomorrow, I'll call. At least he had a goal. Maybe calling her on Wednesday would get him nowhere. Perhaps she wouldn't be ready to speak to him, but he had to do something.

His doorbell rang. Carter glanced at the clock on the microwave to see it was 8:00 a.m. on the dot.

At least the kid is punctual. He opened the door and summoned a smile for Rohen. Their Tuesday internship started today and he wasn't going to let his screwed up emotions over Dena deprive Rohen of a good learning experience. "Good morning."

"Good morning." Rohen squeezed the strap of the bag slung across his chest then wiggled the bag slightly. "I didn't know what to bring so I brought my sketchpad, pencils, and my laptop."

Carter stepped out of the threshold and motioned for Rohen to come in. "Sounds good. I guess I should have made a materials list or something. Forgive me. This is my first time having an intern. I'm sort of figuring it out as I go along."

"Aren't we all?" Rohen gave him a small smile as he walked through the door and past Carter.

"You're wise for a seventeen-year-old."

Rohen sifted out a breath. "I feel as if I've lived for at least forty years already."

"Great, you be in charge then. You'll probably do a better job than me."

The boy set his bag down on the kitchen island. "Anything will be better than PE class."

"Ah, yes. Battling with the jocks is to be avoided at all cost." Carter opened the refrigerator. "Have you had breakfast?"

Rohen shrugged. "Granola bar. The group home's menu doesn't always agree with me. I've got a shitty stomach." The kid shot his gaze to Carter's. "I'm sorry. I shouldn't have used a swear word."

Carter held up his hands. "Hey, man, this is a swear-friendly zone. I don't mind cursing."

"Okay," Rohen said. "But I'll try to keep it tame."

Carter went back to perusing the refrigerator. "So shitty stomach... hmm..." He reached in and pulled out some yogurt and fresh strawberries and blueberries. After getting two bowls from the cupboard, he dished out dollops of yogurt and added cut-up strawberries and the blueberries. He grabbed some cinnamon graham crackers and crumbled them over the yogurt-fruit concoction.

Sliding one bowl toward Rohen and arrowing a spoon into it, he said, "Breakfast of champions."

Rohen stared at the bowl for a few silent seconds.

"What's the matter? Is there something there you don't like? I can put something else together." He backpedaled to the cupboard above the microwave and opened it. "I have cereal."

Rohen shook his head and picked up the spoon. "No, this is… this is actually great. I just… I can't remember the last time someone made me breakfast." He looked right then left. "Or the last time someone didn't try to swipe my food as soon as I sat to eat it."

Carter's bruised heart took another hit. "Oh, man. That fucking sucks."

The laugh that bubbled out of the kid made Carter feel as if a great victory had been won. And he needed some victories. His record with Dena had been plummeting. Maybe Rohen had been sent to him for some balance.

"This, however," Rohen held up a spoonful of yogurt and fruit, "does not fucking suck." He shoveled it into his mouth and Carter didn't miss how the kid's eyes closed for a minute as he chewed and savored the simple food. "Thank you."

"No problem. If you tell me other shit you like, I can get some of it."

"You don't have to feed me. That's not part of the mentor responsibilities." The way Rohen polished off the food, however, told Carter that it definitely should be.

"Take a look around, young apprentice." Carter held his arms out to his sides. "I'm not taking care of anyone else. I think I can swing some breakfast and lunch for you every Tuesday. No big deal. Text me a list of foods when you get a chance, but don't expect lobster."

That squeezed another chuckle out of the boy. "Fair enough."

Rohen slid off the stool at the kitchen island and took his dish and spoon to the sink when he finished his breakfast. He washed and dried both items and returned them to where Carter had gotten them. Carter didn't stop him, understanding the kid wanted to repay him by cleaning up after himself.

"So why don't you have anyone else to take care of?" Rohen held up his hands. "If it's okay to ask that."

"It's okay." Carter finished his own breakfast then Rohen took his bowl and spoon and washed, dried, and put them away. "My... girlfriend," he guessed he could call Dena that because they'd gone way past the making out phase, "is going through some stuff so I suppose we're on a break right now."

Rohen hummed his understanding. "My girlfriend in California said we should take a break while I'm here. I said I'd be back once I turned eighteen, but I don't think she believed me. She probably hooked up with someone right after I left."

"Chicks," Carter said, frowning and shaking his head.

Rohen nodded. "Chicks."

"Too bad they're so hypnotic."

"And they smell good."

"Indeed." Carter rubbed his hands together and headed toward the hallway. "So why don't we start this internship with a tour of our working environment then of the hardware and software I use to do my job. Does that sound good?"

"Sounds like something a mentor would do so it must be right."

Carter spent the next thirty minutes showing Rohen the rest of the cottage, including his office space and his computers, drafting table, movable figures he used to draw different body stances and fight scenes, and the software programs he used to build the various parts of each game he made. He ended by showing the boy some of the character sketches he'd done for the new game he was working on now.

"*Andromeda Rebellion* is one of my favorite series of games," Rohen said as he looked over the sketches of Ergon soldiers. "It's so challenging."

"How long did it take you to beat the first game?" Carter loved hearing about fan experiences with his games.

Rohen swiveled on the desk chair in the office. "Probably a month."

"Wow. You stuck with it for a month?"

"It wasn't any problem to stick with it. Your games are a total experience. Amazing graphics that build the virtual world, perfect soundtracks with music that stays with you after you shut down the game, and killer storylines. It's like getting a concert and a book with the game each time."

"Huh, I never thought of it like that." Carter rocked back on his chair. "I mean, I get to write the story when I make the game and I have a ton of input on the music though I don't make it myself, but I guess I get caught up in the visuals, you know? On designing what everything will *look* like that I forget about the fact that players are getting a story and music too."

He grabbed a nearby notebook and scribbled down *story* and *music* to remind himself to pay more attention to those aspects. If they were important to Rohen as a gamer, other fans probably felt the same.

Carter waved his pen at Rohen. "I knew taking you on would help me as much as it helped you. Maybe even more. Thanks."

"I didn't do anything. Just telling you how it is."

"Yeah, and I wish more people would do that." Instead of hiding behind walls and fear and alone time.

"And now we're back to chicks." Rohen grinned. "Annoying."

"No doubt." Carter ran his hands through his hair. "I thought I'd show you how I take a character from one of my sketches and use the software to Frankenstein it to life. You can help too."

"Awesome." Rohen used his feet to roll the office chair closer to Carter. "It's so cool to get a sneak peek at the Ergon army."

Carter chewed on his bottom lip for a moment as he regarded Rohen. "You won't leak any of this info to the outside world, will you? Like this stuff can't end up plastered on social media or you'll kill the buzz about the new game for me."

Rohen patted the pockets of his jeans. "Have you seen me with a phone?"

Now that Carter thought about it... "No, I haven't."

"That's because I don't have a phone. Can't afford to buy one. The laptop I brought is a dinosaur." The boy stretched out his long legs. "My car's a piece of shit too. It was my aunt's." He folded his arms across his chest. "What I need is a job."

Carter dug out his phone. "I may be able to help with that. I see you know how to wash dishes."

"Doesn't everyone?"

"Not always without breaking them." He held up a finger as he found the contact he was looking for and tapped it.

After three rings, Kyle picked up. "Hey, Carter. Calling to invite me to a gaming party? I could really use one."

"I wasn't, but you're welcome here any time, man. You know that."

"Well, I figured now that you're with Dena, maybe your have-the-guys-hanging-around days were... limited."

"Never." He didn't feel like explaining the whole situation with Dena. Not now, but Kyle might have some advice so Carter made a mental note to hit his friend up about the topic at another time. "We'll schedule a night when Dakota gets back."

"Sweet. So what did you want?"

"Are you still looking for a dishwasher? I remember last week when I picked up a pizza, you were shorthanded in that department."

"Yeah, I'm still looking. Saturday night I actually ran out of dishes and had to resort to paper plates. I was horrified. Customers didn't care, but I'm trying to run a classy place here."

"Well, I have a kid here who is in need of a job and I've witnessed his dishwashing skills in person." He winked at Rohen who had moved to the edge of his chair, leaning his elbows on his knees and listening with great interest. "I think he'd be a great fit."

"How old is he?" Kyle asked.

"Seventeen. He goes to Maplehaven High and is currently my intern. Interning, however, doesn't pay. Dishwashing does."

"He's not a flake, is he?"

"Not at all. In fact, I think he might bring the classiness your establishment needs."

"Are you saying that Mountain View Pizza is not classy?"

"Depends on your definition of classy."

"I'm spitting on your pizza next time you come in."

"Yeah, because *that's* classy." His girlfriend might not want to talk to him, but at least people like Kyle did. Joking around with him lifted Carter's spirits.

A little.

Kyle laughed. "Okay, okay. Can the kid start tonight? I could use him right away."

Carter held the phone away from his mouth. "Do you have prior plans for this evening or would you be able to showcase your dishwashing skills for Mr. Kyle Lennings, owner extraordinaire of Mountain View Pizza?"

Rohen gaped at him for a few seconds.

"Rohen, what do you say?" Carter extended his leg and tapped the boy's knee with his foot.

Blinking and nodding, Rohen said, "I'll take the job. Thank you. Thank Mr. Lennings too."

Carter leaned forward and fist bumped Rohen. "He's available tonight, Kyle. His name is Rohen Sears and he says thank you for the opportunity. What time would you like him to report to the restaurant?"

They figured out the specifics and by the time the phone call had ended, Rohen had thanked Carter a bazillion times.

"No problem," he said. "This is an all-inclusive internship."

Dena might not need him, but Rohen did. And right now, Carter needed to be needed.

Chapter Eleven

Dena's left leg shook as she sat on the witness stand. Having to answer questions and relive her ordeal with Gary had not improved her mental state. Since Friday night, she'd been on a downward spiral, including several bouts of vomiting because she'd made herself so upset.

PTSD is a monumental pain in the ass. Especially when the logical Dena Brenton understood she was experiencing trauma. Why couldn't she rationalize her reaction away? She got the science of what was going on in her mind and in her body, so why couldn't she fucking stop it?

"Ms. Brenton?" the lawyer asked. "Could you please answer the question?"

No. No, I can't because I didn't hear the question. She was too busy falling apart.

"Could you repeat the question?" She focused on the lawyer's face, willing her body to settle so she could get the job done here and retreat to Maplehaven where she could hide.

"Is the man who attacked you in this courtroom now?"

With a quick flick of her gaze toward Gary, sitting beside his lawyer, Dena nodded. She'd spent most of her time in the courtroom so far doing her best to *not* look in Gary's direction. If she was this screwed up from her memories of her time with him in the parking garage, she feared what looking at him would do to her.

But I have to do this. She had committed herself to making Gary get what he deserved so no one else would fall victim to him. Maybe she'd be able to put this all behind her as well if he was locked up.

"Can you point him out to us, please?" the lawyer asked.

She raised a shaking hand and pointed an index finger at Gary. "He's right there."

The glare Gary sent back to her made bile rise in her throat. *Shit.* Puking on the witness stand would not be good. She already felt weak for having gotten into the position where Gary could attack and cut her with a damn knife. She didn't want to give him the added pleasure of knowing he'd made her sick in a crowded courtroom.

The lawyer walked away from her and faced the jury. "Let the record show Ms. Brenton has indicated Gary P. Warner as her attacker."

More questions followed about how Gary had wounded her and exactly where the incident had taken place. Two other women testified as well, and the courtroom portion of the trial wrapped up fairly quickly as the evidence against Gary was solid. The jury filed out to deliberate and the lawyer told Dena they'd most likely know the verdict in a matter of hours.

"Is someone here with you?" the lawyer asked.

Dena nodded. "My sister."

"There's a great café across the street if you want to hang around. I'll call you when the verdict's ready to be delivered if you'd like."

"That sounds good." She shook the lawyer's hand. "Thank you."

"No. Thank you. This guy is going down because of you and the other two women who testified. Another scumbag off the streets."

After parting ways, Dena found Jacy at the back of the courtroom near the exit.

"It was hard not to trip that bastard as he was led out," Jacy said, her arm going automatically around Dena's shoulders. "You did a great job."

"I think I might be sick."

"To the ladies' room we go." Jacy kept her arm around Dena as she navigated them to the nearest restroom. When they got to a stall, Jacy said, "Do you need me to hold your hair?"

"Not this time, but thanks." On shaky legs, Dena pushed open the stall door, entered, and closed the door. As she slid the lock into place, her stomach pitched and she whipped around to face the toilet. Her meager breakfast of a muffin made a repeat appearance, but her stomach felt much better afterward. She rooted around in her purse for a stick of gum, unwrapped it, and popped it into her mouth. The burst of mint helped.

She flushed and emerged from the stall to find Jacy standing right there.

"You okay?" her sister asked, her gaze searching Dena's face. The worry there creased Jacy's eyebrows and tightened her lips. The ball-busting twin was nowhere to be found. What stood in her place was a rock of support.

Dena's throat stung as did the corners of her eyes. *Do not cry. Do not cry.* It was bad enough she'd vomited. Crying like a stupid baby would push her over the edge. She feared she wouldn't be able to climb back to sanity if she let those tears fall.

Squaring her shoulders and sniffing, she said, "Yes. My stomach feels better."

"You know I don't just mean your stomach, Dena." Jacy reached out and knocked her knuckles lightly against Dena's forehead. "I mean in here. Talk to me. I'm all ears."

Dena made her way over to the sinks, washed her hands, and dried them. She glanced at herself in the mirror in front of her and winced. Her hair was frizzy and dull. Her eyes were bloodshot, her gaze distant. A spot of vomit dotted her shirt. She grabbed more paper towel, wet it under the faucet, and dabbed at the stain.

When Jacy came into view behind her, Dena felt as if she were looking at one of those makeover pictures. She was the before picture, Jacy the much improved after.

"Let's go to that café," Jacy said. "Even if you only want water, we should get out of here for a few."

Not sure what else to do, Dena followed Jacy out of the restroom. She was vaguely aware of leaving the building, crossing the street, entering the café, and sitting at a table while Jacy got them some drinks. When her sister returned to the table with a tray sporting two teas and a cookie the size of a large pizza, Dena's stomach did a flip-flop.

"By the greenness of your skin," Jacy said, "I think this tea will hit the spot." She set one of the cups in front of Dena. "I'll handle this cookie. Don't you worry about its welfare."

The steam from the tea—ginger-scented—reached Dena's nose and something in her stomach decided the fragrance was friendly. She picked up the cup and took a tentative sip. Warmth traveled down her throat and spread out to extremities gone cold with anxiety.

"Thanks," she croaked between sips.

"No problem." Jacy broke off a piece of the cookie, popped it into her mouth, and chewed as she stared at Dena.

"What?" Dena tightened her hands around the cup, craving the heat.

Jacy angled her head at Dena. "I think what you're doing is incredibly brave."

"But?"

"But you don't have to keep your shit together all the time."

Dena let out a mirthless laugh and pointed to herself. "You call this keeping my shit together? I was like a robot on the stand. I've been shaking like a goddamn leaf since Friday night. I puked in the ladies' room. Newsflash: My shit is *not* together."

"Your shit is well contained, Dena. It's okay to let yourself crumble. What you went through earns you a free pass to come unglued. I can see you beating yourself up. You think you need to keep everything bottled up because you don't want to burden anyone with your feelings." Jacy reached across the table and put her hand atop Dena's. "Well,

206

newsflash: There are people ready and willing to take some of that burden in order to help you. Me, Dad, Mom, Dakota, Leah, any one of your friends. Carter."

At the mention of his name, Dena squeezed her eyes closed. She'd hurt him again on Friday night when she'd asked to be taken home. When they *hadn't* made love. When she'd pretty much told him to take a hike.

Again.

How many times would he let her push him away before he stayed away for good? Did she want him to stay away? One thought of his compassionate brown eyes, his strong hands that had only touched her with respect, his humor which had made her laugh... he truly was perfect, but if she kept shutting him out, eventually he wouldn't want back in.

Maybe he already didn't want back in. He hadn't called or texted her. She couldn't blame him though.

Dena shook her head. "I can't let Carter waste any more of his time on me."

"Isn't that for him to decide?" Jacy asked. "Maybe he loves wasting his time on you."

"No one loves wasting time." Dena sipped her tea, the heat not as potent as her first sips had been. "He deserves someone who will appreciate him."

"Are you telling me you don't appreciate him?"

"I do, but he's not getting the most out of this relationship." She folded and unfolded the small square napkin Jacy had given her with the tea. "I'm sure there are women out there who would make him far happier than I can."

"You're probably right."

Dena's eyes widened as she looked at her sister. "Ouch."

Jacy leaned back in her seat as she squeezed the water out of her teabag and placed the bag on the saucer. "Look, I'm trying to be straight with you. It's my duty as the twin to not sugarcoat anything to spare your feelings." She slapped her phone on the table between them and pointed to it. "And, for the record, Carter has texted me three times today. If he didn't want to wait for you, he wouldn't be asking if you're okay."

Dena stared into her teacup. She pictured Carter at his cottage, working in his office, but taking breaks to check on her. "Ugh. I'm such a jerk."

"Absolutely not. You went through something that sucked ass. Big time. Carter understands that, however, he also wants to be there for you. He's the kind of dude who has the magic necessary to slay your dragons. Not *for* you, but *with* you. He's definitely one you want by your side."

Jacy was right. The only time Dena had allowed the Gary incident to truly fade away was when she was with Carter. His presence soothed, supported, empowered. Her first instinct when Tim had grabbed her at *Beyond* had been to freak out, but Carter had been right there, ready to defend her if necessary, ready to talk her off the ledge.

And I retreated instead of thanking him. She hadn't even given him a chance to comfort her. She could admit that comforting was what she needed. A man like Carter was the guy for the job.

The guy for her. Why hadn't she been able to see that on Friday night when it mattered?

Dena puffed out a long breath. "I need to call him."

"Yippee!" Jacy clapped. "I'll be over here with this ginormous and delicious cookie."

Grabbing her purse, Dena fished out her phone. "Be right back."

She left the café, and judging the street busy enough that an attack by a stranger was unlikely, Dena tapped Carter's contact on her phone. She meandered away from the café a bit as she listened to the ringing. The call went to voicemail and the sound of his voice on the message made her smile.

She ended the call, figuring what she had to say needed to be said to him directly and not left on a message.

"That was way too fast," Jacy said when Dena entered the café again. "What happened?"

"Nothing. It went to voicemail." She checked the time. 1:30 p.m. "He's probably working."

Jacy swiped her phone and opened her messages. "He did say he had his intern over, so that's a fair guess. Call him later though. Don't let what needs to be said go unsaid."

Dena regarded her sister. "When did you become the wise one?"

"Oh, me? See, I have all this free time because I'm not marrying my soul mate like our brother did or dating anyone dreamy like you are. I've decided to offer my counsel to others instead." She rolled her eyes and ate another chunk of cookie. The monstrous dessert was about a third gone at this point.

"There's someone—"

Jacy lasered a glare her way, effectively cutting Dena off. "If you say 'there's someone out there for you, Jacy,' I will scream."

Dena held up her hands. "Okay, but it'll happen for you. You're a great person with so much to offer, and I'll be the first to say you're gorgeous."

"Oh, identical twin, you are a funny gal."

"When I'm not paralyzed by trauma, yeah, I'm pretty amusing."

Jacy rubbed her hand on the table. "That trauma will fade when you fill up the space with Carter-infused moments. When you make new wonderful memories to replace the shit ones."

Dena reached over and broke off a piece of cookie. The scent of chocolate chips didn't send her stomach into a spiral so she took a nibble and realized she was starving. "Does this place have actual food?"

She got up, went to the counter, and ordered a BLT grilled cheese and a ginger ale. Demolishing the tasty sandwich in a matter of minutes, she sat back and patted her stomach.

"Let's hope that stays put," Jacy said.

"I think it will. What have I got to be sick about?" She sat up straighter. "We're about to get news of a guilty verdict. I'm going to talk to Carter when we get back to Maplehaven. Things will be good."

"There's my goal-oriented, let's-get-control-of-the-situation sister. Welcome back." Jacy held up her teacup.

Dena tapped her ginger ale glass to it. "Sitting here with you shook things back into place. Thanks."

"What are twin sisters for if they can't hit the reset button on each other when needed?" Jacy wrapped up what remained of the cookie. "We can chow down on the rest of this tonight at the hotel as we do our victory dance over Gary's incarceration."

As if on cue, Dena's phone buzzed. She swiped the screen to find the lawyer's number.

"Ms. Brenton?" The lawyer's voice was upbeat. That had to be good.

"Yes. Is the jury ready?"

"Indeed they are."

"We'll be right there." Dena tapped the screen and dropped her phone into her purse. "Let's finish this."

"Amen."

After they cleaned up their rubbish, Dena led them outside, but before they headed for the courthouse, she turned around to face Jacy. "Thanks for coming with me today. I know you're busy at the sawmill and whatnot."

Jacy pulled her into a hug. "I'm never too busy for you."

That was the thing about Brentons. They stood by each other. Always. Being able to count on that reminded Dena how lucky she was.

****

Carter sat in his office by himself as he studied the three drawings Rohen had done during their interning session today. The first was a rendering of Theo—the real Theo, whom Rohen had taken an instant liking to and vice versa. The bunny had allowed the boy to pick him up and set him in his lap. When Carter had told Rohen about the rabbit's injury and surgery, the kid had stroked the bunny's soft fur in such a soothing, compassionate way. Theo had eaten up the attention.

"You can tell a lot about a person who is accepted by animals," Carter had said.

Still gazing at the bunny, Rohen had said, "We had a bunch of animals at our home in California. My parents were both veterinarians. They took abandoned, injured animals home on a weekly basis." He'd smiled at Carter. "They always said it was until they could find the animals a good home, but we always ended up keeping the creatures. Sometimes it felt as if we lived in a zoo." The boy's eyes had closed as he'd petted Theo.

"And you'd give anything to go back there, wouldn't you?" Carter had asked as he'd lowered to sit on the coffee table.

"Yeah." Rohen had cleared his throat. "But some things can't be undone no matter how much you wish they could be."

"What happened to your parents?" Carter had held his breath, hoping he wasn't making the kid uncomfortable.

"Wildfires. They both volunteered to help, mostly with the animals. They stayed too long, got too close, and then they were gone." Rohen's voice had gone scratchy, his hand shaking as he'd stroked Theo's back.

"I'm so sorry, Rohen."

"Thanks." Rohen had kept his gaze trained on Theo. "When I get sad about them, I try to remember they were heroes."

"Truly. My brother was a firefighter, so a hero as well, but losing ones you love fucking sucks, hero or not."

Rohen had nodded. "Fucking sucks."

The drawing of Theo that Carter looked at now was remarkable. Rohen had managed to make the two-dimensional figure leap off the page. Carter swore he could reach into the picture and hold the bunny in his hands. The white fur looked touchable. The kid had somehow made the rabbit have a knowing expression on its face—as if Theo was a genuine sacred bunny with a great many secrets filed away in his brain.

Carter picked up the drawing of an Ergon general. Rohen had examined many of Carter's completed character sketches and had asked if he could play around with making an Ergon. The final result was actually usable. Carter had shown the boy how to scan the picture and make adjustments.

"You mean you'll really use this in the finished game?" Rohen had asked, a new light in his blue eyes.

"If you give me your permission to, yeah," Carter had said. "I'll put your name in the end credits too."

"Sweet." Rohen had immediately turned to a clean sheet of paper in his sketchbook and set to work on the last drawing of the day.

An insane depiction of Dena.

The kid had captured her... her *Dena-ness*. That something extra that made Dena so special. He'd used a picture Carter had on his computer screen. In a matter of moments, he'd had an amazing pencil drawing, but when he'd added some color—especially green-brown at the eyes—the entire picture came to life. It was almost like having Dena there in person.

If only.

Working with Rohen all day had been an excellent distraction, but a huge chunk of Carter's brain had been on Dena. He was fortunate Jacy had given him updates. He was also a little miffed Dena had gone to Providence for the trial without him. He'd made a promise to go with her for support, but she'd slipped away to Rhode Island with Jacy instead.

Carter understood that perhaps she preferred to have her sister with her. He couldn't compete with the bond between sisters, especially *twin* sisters, but didn't she know he'd be worrying about her? Didn't she know how much he wanted to be there for her as she went through this court process? Didn't she know he loved her?

No, she doesn't because I've never told her. He'd never said the words to make his feelings for Dena official. He'd thought the words, felt the sentiments, even gone so far as to dream about a future built on his feelings for her. But that wasn't the same as saying it to her.

Is it too late?

Would Dena want to hear those words? Was he a fool for hoping a relationship with her was still actually possible?

He glanced down to the picture of her. Tracing her lovely mouth with his index finger, he became full with missing her. He picked up his phone from his desk and swiped the screen. No more messages from Jacy.

None from Dena.

Grumbling to himself, Carter set the drawing on the desk and stood. He pocketed his phone and stretched. He'd been sitting way too long today and while he hadn't noticed because Rohen's conversation and presence had distracted him, he was extremely aware of how quiet his cottage was now.

He walked out to the kitchen, pulled open the refrigerator, and scanned the shelves. The bare shelves. "Well, this won't do."

He let the door close then swiveled on his heel to face the kitchen island. After checking on Theo, who was resting in a nest Rohen had made of an empty box and a blanket, Carter pulled on his coat and stepped outside.

A walk. He'd go for a walk, clear his head, and… and what? The long night stretched before him and he had nothing to fill it. He could work some more, but his poor eyes were tired after going at it all day with Rohen. He needed a break.

And some sex. Making love to Dena would have been the perfect way to pass the hours from sunset to sunrise, but she was in Providence and he was in Maplehaven. According to his last communication with Jacy at a little after noon, she and Dena were planning to stay in Rhode Island overnight. The earliest he'd be able to see Dena was most likely tomorrow afternoon.

Puffing out a breath, he zipped up his coat and walked down the street. He didn't have a destination in mind so when he came upon Freddie's Liquor, he milled about in the parking lot for five minutes before deciding to go in.

A voice in his head that sounded so much like Chase's cautioned him to march out of that store. To not be tempted. To go home and get more work done. Snuggle poor Theo. Watch a movie. Go to bed alone.

And sober.

He ignored that voice. Dead men didn't get to tell him what to do.

After purchasing a bottle of his favorite whiskey, Carter power-walked home, as if he were afraid he might run into someone who would try to stop him from self-medicating with alcohol.

Once inside his cottage, he cracked the whiskey bottle open, dropped ice cubes into a glass, and poured himself three fingers of whiskey. He took the glass—and the bottle—over to the couch and plopped onto the center cushion. Grabbing the remote, he turned on the TV, but within the hour, it didn't matter what was on the screen. The only thing that mattered was how the whiskey burned the back of this throat and blurred the setting around him.

Being alone wasn't that bad if he dulled his senses and didn't give a shit. He'd gotten over Chase's death with a little help from Mr. Whiskey and friends. He'd get over Dena pushing him aside the same way. He didn't need anyone. He could take care of himself.

Or he could forget the world for a while. He could get to the bottom of that whiskey bottle and not give a shit about anything or anyone. He'd take a break from being the nice guy.

Each sip of whiskey chased the next and soon Carter had a solid buzz going. He stumbled to the hall closet and rummaged around, finding a bottle of wine Leah must have left behind when she'd moved.

Perfect.

He was just a bachelor, living on his own, getting wasted as was his single-guy right. Around this point in a drinking spell, he usually was itching for a fight with someone. The last time he'd gotten smashed, he'd been at a bar in New York City and had nearly been arrested for his unruly behavior. Not something he was particularly proud of, but it had been a wakeup call for him. Soon after that event, he'd called Leah, arranged to visit Vermont, then completely fallen for the state, specifically Maplehaven.

Specifically Dena.

But Dena wasn't his right now. Would she ever be his? How long could he wait? How long did he want to wait? He was tired of waiting. So tired.

Carter sat on the couch and pulled his legs up to recline across the cushioned length. He wedged his hands behind his head as the ceiling spun above him. Why didn't he want to pound on someone? Why was he so sleepy instead? Where had all the fight in him gone?

Crap. He was acting like a grown up, wasn't he? He knew he was a little trashed and instead of rushing out to piss someone off, he was preparing to sleep off what he'd imbibed.

Because of Dena.

She wouldn't approve of him going off half-cocked and stirring up trouble. Drunken trouble. He couldn't bear the thought of her being disappointed in him.

How will she be disappointed if she never knows? She wasn't around. She clearly didn't want him around. It was quite possible they wouldn't be around each other ever again though that was unlikely. Maplehaven was a small town. His best friend had gone and married Dena's brother. He wasn't about to stop hanging with Leah… or Dakota for that matter. Of course he'd still see Dena. Probably often. Often enough that falling on his old defense mechanisms of getting shitfaced and sniffing out a brawl wouldn't do.

If he wanted to win Dena back, he'd need all his brain cells to function, to work together as a team, to help him come up with a plan of attack to make her see she couldn't live without him.

But first a nap to stop the spinning. Usually the spinning was the best part. That whirlwind of carefree abandon where he didn't give a shit about anything other than keeping his glass full.

Tonight, however, his muddled thoughts kept circling back to Dena and being a man who deserved a woman like her. Sure, she didn't want him right now, but Carter could understand why.

He could also hope it was a temporary situation.

She'd pushed him away once already and had come around to see him again. He wasn't crazy to wish for that again, was he?

His phone buzzed in his pocket and he fell off the couch trying to maneuver it out. Getting to his knees, he squinted at the screen and seeing Leah's name, he answered.

"Leah!" he roared.

"Carter? Why are you yelling?"

"I'm happy to talk to you, buddy." He was still shouting, but he couldn't seem to lower the volume.

"Are you... shit, Carter, are you drunk?" Leah's voice had that teachery vibe to it. As if she were judging him and he wasn't earning high marks.

"So what if I am? I can be drunk. I'm an adult."

"If you have to declare you're an adult, chances are you're not an adult," Leah said. "I'm coming over."

"I didn't invite you over."

"I know. I'm coming anyway. Do not leave your house."

"You're not the boss of me."

"I'm aware of that, Carter, but I don't like what's happening here." Leah's voice softened. "Is this because of Dena?"

"No. I'm kicking back on a... on a..."

"Tuesday night?" Leah puffed out a breath. "Stay put."

"I'm okay, Leah. Really. You just got home from your moonhoney."

"Honeymoon."

"Whatever." He yawned and got back onto the couch. "You have your own shit to do and I'm going to go to bed now."

Leah was quiet for a minute and Carter closed his eyes, his desire for sleep growing exponentially by the second. "You promise you'll go to bed and not go looking for trouble?"

He let out a short laugh. "I promise. Besides I never go looking for trouble. It finds me. Sometimes in the form of a douchebag that needs his face rearranged." *Like that Gary asshole.* "Other times in the form of a chick that doesn't dig me as much as I dig her."

"Dena digs you, Carter. Everyone who has seen the two of you together knows this. She needs—"

"Some time." He sighed. "Yeah, I've heard." His pleasant buzz was becoming less and less pleasant. Instead his stomach felt crampy and he could barely keep his eyes opened. "I gotta go, Leah."

"Are you sure I shouldn't come over and check on you?"

He smiled despite the fact that being sick was entirely possible. "I can take care of myself, and you now have a husband to take care of. Settle in after your trip. We'll catch up tomorrow when you can bore me to death with pictures of beautiful... where the hell did you go again?" His brain was too foggy to remember.

But it did remember there had been a bottle of tequila in the hall closet next to the wine.

"Fiji."

"Right. Fiji. Can't wait to see." He yawned again. "Good night, Leah."

"Good night, Carter."

He was pretty sure it wouldn't be a good night. Not with Dena in a whole other state four hours away and a raging hangover headache on his horizon.

Christine DePetrillo

Chapter Twelve

With a guilty verdict and some jail time for Gary, Dena and Jacy arrived back in Maplehaven by mid-afternoon on Wednesday. Jacy put her blinker on to turn onto Dena's street, but Dena pointed out the windshield.

"Can you take me to Carter's instead?" she asked.

Jacy clapped her hand against the steering wheel. "Yay! I'd be delighted to take you there. Are you going to throw yourself at him?"

"Umm... probably not," Dena said. "We need to talk first."

"Talking is boring."

"I owe him an apology, Jacy." She'd thought about what she would say all night as she attempted to sleep in an uncomfortable hotel bed. She'd been overjoyed about the verdict and punishment handed down to Gary, but she couldn't truly celebrate until she saw Carter and made things right. Asking for another chance was probably pushing it, but she was going to do it anyway. She hoped he'd agree.

"I don't know of another apology better than getting naked," Jacy said.

"If it all goes well, we will get naked."

221

"Okay. Make your apology short then. The tension in your shoulders is insane. You need something to help you unclench."

Dena rubbed the ache in her left shoulder. "How do you know there's tension in my shoulders?"

"Because they are up in your ears, dear sister." Jacy scrunched up her own shoulders. "You also tossed and turned all night last night."

"Sorry if I kept you up."

Jacy waved a hand. "I would have been up anyway. I was amped about the verdict and the thought of that scumbucket going behind bars. I do love a good victory."

"Yeah, I'm happy with the way things turned out. It sucks that it happened, but at least there's a sense of justice."

"And that sense will set you free. Allow you to move on." She turned onto Carter's street. "Move on with the hunk in that cottage." She pointed toward the cottage then pulled into the driveway. "Want me to beep the horn?" Jacy put her hand over the horn on the steering wheel, an eager smile on her face.

Dena grabbed her sister's forearm and wrenched her hand away from the horn. "No. I'd prefer a more subtle approach."

"You're no fun." But Jacy was smiling. "Well, get out of my car already and get your man. Call me if you need anything."

"Thanks so much for coming with me." Dena leaned over and hugged Jacy.

"Anytime. For any reason," Jacy whispered before pulling back from the embrace. "Now scoot. Good luck."

Dena climbed out of the car, grabbed her small suitcase, and waved to her sister. As she walked up the front steps of the cottage, Jacy pulled out of the driveway. Dena watched her taillights disappear then turned to the front door. Raising a hand, she knocked once, twice, three times with no evidence of any stirring inside.

Shit. Was Carter not home? Great. She'd have to call Jacy and tell her to come back to pick her up. She'd have to delay seeing Carter. That was what she got for being spontaneous.

She wandered over to the bay window to the left of the door and peeked in. The first thing to catch her attention was a set of... rabbit ears. She squinted and yes, two rabbit ears as white as snow twitched at her. The bunny sat on the bay window's sill, his big dark eyes looking at her as if she were an intruder.

Open the door, Theo. If only the bunny had opposable thumbs and could reach the doorknob.

Dena looked beyond the bunny and caught sight of Carter sprawled out on the couch. His long legs were propped up on the armrest and his left arm hung off the cushion, his hand almost touching the floor.

She backed up and pulled out her phone to check the time. 2:30 p.m. Why in the world was Carter sleeping at two-thirty in the afternoon? He often worked unusual hours, but he didn't sleep mid-afternoon as far as she knew.

Something wasn't right.

Her gaze traveled to the coffee table where three bottles—three *empty* bottles—lay on their sides. She shaded her eyes to see better through the window and instantly realized she was looking at liquor bottles. *Jesus.* Had Carter consumed all three in one sitting?

More importantly, was she the reason he'd turned to alcohol? Had she jerked him around too much?

I won't get answers to any of these questions standing out here.

And what if he wasn't merely sleeping off a hangover? What if he was sick or hurt in there? Her worry propelled her into action. She jogged back over to the front door and pounded her fist on it. Over and over and over.

"Carter! Open up, Carter!" she shouted. "I see you in there! Wake up and open the door!" *Pound, pound, pound.* "Carter! It's Dena!" *Pound, pound, pound.* She jabbed at the doorbell, but that didn't garner any results either.

She tried calling him, but he didn't pick up. How was she going to get in there and make sure he was all right? Shouldn't he have awakened amidst the ruckus she was creating? If only she had a key.

A key. Who would have a key? Leah maybe? Dena texted Leah.

At Carter's. Can see him inside, but he won't wake up. Do you have a key to the cottage?

She paced the length of the front porch as she waited for a reply. The moment her phone buzzed in her hand she swiped the screen.

Have key. Ten more minutes until school gets out. Be right there. Knew I should have checked on him last night.

224

That last sentence worried Dena even more. Why had Leah felt the need to check on Carter? What did she know that Dena didn't? She hated bothering Leah, especially since the woman had just returned to work after being on her honeymoon. This was an emergency though. She needed to get in that house.

Dena banged her fist on the front door again, needing to do something while she waited for Leah and the key. "Carter! Please wake up!" She pressed her forehead against the cool surface of the frosted glass on the door, wishing like hell she had the ability to walk through walls.

Could this have been avoided if she hadn't pushed Carter away for a second time? Had her treatment—*mis*treatment—of Carter caused him to fall off the wagon? Did he get violent when he was drunk?

She pushed off the door and took a few steps away from it. She had a hard time picturing Carter being violent, but alcohol did bad things to good people. It changed them. It made them lose control. Made them unpredictable.

Aggressive.

Dena's stomach did a sick roll and she lowered to sit on the front steps. Leaning her elbows on her knees, she held her head in her hands and massaged her temples. Maybe she didn't know anything about Carter at all. Perhaps he was a completely different man than she'd thought. Possibly he'd played a good role and had lured her in only to turn into something harmful later. Gary had seemed harmless during the conference workshops and then had morphed into a knife-wielding maniac in the parking garage. People were misleading.

Shaking her head, she sat upright and squared her shoulders. This was ridiculous thinking. Carter had only ever been sweet to her. Patient. Comforting. Loving. Every single touch from him had been powered by respect and gentleness.

He was no Gary.

"Carter Bennett would never hurt me." She made the statement aloud as if checking to see if it sounded right. It did. It totally did. The man inside that cottage was made for her. Whatever had happened while she was in Providence had an explanation. One she was going to get as soon as she got the damn front door opened and woke Carter up.

She got to her feet and walked through slushy snow around the perimeter of the house, peeking into windows and relieved to find no signs of a struggle. It didn't appear as if there had been a break-in or anything. Carter hadn't fought off a burglar so chances were he was merely asleep on that couch.

Please be asleep.

She didn't know if he had any medical conditions. They'd never talked about that stuff. They'd been too busy making out and more recently making love and even more recently being apart thanks to her. Maybe he wasn't physically well and she had no idea because she'd been far too wrapped up in herself to learn more about him.

As she recalled all her interactions with Carter, she realized that after he had told her about losing Chase and let her know his parents were also gone, she hadn't afforded him the opportunity to tell

226

her anything else about himself. Sure, she knew he designed video games for a living and he had the ability to set her body on fire with his lovemaking, but other than that, what did she know about Carter Bennett?

I'm an awful person.

She made her way back to the front of the house and contemplated calling Jacy to come get her. Leah would arrive with the key and check on Carter. He'd get help if he needed it. She could let the gap between them widen until he forgot about her and found someone who would be way better for him than she was. Someone who would make the effort to get to know the real man behind those glasses. She was better suited to crunching numbers in the impersonal manner of a financial manager than developing intimate relationships with other humans. Dena was close to her family and her few friends, but she didn't really *do* people.

And now it was obvious why. You couldn't write people down on paper or enter them into a spreadsheet, calculate their totals, and then forget about them. People needed care and interactions and conversations. She sucked at all of that. Give her a big old pile of numbers and she knew what to do.

Give her a man's heart and she was a complete idiot.

She swiped her phone, intent on calling Jacy and getting the hell out of there, but the sound of a car engine made her look to the driveway. Leah barely shut off the car before hopping out and taking the front steps in one leap.

"Where is he? Inside?" Leah had a semi-panicked expression on her face, her eyes wide and worried.

"Yeah. On the couch. I can't get him to wake up."

Leah flicked through keys on her keychain and poked one into the doorknob. "Good thing I kept this."

"Wait." Dena squeezed Leah's arm, making the other woman look up at her. "Does Carter... Does he have a drinking problem?"

Leah's face softened. "I should let him answer that, Dena."

With a quick turn of her wrist, the front door was open and Dena was stuck between taking a step inside or bolting down the front steps. She could run down the road a bit then call Jacy. She could be back at her own house, unpacking, doing laundry, hiding behind mundane tasks.

Hiding.

No. She wasn't a hider. She may not know a great deal about maintaining intimate, serious relationships with a guy, but she didn't ignore problems. She was a problem solver by nature. Usually she solved problems with numbers, but she could make an effort to solve a problem with a person.

A very important person. One she couldn't deny she wanted in her life.

Dena followed Leah into the cottage and to the living room. They both stood by the couch for a silent moment.

Carter's glasses were askew, his black hair wild about his head. The T-shirt he wore had ridden up, exposing his abs and reminding Dena what it had been like to trace her fingers along those toned muscles. Her fingers were interested in doing that again.

His chest rose and fell in a steady rhythm that told her he was, in fact, sleeping. She sifted out a breath of relief and kneeled beside the couch.

"I'm going to go," Leah whispered as she gave Dena's shoulder a light squeeze. "He's in good hands with you."

"But…" Dena started, but Leah was heading for the door which was still open.

What if Carter *wasn't* in good hands? She looked back at him after Leah closed the door. His lips were slightly parted and when she leaned forward a bit, she could smell the liquor on his breath. Tequila if she wasn't mistaken. Glancing over her shoulder to the coffee table, she confirmed tequila was among the three bottles. Whiskey and wine were the other two and not a drop of liquid remained in any of them.

She couldn't help but feel responsible.

As she slowly reached out her hand to cup his cheek, something hopped into her lap and she let out a squeak, forgetting all about Theo.

"Hey, little guy." She ran her hands over the soft white fur of its back and the bunny nestled itself against her stomach. Dena rubbed the rabbit's long ears right to the tips then she leaned toward Carter and pressed her hand to his cheek. "Carter," she whispered. "Carter, wake up. It's me. Dena."

When he didn't respond, she set the bunny on the floor and scooted closer. She dropped a soft kiss to his cheek then along his bearded jaw then on his parted lips.

After a few seconds, a moan emerged from Carter's throat and he joined in the kiss. He tasted like tequila which had always been one of Dena's favorite liquors. His arms came around Dena's sides, urging her onto the couch with him.

She climbed atop him, her body a long line against his, but when Dena looked at his face while maintaining the kiss, she realized his eyes were still closed. Did he think he was dreaming?

Was she?

****

A flowery fragrance filled Carter's nose. Vaguely familiar. Extremely pleasant. He inhaled deeply and continued kissing. Kissing dreams were among his favorites. Certainly better than the ones where he fell and then *smacked* down onto hard, unforgiving pavement. Or dreams about Chase's death.

He loathed those dreams.

But this one? Right now? *Sweetest dream ever.* The mouth he explored tasted like spearmint, the tongue soft and velvety as it brushed against his. A pleasant weight rested atop him and his arms were full of curvy woman. His dick hardened, wanting to bury itself somewhere wet and warm.

The only bad part about this particular dream was the headache slamming into the walls of his skull. It pierced through his brain like a sword and distracted him from giving his all to the dream kiss.

Unless…

His eyes shot open and the little bit of daylight spilling into his living room was enough to make him clamp them shut again. In the two seconds they were open, however, he'd gotten a quick glimpse of wavy brown hair and foresty hazel eyes.

"Dena," he rasped against what he now realized was *her* mouth.

She stopped kissing him, ending whatever illusion of a dream still lingered. "You're awake."

"I am." He lifted a hand which felt as if it were made of granite and stroked her cheek. "When did you get here?"

She shifted to sitting on his lap, a leg on either side of his still reclining body. "Well, I've been outside worrying about you for about fifteen minutes and then in here, kissing you, for maybe three minutes." She smiled, but the worry in her gaze was clear.

Carter turned his head to the left and yep, the empties were still on the table. *Fuck.* He sat up, immediately regretting it. The room spun and the sword in his skull turned into a jackhammer.

His throat tingled.

His ears rang.

His stomach pitched.

He basically threw Dena off his lap as he struggled to his feet, stumbled down the hallway, and dove into the bathroom, slamming the door behind him. A moment later, he was hugging the toilet and retching up his mistake—correction, *mistakes*—from last night.

Ugh. He was a piece of shit for drinking like that. At least he had stayed true to his promise to Leah and hadn't gone out looking for a fight.

Had he?

He looked down at his clothes which were the same as what he had worn yesterday. He wasn't wearing any shoes and he didn't appear to have any new bruises on him. He also didn't have the sense he'd seen anyone or punched anyone's face in last night.

Then again, his senses were significantly fucked up at the moment. They'd been pretty tuned in to Dena kissing him though. Despite the fact that he was currently inhaling the scent of his own vomit, he had to smile about that kiss.

The smile only lasted a millisecond. He had to get out there and explain before Dena came to her own conclusions and left.

He flushed the toilet, got to his feet on shaky legs, and brushed his teeth. He washed his face and finger-combed his hair into submission. Leaning toward the mirror, he inspected his bloodshot eyes and wondered if he should grab his sunglasses.

Fool. One didn't share dirty secrets from behind the veil of shades. Would only make it seem as if he had more to hide.

Brushing the wrinkles out of his T-shirt, he opened the bathroom door to find Dena right on the other side of it. "Oh, hey."

"Hey." Her arms were crossed and she looked a lot like Leah did when she had to discipline her students. He deserved that. He really did.

232

Christine DePetrillo

"Listen, I… umm…" He raked his hand through his hair and puffed out a long breath, which he hoped smelled like toothpaste and not tequila.

Or wine.

Or whiskey.

Dammit.

Dena held up a hand. "Hang on with the explanations. First things first. Are you okay?" Her beautiful eyes held no judgment now. Just concern. For him.

He leaned against the doorway to the bathroom, partly to seem casual, partly to keep from swaying like a sailor on stormy seas. "I am okay." He arrowed a thumb to the bathroom behind him. "I reset time by puking up my guts." He patted his stomach. "All clear now."

She narrowed her eyes at him. "Your stomach may be fine, but the squinty nature of your eyes tells me there is pain elsewhere in that body of yours." She turned and headed down the hallway. "Come on. Let's get some water and aspirin in you."

If she was willing to take care of him, was she willing to forgive the state in which she had found him today?

He followed her out to the kitchen and slouched onto one of the island stools. Not the most comfortable seating in the cottage, but maybe some discomfort would help him get his shit together.

For Dena.

She was here and he wasn't going to let this opportunity go to waste.

"Drink this." She handed him a full glass of water then turned in a circle. "Where are the aspirin?"

He pointed to the corner cabinet. "Second shelf." He took a few tentative sips of water and when his stomach didn't revolt, he drank more heartily.

Dena took the glass and refilled it. She shook aspirin out onto the counter and pushed the tablets toward him. "Down the hatch."

"So bossy," he said, but he took the aspirin and gulped them down with water. After he set the glass on the island, he met Dena's wary gaze. "Before we get into this mess," he waved his hand over himself, "tell me Gary is in jail."

"He is."

"Good." He reached for her hand and silently rejoiced when she met him halfway across the island and clasped his hand. "How are you doing? Was the trial awful?"

Dena shook her head. "It wasn't too bad. I mean, seeing Gary again was difficult, but watching him get carted away to jail was fabulous."

"I'm glad Jacy went with you." The thought of her facing Gary alone made him feel hollow inside.

"Yeah, it was good to have her there."

"I would have been there for you," he said.

"I'm sorry I pushed you away," she said at the same time.

A heartbeat of quiet hung between them until Carter squeezed her hand and said, "It doesn't matter how many times you push me away, Dena. I'll keep coming back for more. I'm hooked."

Still holding his hand, Dena came around to his side of the island and stepped into the space between his knees. She rested her hands on his shoulders and gazed directly into his eyes, her lips turned up at the corners. "I'm so happy to hear you say that. I don't plan to push you away again, but I think my experiences in Providence can creep up at any time. I can't promise that I won't need some alone time now and then." She cupped his cheek. "But I can promise I will give my all to this." She gestured between them. "It seems I've fallen in love with you, Carter Bennett, and it's time I dedicated myself to showing you how much I love you."

Carter opened his mouth several times, but no words came out. *Had Dena just told him that she loved him?* Or was he so hungover his imagination had taken him on a fictional journey that manifested what he *wanted* to hear?

"You love me?" The only way to be sure was to ask.

Dena nodded. "I love you. Is that okay?"

"Okay?" He let out a laugh. "It's more than okay. It's amazing. It's unbelievable." He wrapped his arms around her, hugging her close. When he released her, he met her gaze, his hand hooking on the back of her neck. "I love you too, Dena. And you should know I've never said that to another woman."

"Never?" Her brows crinkled adorably.

"Never. You are the first. You're the only one I've wanted to say it to." His gaze coasted down to her lips then he leaned forward and captured that mouth.

The kiss that followed went supernova in no time. His hand somehow ended up on her thigh which he was pressing to his hip, bringing her closer to his raging erection. If he didn't get her naked in the next few moments, he might go insane.

But he still had some explaining to do.

He managed to break the kiss and look up into her eyes. "The bottles..." he began, "I... sometimes I... get carried away when something has upset me."

"Something like me pushing you away?" Dena took a few steps back. Whether it was to be able to have the conversation or out of disgust, Carter wasn't sure yet.

"It's a horrible coping strategy," he said. "I did it after Chase was killed. When I first came to visit Leah here in Vermont, it was because I'd had enough of getting drunk, getting into fights, getting arrested." He let that last word hang out there for a moment. When Dena didn't recoil, he said, "I was tired of the cycle, so I came here. I met you and things were good. My mind was off losing Chase and on better things."

"When I pushed you away, I took the better things away," Dena said. "I'm sorry, Carter."

He shook his head. "It's not your fault, Dena. It's me. I should be able to control myself. And I had been. Last night... I don't know what happened." He took both of her hands in his now and held them tight against his chest. "I let myself lose it. I can't promise it won't happen again." He looked down at her hands, running his thumbs over her knuckles. "I can promise to get help though. I want to be the man you deserve. I'll do whatever it takes."

Dena brought their joined hands up to her lips. She pressed soft kisses to the backs of his hands. "I need some help too. That Gary thing fucked me up more than I wanted to admit. Handling it on my own isn't working. Maybe we can help each other."

236

Christine DePetrillo

"I would like that." Carter stood and pulled her against his body. He rested his chin on the top of her head. "I would like that a lot."

"It's a deal then." She squeezed him around the waist.

He nosed around in her hair. "You know the best way to seal a deal?"

She ground her hips against his. "I have an idea."

"God, I missed you." He swept her up into his arms, laughing when she squealed. He headed for the bedroom, coming to an abrupt stop when Theo hopped into his path. Carter ran his foot over the bunny's back while still holding Dena in his arms. Now that he had her, he wasn't letting her go until he'd had his fill.

So never. I'm never letting her go.

"Game design is still going well?" she asked.

"It is." He jiggled her in his hold. "But I have a different game in mind right now."

"Hey, just press start."

She kissed his jaw and that propelled him back into a walk. Okay, it was more of a jog to his bedroom where he set her down on the bed, loving how she corralled him with her legs so he couldn't get away.

Not that he wanted to get away.

She propped herself up on one elbow. "Are you sure you're up for this? You were sleeping off a hangover like thirty minutes ago."

"I'm awake and more than... ready." He angled his hands toward the bulge in his jeans.

Dena's pupils zipped open, huge black pools drinking in the sight of what was waiting for her beyond a layer of denim. "Let's free that, shall we?" She scooted to the edge of the bed and popped the button at his waist. An unzip later and he was in her hands.

Her capable hands. *So capable.* She stroked him once, twice, three times and he was panting her name.

He shoved off his jeans and boxers and immediately set to work stripping off Dena's tights and dress. "This is a nice outfit, by the way."

"Thanks."

"It looks better in a pile on the floor though."

Dena relieved him of his T-shirt. "As does this." She threw the shirt to the pile then grabbed Carter's wrists. "Love me, Carter."

"I plan to."

Chapter Thirteen

Everything about having Carter kiss her all over felt right. Yes, he'd been drunk. Hungover. Nearly unconscious in his slumber. But she was far from perfect as well. They'd both admitted to needing help and together they could find the courage to get what they both needed. They could stand by each other in support and in care.

In love.

Dena still reveled in the afterglow of hearing Carter say those words back to her. She'd had guys tell her they loved her in the past, but she'd known all of them were playing the game, telling her what she wanted to hear so they'd be granted access to her... goods. Sometimes she'd given in. Most times she'd lost interest soon after.

With Carter, however, it was all different. Telling him she loved him had rolled out of her without having to obsess over it or plan it out. One look at him and her heart knew. Knew like she knew the satisfaction of all her columns of numbers balancing in her spreadsheets at the sawmill.

His body slid over hers and she kneaded the muscles of his shoulders and back as he nibbled on her collarbone, her neck, her earlobe. When he traveled down to her breasts and used his tongue to bring her nipples to attention, she arched her back, eager to have him inside her right where she wanted him.

Carter pressed gentle kisses to the area around where Gary had sliced into her. She wasn't wearing a bandage today because it appeared to be healing nicely.

"You're so brave," Carter said softly, his fingers gently tracing a wide circle around the slice. "You faced Gary and put him where he belongs."

"Not all by myself," she said. "Two other women came forward."

Carter rested his chin on her hip. "Were those women planning to come forward before you said you would?"

She shook her head.

"See? Brave." He reached a hand up and put it over her mouth when she denied her courage. "Brave like an Ergon warrior." He sat up abruptly and snapped his fingers. "That's it."

"What's it?"

"I've been drawing the leader of the Ergon army as this big, beastly troll-like character with horns and fangs, but that's like all my other games." He smiled so widely his eyes scrunched closed a little. "This new game needs an all different brand of leader." He pointed to her. "You."

"Me?"

"Yeah, a female leader who isn't ghastly, but beautiful, and the army follows her command not only because she is skilled in battle but because each warrior is trying to win her heart." He popped off the bed, but she grabbed his arm before he could go.

"Where do you think you're going?"

240

"I need to—"

"Make love to me. Then you can draw, write, whatever." She tugged on his arm and he climbed back onto the bed. "As leader of the Ergon army, I command you to make my body sing, warrior."

His eyes widened behind his glasses and his mouth dropped open. "You have no idea how hot that order is."

When he kissed her with fevered intensity, making her entire body tingle with desire, she had an idea how hot that order had made him. "It's time to sheath your sword, Player One."

He laughed against the thigh he was kissing then put his mouth right where she wanted it. He teased her until she was so ready she could scream. Carter took a few seconds to roll on a condom, then he drove himself into her like any good invading warrior would.

With each thrust, she fell more in love with him, their bodies saying things words never could. Some things went beyond words. Some things were felt on levels that could not be described, quantified, calculated.

Some things were just magic.

"Carter…" His name slipped out of her mouth on a breathy rasp.

He closed his mouth over hers and they rode that kiss to the stars, their bodies pumping in a rhythm only they could create together. At the apex, they both teetered over the edge, the fall leaving her vibrating like a spiderweb in a breeze. One touch and her entire body reacted.

Carter collapsed beside her, his arm draped over her hips, and she raked her fingers through his hair. "That... that..."

"Doesn't go in the game," Dena finished.

He pressed a kiss to her overheated skin. "No. That's only for us special VIP players with the access codes."

"Video games are a lot sexier than I thought." She snuggled into his side and he maneuvered the comforter over them.

"Well, when you add a smokin' hot female leader, what do you expect?"

"Who will win her heart in the game?"

"Hmm..." Carter puckered out his lips and she wanted to kiss them again. "I'll need to add an Ergon warrior with glasses."

"Ah, yes, a dorky Ergon warrior."

"Hey, this dork has a smokin' hot female in his bed. Dorks do okay."

She nipped his bottom lip. "Dorks do more than okay." She slid her leg up his and hooked it around his hip, pressing him closer to her body. "Dorks earn very high scores."

"Yeah?" He kissed her until they had to come up for air. "Dorks also have incredible recovery times." He moved his hips, letting his erection rub against her thigh.

"Go, dorks."

After another round of epic lovemaking, they fell asleep in each other's arms and Dena had never slept better.

Until she felt Carter get out of bed beside her.

"Where are you going?" she asked, her words muffled by the pillow her face was currently smooshed against.

"Someone is at the door," Carter said.

"Oh." She sat up and Carter groaned when the covers fell to her waist, revealing her breasts.

"I want to draw you like that. I will get rid of whoever is at the door. Don't move."

She probably couldn't move even if she wanted to. Her body was still ultra-relaxed from the attention Carter had given it… last night? *What time is it anyway?* Dena looked at the clock on Carter's side of the bed. 8:00 p.m. Judging by the fact that she wasn't famished, she assumed it was Wednesday night. She still had time to spend with Carter before having to go to work tomorrow where she'd have her first session with her intern, Nikolas.

Flopping back down on the bed, she closed her eyes, still caught in a sleepy fog. She rolled to her side and let her head rest on Carter's pillow. Inhaling deeply, she enjoyed the pure scent of him as she ran her hand over the wrinkled sheets he had occupied. How could she have pushed him away—*twice*—when he had the ability to make her feel as she did right now?

And it was more than the physical bliss he created. He stimulated her on so many levels. More than any guy she'd ever dated.

Perhaps she stimulated him too. He'd been inspired by her for his game and that made her all squishy inside because video games were such a big part of his life. She'd seen Carter's artwork and had no doubt the character he made based on her would kick ass. She couldn't wait to see it.

She also couldn't wait for him to come back to the bedroom. *Where is he?* She strained her ears, listening, and voices wafted back to her. One was Carter's. The other was a male's that she didn't recognize.

I can go if you want me to, the unfamiliar voice said.

You're not going anywhere, Carter said. *Give me a minute, okay?*

His footsteps sounded in the hall then the bedroom door opened. He slipped inside and smiled at her. "God, I love seeing you in my bed."

She nestled deeper into the covers. "It's a comfy bed, but it's not as fun without you in it too."

His brown eyes darkened to almost black. "You fog my glasses, woman." He leaned over the bed and kissed her forehead. "But is it okay if we put this on hold for a few? My intern, Rohen, is out there. Some kid at the group home where he lives ripped up some of his drawings. He needs a place to hang for a while. Thought we could make some dinner. Are you cool with that?"

"Of course I am." She slid her legs over the side of the bed. "Poor kid." She got up and went for her clothes on the floor.

"Yeah, I got him a job at Mountain View Pizza, which he went to tonight, and while he was gone, some jerk got into his things." Carter frowned. "I used to hate it when Chase got into my things, but he never destroyed anything. And he was my brother so I had to forgive him. These other kids aren't even related to Rohen."

"What's his deal?" Dena asked as she slipped on her dress, undergarments, and tights.

Carter filled her in on how Rohen had lost his parents and ended up in a group home in Maplehaven. Her heart broke for the kid.

"Jeez." She leaned against Carter. "It's a good thing he found you."

"Well, I know a thing or two about not having any real family left. I wasn't as young as him, but I can understand what he's feeling." He took her hand. "Thanks for being so understanding about the intrusion."

"No intrusion. I'd like to meet him." She rose up on her tiptoes and brushed a quick kiss to Carter's lips. "Besides, we have oodles of time to do more of that." She arrowed a thumb over her shoulder to the rumpled bed.

"And there will be more. I can promise you that." He kissed her and led her down the hallway by the hand.

When they arrived in the kitchen where Rohen was sitting on one of the island stools, the boy immediately stood. "Oh, shit, Carter. I'm sorry. I didn't know you had... company." His cheeks pinked and he started packing up the colored pencils he had strewn about the island.

"Now he has more company," Dena said, taking in the kid's lanky build and worn sweatshirt and jeans. "You don't have to pack up your stuff." She extended a hand to him. "I'm Dena. It's nice to meet you."

245

The boy's blue gaze flicked to Carter as if to ask *Are you sure I can stay?* Carter nodded and Rohen looked back at Dena's still outstretched hand. Slowly he raised his own hand and shook hers.

"I'm Rohen. Carter told me about you."

"Did he now?" Dena shot Carter a grin. "What did he say exactly?" She leaned against the island, resting her chin on her fist and giving the boy her full attention.

Rohen smiled and scratched at the back of his head where his blond hair was shaved close. "That his life wasn't complete until you were a part of it."

Dena clapped. "Oh, this kid is good. He's learned so much already as your intern, Carter."

"How to be Charming 101." Carter pretended to have a clipboard and pen in his hands. "A+, Mr. Sears."

All three of them laughed, then Dena asked, "Someone ruined your drawings?"

At that question, Rohen's face grew serious. "Yeah. The group home has an abundance of a-holes."

"You should booby trap your stuff." Dena opened the refrigerator to survey Carter's inventory.

"Booby trap?" Rohen sat back on the stool, but he moved his supplies and bag to the floor between his feet.

"Yeah. I used to keep a diary when I was a teenager. My sister and brother were always trying to read it. I would catch them with it and they would think they were so funny. They'd tease me about whatever I wrote… which was usually about Ralphie Monnors, my first love."

"Ralphie?" both Carter and Rohen said together before bursting into laughter.

She let the fridge door close and put her hands on her hips to face the two of them. "Hey, I'll have you know Ralphie was a hunk and a star baseball player." She waved a hand. "Anyway, back to the booby trapping. I put a book cover on the diary once and coated it with honey. When Dakota went to sneak a peek, he got sticky honey all over his hands. Then I called his name from where I was waiting on the floor on the other side of my bed. When he turned around, I threw a ball of lint from the clothes dryer at him. Instinctively, he raised his hands and the lint stuck to the honey. Twenty minutes later, he was still trying to wash it all off."

She chuckled remembering how mad Dakota had been. Served him right for snooping. She'd gotten Jacy good a few times too and soon both of her siblings knew to keep their mitts off her diary.

"Do you have any—" Rohen started.

Carter put a plastic bottle of honey on the island in front of him. "Use it well, young apprentice."

"Thanks." Rohen put the bottle in his bag.

"So Carter tells me he got you a job at Mountain View Pizza. Do you like it?" Dena asked.

"I only went twice so far, but yeah. Kyle is really nice." Rohen glanced over to Carter. "Thanks again for getting me the job."

"No problem." Carter stuck a large pot in the sink and turned on the faucet. "I'm just sorry your shit got destroyed while you were working."

Rohen gave a small, one-shoulder shrug. "I can always draw more stuff. Whatever."

Carter set the pot on the stove and turned on the burner. He pulled out a box of pasta and a jar of tomato sauce, holding them up with raised eyebrows as if looking for Rohen's approval.

After the boy nodded, Carter said, "If you want, I can clean out a drawer in that big filling cabinet in my office. You can store shit you absolutely don't want anyone touching there."

"That'd be cool."

"Bring whatever you want over. It'll be safe here." Carter took out a loaf of bread and set it on the small dining room table while Dena made a subtle sweep of the living room, clearing away the empty liquor bottles.

Back in the kitchen, she opened a few cabinets until she found the dishes and passed three to Rohen who automatically brought them to the table. The three of them moved around the kitchen and dining room areas as if they were accustomed to doing this routine every night.

Dena couldn't help thinking she'd love that routine.

****

Watching Dena and Rohen move about his normally quiet cottage with a strange familiarity did much to lift Carter's spirits. How could he have been so down last night that he'd drunk himself into oblivion? Right now he felt completely different—completely better—than he had hours ago. His headache was gone as was his heartache. Making love with Dena had given him new hope and having

248

Rohen around gave him a purpose beyond making video games. He rather liked hope and purpose.

As he stirred the boiling pasta, Dena assembled a tossed salad while Rohen mostly stole stray veggies that she'd cut. Carter wondered how well Rohen was fed at the group home. The kid couldn't weigh more than a hundred twenty pounds, yet he was almost as tall as Carter's six feet two inches. He knew the kid said his stomach was shitty, but that was no excuse for the group home to not make accommodations for him. Carter made a mental note to ask Kyle about sending food home with the boy on the days he worked at Mountain View Pizza.

"So I've been thinking about the Ergon army since yesterday," Rohen said as he crunched on a celery stalk.

"So has he." Dena motioned to Carter with her chin.

"I can't help it," Carter said. "Once an idea takes shape, I have to let it consume me until it's finished."

Rohen nodded. "Yeah, I get like that when I've got something I need to draw. As if I can't rest until it's all down on paper."

Dena angled her head at the boy. "I guess I know what you guys mean. For me, it's numbers. I can't walk away from my computer until all my calculations are complete and everything is balanced."

"And you called me a dork." Carter shut off the burner on the stovetop and drained the water out of the pasta pot. Steam rose in a gush, causing his glasses to fog. He paused for a few seconds until the lenses cleared. Many things seemed clearer today.

Dena put the salad ingredients in the refrigerator. "I never said I wasn't a dork too."

"Dorks are better than any other kind of person," Rohen said quietly. "In my experience anyway. My parents were huge dorks and they were the greatest."

"My parents were dorks too." Carter added sauce to the pasta and brought the bowl to the dining room table. "My dad was a journalist and my mom was a librarian. Dad went around correcting everyone's grammar and Mom liked to catalog pretty much everything in the house."

Dena laughed and that sound was one Carter wanted to hear again and again. Especially in the cottage. Especially when he was the cause of it. A woman like Dena deserved nothing but days filled with laughter and he wanted to be responsible for such days.

He'd seen her gather the empty liquor bottles before Rohen could see them and he loved her all the more for that simple action. He was more than embarrassed by his behavior, but Dena had truly meant what she'd said about them helping each other heal. He planned to keep up his end of the bargain too. Whatever she needed, he'd be all over it.

Hope and purpose. His new life direction.

"What about your parents?" Rohen asked Dena, and Carter noted how the boy appeared to feel comfortable around her. "Are they dorks?"

Dena puckered out her lips in thought, making Carter want to kiss that mouth. "Yeah, I guess they are. My dad owns the sawmill and he's pretty meticulous about how everything runs over there even though he's semi-retired. My mom is retired now, but she was a nurse so she had to know a bunch of medical stuff." Dena shook her head. "I don't know how she could stand to be around blood and guts. Not for me at all."

"Delicate stomach, Miss Brenton?" Carter asked as he brought the salad she'd made to the table and corralled her and Rohen into the dining room.

"Super delicate. I don't like to be grossed out which probably sounds silly to you two who are into video games."

"I'm not into the bloody ones so much," Rohen said as he went to the other side of the table and sat across from Dena. "I like his games." He pointed to Carter.

"And yours aren't bloody?" Dena asked, her brows furrowed as she regarded Carter.

Carter shook his head. "No. Although I have warfare in my games, it's usually through sword combat and the player has to outmaneuver or outsmart the opponent. I don't do killing in my games."

"Wow. I never knew that." She passed the pasta bowl to Rohen so the boy could fill his plate first.

"His games are still awesome though. I had friends back in California who were into the more brutal games, but we always turned back to Carter's. All that violence gets to be too much after a while. I'd rather see amazing graphics and have to use intellectual skills to beat a game than just hit the controller and lob someone's head off. Where's the challenge in that?"

"This is why I like working for myself," Carter said as he heaped pasta onto his dish after Dena had taken her serving. "I say what kind of games I make. I've had big vid companies want to hire me, but I always say no because I don't want to be forced into making content I don't believe in. Kids don't need more violence in their games. Real life is violent enough."

Ask Chase. Oh, no… wait. No one could ask Chase because real life violence had stolen his brother away from him years ago. The best Carter could do was create games that were fun but hopefully instilled honor and problem solving that didn't involve exposing kids to bloodshed every time they played.

Conversation continued around the table and Carter was surprised by how much life Dena and Rohen brought to dinner time. Normally he ate something quick and on the couch in front of the television or in his office while still squeezing in some work time. Perhaps he'd avoided actually eating at the dining room table because it reminded him of how his family had shared special time at dinner each night. It was better to be busy while eating so he didn't have to feel the emptiness.

Nothing empty about tonight.

Tonight his house was full as was his heart. The cottage felt like a home for the first time since he'd moved from New York.

"This is nice," he said before he could stop himself.

"Yeah," Dena said. "This pasta is good for jar sauce."

Carter shook his head. "I didn't mean the food." He motioned to the three of them at the table. "I meant this. Having you guys here. It can get rather quiet here all by myself."

"We can make more noise if that would please you," Rohen said with a grin.

"Yeah," Dena added, a devilish look in her hazel eyes, "why don't we turn on some tunes? Get this party going."

Carter popped up from his seat. "Now you're talking." He made his way into the living room and picked up his phone from the coffee table. "What kind of music do we want?"

"Nineties hip-hop!" Dena and Rohen said at the same time.

Carter looked up to find the two of them staring at each other across the table. "Wow. You both like nineties hip-hop? Uncommon to have a teenager like the music an old lady likes."

"Watch it, Carter Bennett." Dena held up a fist. "I believe you upgraded me to leader of the Ergon warriors earlier today. I can crush you, puny human."

"Wait a minute." Rohen held up his hand then looked at Carter still standing in the living room. "A female leader?"

"Yeah," Carter said. "What do you think?"

Rohen's eyes lit up. "Brilliant!"

"You think so?" Carter had been excited about the idea when it had occurred to him, but Rohen was his target audience. If Rohen liked it, the notion might actually work.

"Oh my God, yeah," Rohen said. "It's perfect. A female leader will surprise all your current fans *and* if you can market with her, you'll likely pull in more girl gamers."

"That's what I was thinking too. She's going to need a good back story so players will believe in her ability to lead the army, but I think I can swing it." Carter selected a nineties hip-hop station and dropped his phone into the speaker base. As a thumping beat filled the living room in the background, he said, "Plus, I'll have you to help me."

"I had a few new sketches to show you," Rohen said as he brought his dish and glass to the sink. "They are unfortunately torn to shreds now."

Carter nudged the kid aside when Rohen made a move to wash the dishes. "Put them in the dishwasher. We're not wasting our time washing dishes by hand tonight." He opened the dishwasher and put his own dish, glass, and silverware in the racks. "Hopefully you can recreate the drawings then leave them here."

"I hate not having any privacy at the group home," Rohen said as he took Dena's dishes and glass, rinsed them, and put them in the dishwasher. "I'm not used to living with a bunch of people. In California, it had been just me and my parents. At the group home, everyone is in everyone's business."

"That has to be a difficult adjustment," Dena said. "Especially because none of those people are your family."

"I have no family." Rohen sifted out a long breath, sounding like a man of about a hundred years old instead of a teenager. "It's a weird thing to know you're the only one of your kind out and about in the world."

"Amen." Carter squeezed Rohen's shoulder. "Especially when you figured you'd have years and years with your family."

Rohen nodded. "No one expects to be an orphan."

"You look as if you could use a hug," Dena said. "I'm not a huge hugger, but I can make an exception."

Rohen opened his arms and motioned with his fingers for Dena to come to him. "If there is one thing my father taught me it's that if a pretty woman wants to hug you, you let her."

"Smart man," Carter said as he finished filling the dishwasher.

He watched out of the corner of his eye as Dena embraced Rohen. She rubbed her hand up and down his spine and the kid's shoulders relaxed a bit as if a weight had been lifted from him.

"Thanks," Rohen said as he took a step out of the hug.

"No problem." Dena's face looked peculiar, as if she'd expected the hug to be awkward and was surprised it hadn't been. She rubbed her hands together then grabbed a washcloth to swab the dining room table.

"Does Theo need dinner?" Rohen picked up the bunny and cuddled it against him.

"Yeah," Carter said. "I put a bowl in the corner by the sliding door over there." He pointed to the doors at the far side of the living room. "I should probably have a cage or something, but he's a wild bunny. I felt weird about containing him."

"Where is he... ah, you know... relieving himself?" Dena asked.

"I put a container of shredded paper on the other side of the sliding door and he's been going over there. I haven't found any surprises anywhere else in the house so I guess that's working."

Dena nodded. "Good. How long is it supposed to take for his leg to heal?"

"A couple weeks," Carter said, coming into the living room and sitting on the couch while Rohen put some lettuce and veggies in the bowl. "Then I'll set him free."

"Won't you miss him?" Rohen asked.

"Sure, but he's a wild rabbit. He needs to live his life outdoors. Our paths have crossed for now and I'll enjoy him, but he's not meant to be my pet." That speech sounded grown up and reasonable, but Carter knew when the time came, he'd no doubt get a little choked up watching Theo leave. Maybe he'd keep a bowl of food on the deck. In case Theo wanted to drop by from time to time.

"You could get an actual pet," Rohen said. "My aunt took me to the shelter in town to volunteer. She thought it would help me feel close to my parents. It didn't, but there were a ton of pups and kittens there. I'll bet any one of them would love it here."

Carter could almost hear Rohen say *he* would love it here.

"I have to second Rohen's motion for you to get a pet." Dena sat beside Carter on the couch while nineties hip-hop continued at a low volume.

"You don't have any pets, right?" He hadn't seen any in the time he'd known Dena.

She shook her head. "But I had many growing up."

"Why none now?" Rohen asked.

"I guess I didn't want to have to take care of one. Taking care of myself is enough work."

"True that," Carter said. "Adulting is hard work, Rohen."

Rohen laughed. "Teenaging isn't much easier."

"I suppose that's true," Dena said. "I don't remember high school fondly."

Carter angled to face her. "You mean you weren't, like, so popular?"

She elbowed him. "Not at all. I was always invisible. Jacy's the bold one."

"You have a twin, right?" Rohen settled on the recliner perpendicular to the couch and Theo attempted to climb up his denim-clad leg. The boy picked up the rabbit and let it find a comfortable spot on his lap.

"Yeah, Jacy is my twin."

"Identical?" Rohen asked.

"Yup."

"But they're nothing alike," Carter said. "I mean, they *look* the same, but..." He shrugged. "I can't put it into words." He'd much rather show her what he'd been thinking.

Later.

"Did you and your sister ever trick anyone with the twin thing?" Rohen asked.

"We did. What's the use of having a twin if you can't play some tricks, right? We got my dad good once. I wonder if he remembers that." Dena told Rohen the story and settled deeper into the cushions beside Carter as if she meant to stay awhile.

Never go home. Carter would be perfectly content if she stayed. Rohen too.

Forever.

Chapter Fourteen

Rohen had fallen asleep with Theo in his lap, both the boy and the rabbit looking as if they were beyond comfortable in that recliner in Carter's living room. Dena could understand that feeling. She'd felt amazingly at home moving about Carter's kitchen, eating at his table in the dining room, and lounging in his living room. While she loved her house, it wasn't as cozy as the cottage.

If she were being honest, it was Carter who made the place cozy. All through dinner, she'd caught him staring at her as he chewed. She had to give him credit for being able to converse with Rohen while he was clearly picturing her naked. The slight blush on his cheeks told her all she needed to know about where Carter's thoughts were.

Hers were in the same place.

"He seems like a nice kid," she whispered to Carter seated beside her on the living room couch.

"I haven't known him that long, but yeah. There's something real about him, you know? As if he doesn't play games with people. What you see is what you get. I like that," Carter said.

"Me too. No drama or pretending." She wished all people were like that. It'd be so damn handy if people didn't try to put on so many faces. If they didn't try to hide that they were secretly into assaulting women, for example.

But that chapter is over, Dena reminded herself. She'd done what she could to get Gary locked up and she'd succeeded. Obviously, there would be other douchebags to cross her path over the years, but at least she'd put one behind bars. Justice had been served and she could move on.

With Carter. That thought warmed her from the inside out.

She snuggled up to him and he slid his arm around her shoulders. "Are there any rules about only having one day for internships? Is it possible you could have Rohen on more than one day each week? Or would that be too much?"

Carter angled his head. "I was actually considering the same thing. It would be cool to have access to him more, but I wonder what core subjects he can miss." He rubbed his whiskered jaw, drawing attention to his lips. Lips Dena was looking forward to tasting once again tonight.

Maybe more than once.

"I'm sure you could talk to his guidance counselor. Do you know which counselor he has?"

Carter nodded. "Mr. Prentiss."

"Oh, he was my favorite. When we had a career project, he let me follow him around for a whole day to observe and take notes." She chuckled softly, not wanting to wake Rohen... or Theo. "A vein in his temple pulsed when I told him I wasn't interested in being a guidance counselor because I didn't want to listen to anyone complain about stuff.

He'd done quite a bit of listening to complaints on the day I'd watched him."

"What made you want to become a finance manager instead?" Carter asked as he took her hand and wove his fingers with hers. He looked at their joined hands resting on his thigh.

What is he thinking?

His facial expression said he was happy. Happy to have her there. Happy they'd come to the other side of being apart. Happy she'd apologized and now they could be together.

The tension in his hand as he held hers, however, made an uneasiness swell around him. Perhaps he was still thinking about how he could help Rohen more.

"I became a finance manager because I'd always been a wizard with numbers and because I knew the sawmill would always have a need for one." She shrugged. "I wanted to be useful to my dad."

That uneasiness drained from his gaze, replaced by a warm glow in his eyes. "Just when I think you can't get more adorable, you get more adorable."

"Adorable?" She huffed. "How am I supposed to lead the Ergon army if I'm adorable? Not very warrior-like."

"Dena Brenton can be adorable." Carter pressed a kiss to her forehead. "Dena, the Destroyer, can make her enemies bow before her."

"Oh, I like that. I might be dangerous with this new power."

"Not new power," Carter said. "I think you've always had the power to make anyone bow before you."

"Maybe. That power waned a little recently." The Gary Ordeal had given her power a beating, but she was collecting the pieces and putting them all back together to form something new. Something that could be happy for the rest of her life with Carter.

Carter pulled away a little so he could see her better. "Your aura is definitely brighter since you put Gary in jail."

"Justice will do that for an aura."

He squeezed her close again, and she could be content living in that space beside him. She was about to tell him so when Rohen let out a shout, snapped awake, and caused Theo to pop off his lap and hop to the armrest of the recliner. The boy's gaze darted around the living room, his blue eyes wild and wide as if he had no idea where he was.

"It's okay, dude," Carter said calmly as he got up and went to sit on the edge of the coffee table closer to the recliner. "You just had a dream."

Rohen rubbed his eyes. "The same one I always have whenever I get comfortable."

"What's it about?" Dena asked, her heart breaking for the kid. When she thought of her own carefree teen years, she wished Rohen could have experienced the same.

Rohen got to the edge of the recliner and rested his elbows on his knees. "Fire. All around our house. I always wake up when it closes in and I can't breathe." He puffed out a breath and scraped at the sides of his head with his fingers. "Stupid. That's not how it happened with my parents. They weren't in a house and I wasn't anywhere near the fires myself."

"The mind sometimes fills in its own details when dealing with a traumatic event," Carter said. "I used to dream of a car accident after my brother was killed, but it wasn't like how he really died. I'd snap awake too, right at the moment of impact. Sucked."

Rohen nodded. "It's like I can't ever—"

"Get a full night's sleep?" Carter finished.

"Yeah. I'm tired all the time. I actually fell asleep in Mrs. Reade's math class today."

Dena waved a hand. "It doesn't take much to fall asleep in Mrs. Reade's math class."

"I thought you loved numbers," Carter said.

"I do, but Mrs. Reade is like a billion years old and has this voice that doesn't change tone." She said the words in a monotone, robotic-like.

Rohen laughed. "Legit."

"I never fell asleep, but I watched many, many of my classmates catch up on a wink or two in her class. She doesn't turn around from writing on the board long enough to see if people are conscious."

"And she does love writing on that board. She still uses chalk."

"Oh my God." Dena giggled. "Does she still wear half of her calculations on the back of her cardigan sweater because she leans on it when she does turn around to face the class?"

"Yes!" Rohen was really laughing now and Dena was glad to be the cause of it. His face totally changed when he was jovial.

"This kid in my class, Steve, secretly took a picture of her sweater and circulated it to everyone," Dena said. "We cracked up over it for days."

"And that was before everyone had phones and social media," Carter said. "You literally had a hard copy photo, didn't you, grandma?"

Dena narrowed her eyes at Carter. "Um, correct me if I'm wrong, but aren't you older than me by four whole years, *old man*?"

Carter grinned back at her. "Yes, but I'm so hip that it seems as if I'm super young."

"Not if you still say *hip*," Rohen said, rolling his eyes.

Dena got up and high-fived Rohen. "Nice one, kid."

"We'll see how nice it is when someone wants his internship completion forms signed and I can't find a pen." Carter patted himself down as if searching for a pen.

"By then, you'll be dying to sign them and get rid of me," Rohen said.

Carter shook his head. "Being a Jedi Master is for life, my man." He stood. "Our paths don't suddenly veer away when your internship finishes."

Rohen looked up at him and Dena loved that Carter had said that. Carter always knew the best things to say.

"Thanks," the boy said quietly.

"Besides, you've got talent. If I sever all ties with you, someday you'll be a big, super successful game developer and my competition," Carter said. "Better if I keep a good relationship going and save myself some headache later." He walked toward the kitchen. "Anyone want hot cocoa? I feel as if this night needs to have hot cocoa."

Dena raised her hand and popped off the couch to follow Carter. "I'm in!"

"Me too," Rohen said. "Then I should get going. It's probably been noted that I'm not around at the group home by now."

"Will you get in trouble for not being there?" Carter asked as he pulled mugs out of the cupboard.

Rohen gave a shoulder shrug. "Probably. Funny how those pricks that tore up my drawings won't get in trouble though."

"Why not?" Dena asked. "They touched your shit and destroyed it."

"But they've all been there longer than me. They've got this insider family thing going on." Rohen waved a hand as if he didn't care, but Dena could tell he did care. More than he wanted to admit.

"Things are better at school though?" Carter asked. "You've got some buddies there, don't you?"

"Sure. My art class is filled with kids I like. I've hung out with a couple of them outside of school too, but it's not as if I can invite them over to the group home to chill."

"You can bring them here. I've got video games." Carter paused then turned around slowly to face Rohen. "That came out as if I'm a creepy guy." He held up his hands. "I didn't mean it like that. I'm not a creepy guy. I just meant my house is your house. Okay?"

Dena rested a hand on Rohen's shoulder. "Besides, I wouldn't hang around here if he *was* a creepy guy. Trust me. I've had enough of creepy guys."

"I know you're not creepy," Rohen said to Carter. "I'm not sure how I know. I just do."

"He does give off this nice guy vibe, doesn't he?" Dena found the cocoa mix and took out three packets while Carter pretended to fall.

Grabbing the counter, he gasped out, "Not… the… nice guy… label." He slid down to the floor, a look of pure disgust on his face. "I'm… doomed…"

"Oh, stop it," Dena stood in front of him, her hands on her hips as she looked down at him. "You're a super hot nice guy. That's the best kind."

He winked up at her. "And don't you forget it." He held out his hand. "Now help me up."

She reached down and the moment Carter's hand touched hers, Dena wanted to tug him down to the bedroom.

"Later," he whispered when he was on his feet. To Rohen, he said, "Marshmallows or no marshmallows."

Rohen scrunched up his nose. "No marshmallows. Those things are gross."

"Agreed," Dena said.

"You guys are no fun." Carter took a handful of mini-marshmallows and shoved them into his mouth. He made a big show of chewing with his mouth open.

"I may have said he was nice," Dena said, "but I didn't say he had any manners."

A lone marshmallow sailed in her direction and she caught it before it hit her.

"Wow," Rohen said. "Sick reflexes. Carter has wisely chosen you as the Ergon leader."

"Yeah, if the enemies attack with marshmallows, we'll all be saved." She threw the marshmallow back at Carter who had turned back to make the hot cocoa. The marshmallow bounced off his shoulder and dropped to the floor.

Theo hopped over to investigate, but Rohen scooped up the marshmallow before the rabbit could make a snack of it.

"No marshmallows for sacred bunnies." He threw the marshmallow into the trash bin then grabbed the bag. "We should probably get rid of this entire thing."

"I'll second that," Dena said.

Carter plucked the bag out of Rohen's hand. "Give me those. You two can be party-poopers with your *plain* hot cocoa, but I'm letting loose." He filled one mug with marshmallows to overflowing. A few stray ones fell to the countertop and he ate those as he set the other two mugs in front of Rohen and Dena. He grabbed his own mug which looked as if it had a cloud atop it and held it aloft. "To disagreeing over the marshmallow's place in the food hierarchy, but agreeing that Dena should lead the Ergon army."

Rohen was the first to clink his mug to Carter's. "To lucky internships and nice guys."

"But not creepy ones," Carter added.

Dena knocked her mug to Carter's. "To cozy cottages and being right where you're supposed to be."

****

Hot cocoa never tasted this good. When Carter drank it by himself, he usually remembered all the times his mom had made hot cocoa after he and Chase had played outside on snow days. Then he'd feel shitty because he missed his family.

Tonight, however, his cottage was full of laughter and conversation and a woman he loved with a side bonus of a cool kid who belonged in Carter's circle. He might not have any actual family left, but he understood now that he could *build* a new one. All he had to do was open his heart.

Thirty minutes later, the hot cocoa was gone, but the conversation continued. Unfortunately, Rohen had to go.

"If I don't get back right now," the boy said, "I'm going to get stuck with extra chores. Possibly bathroom duty. I can't have bathroom duty. I just can't."

Carter took the kid's empty mug. "That doesn't sound like a good time." Nothing related to that group home sounded like a good time and it pained Carter to let the kid go back there. "Well, I'll say it again, you can hang here whenever. I'm home most of the time."

"And if he's not home, he's with me," Dena said as she sidled up next to him and put her arm around his waist. "That's the plan anyway."

"I like this plan." Carter slid his arm around her shoulders and gave her a quick squeeze.

Dena stepped away and rummaged around in her purse. She pulled something out then walked back toward Rohen who was putting on his jacket and gathering his bag. "Take this. It's my card. It has my

Christine DePetrillo

cell phone number on it so if you need Carter and can't find him, or if you need me, just call."

Rohen took the card and fingered the edges. The boy's throat muscles worked a little extra before he managed to say, "Thank you."

"No problem." Dena gave him a smile as Rohen put the card in the pocket of his jeans as if he wanted it directly on his person and not where someone at the group home could get at it. "Hey, maybe we could get my brother to give us an adventure."

"Oh, that's a great idea!" Carter had been searching his mind for something that would ensure Rohen would have a legitimate reason to not be at the group home.

"An adventure?" Rohen's eyebrows furrowed. "What does that mean?"

"My brother, Dakota, owns Birch Peak Adventures," Dena explained. "He takes people out on trips like snowmobiling, cross-country skiing, hiking. There are different activities for different seasons." She went back to her purse and pulled out her phone. Tapping and swiping the screen a few times, she motioned for Rohen to come closer. "Have you ever been snowshoeing?"

Rohen shook his head as Dena showed him a picture from the Birch Peak Adventures website. "No snow in California where I'm from."

"Right. Are you interested in seeing the great Maplehaven woods on snowshoe?" she asked. "There's still enough snow."

"I… I would love that, but…" Rohen looked at her then glanced to Carter. "You guys don't have

269

to, like, babysit me. You've got your jobs and shit to do. I can deal with my... situation."

Carter walked over to the boy. "Of course you can deal with your situation, but why should you when we're more than willing to hang out with you?"

"Yeah," Dena said. "Unless it's not cool to hang out with us." She looked up at Carter. "Maybe we're not cool."

"No, that's not it." Rohen held up his hands. "Not at all. You guys are like the coolest people I've met in a long time. A *long* time." He rubbed his forehead. "I don't want you to think I'm taking advantage of your kindness."

"Taking advantage?" Carter blew out a breath. "You can't take advantage if we're offering. We asked you freely and you should feel free to accept."

"If you want to," Dena added. "We're not forcing you. I mean, we'll sit here and be pathetic if you don't accept, but no big deal."

Rohen laughed and Carter loved how easy it was for Dena to crack the boy's exterior.

"Okay, okay," Rohen said. "I'd love to go snowshoeing if only to save you two from being pathetic."

"Great!" Dena swiped her phone. "I'll call Dakota now. When do you want to go?"

"I'm free whenever," Carter said then looked at Rohen. "When are you working at Mountain View Pizza?"

"Friday night, Saturday night, and Sunday afternoon."

"Wow, Kyle's keeping you busy," Dena said.

270

"I told him I wanted as many hours as possible. I'm trying to save up some money for a phone and a car." Rohen arrowed a thumb over his shoulder toward the front door. "My aunt's car is running on borrowed time."

"How about Saturday morning then?" Dena asked. "We can have you back in time for work."

"Okay." Rohen's smile was wide. "Thanks. I'll see you Saturday morning then. I'll come here?"

"Yeah," Carter walked Rohen to the door.

"Bye, Rohen," Dena called before wandering back to the couch after Dakota answered the phone.

"She's pretty awesome," Rohen said quietly to Carter at the front door.

Carter glanced over his shoulder to see Dena resting her feet on the coffee table. God, he loved seeing her all comfortable in his cottage. He couldn't wait to strip off her clothes and kiss every inch of her delectable body.

"Yeah. She is pretty awesome. I'm glad she's giving me another shot."

"Well… you're pretty awesome too, so the two of you together makes sense." Rohen gave him a wave. "See you on Saturday. And thanks."

Carter waved back and stood in the doorway while Rohen walked to his car. The engine roared to life, sputtered to a dull hum, then cranked back up to a clanking rumble when the kid backed out of the driveway. One of his headlights blinked, ready to go out for good. Rohen rattled down the road into the darkness and Carter stood there for a few seconds, wishing he could do something more for the boy.

Arms wrapped around his waist from behind. "You're the hero that kid needs." Dena pressed her head against Carter's shoulder blade.

"I'm not a hero," Carter said as he turned around in her hold and put his arms around her. "A hero wouldn't have let him go back to the group home."

"They're expecting him to go back. You can't keep him. He's not an injured bunny you found in the woods," Dena said gently.

"I know." Carter walked her back a couple of steps so he could close the front door against the cold night air outside. "But I wonder what I *can* do."

"Like… legally?" Dena looked up at him, her eyebrows raised over those hazel eyes.

Carter nodded. "He's got no one looking out for him."

Dena tightened her hold around his waist. "You've got such a big heart, Carter Bennett. I love that about you."

"What else do you love about me?" He'd gone long enough without making love to her. It'd been hours at least. Time to touch her all over. Touch her until she gasped his name on every breath.

"Hmm… you're a talented artist."

He nibbled on her earlobe. "What else?"

She let out a soft moan that instantly hardened him. "You're funny and clever and smart."

"What else?" Carter inched up the hem of her dress and cupped her phenomenal ass in his hands.

Dena ground her hips against his as she lifted his T-shirt up over his head and let it drop to the floor. "You're the sexiest thing I've ever seen in my life."

"Likewise, Miss Brenton. Likewise."

"It is so time to get naked."

"I was hoping you'd say that." Carter rid Dena of her dress. "I like Rohen and all, but sometimes a guy just needs some R-rated time with his woman."

"Only R-rated?" Dena pouted. "I was hoping for X-rated."

Carter let out a groan as he stripped off her tights. "You know all the right things to say."

Dena hooked her fingers on the waistband of Carter's jeans and walked backward as she tugged him along down the hallway toward the bedroom. "And you know all the right places to touch me."

"I love touching you." He picked her up when they got to the doorway to his bedroom and she wrapped her legs around his waist, her arms coming around his neck. "It's hard to be near you and *not* touch you."

She dropped a series of light kisses along his jaw that only served to make him want her more. He positively ached to be inside her.

"I know what you mean. I think that's why I keep coming back to you," Dena said. "Even with what happened in Rhode Island and how I got scared that night at *Beyond*, I keep craving you. Your touch is the only touch that makes everything okay again."

Carter walked to the bed and let her slide down his front so she sat on the still messy blankets from their earlier lovemaking. "It makes me feel so special, that you feel that way." He sifted out a breath. "My touch is full of love for you. My touch is the only way I can show you what you mean to me. Words are not enough."

She made quick work of unzipping his jeans and peeling them off his legs. "You're pretty good with words too, Carter. Your talents are many." Her eyes were huge green-brown pools. Their depths drew him in and he could wait no longer to be inside her, to feel her heat pulse around him.

After rolling on a condom, he slid into her, loving how her eyelids fluttered then closed upon his entry. She wrapped her arms and legs around him, possessively accepting him to the hilt. The stillness as he hovered above her, buried so deeply, made him lose his mind.

"Being this close to you," Dena whispered, "is one of my favorite things."

He'd agree if he was capable of forming words right now.

She shifted slightly and that was enough to get Carter moving in and out of her, slowly at first, then building up momentum. When she arched her back and thrust with him, he captured her mouth and gave everything he had to the kiss, to the lovemaking, to her. He was convinced no two people had ever been more perfectly matched. Being with Dena like this filled his heart, flowed into every empty space, brought him back to life in a way he hadn't thought possible a few months ago.

When he'd left New York, he'd never expected to find someone like Dena. He'd been in a bad headspace then. The drinking. The fighting. The not being able to focus enough to work on his games. There was a time when he thought he might not make it. Where he'd considered drinking until something tragic happened. It wasn't as if anyone would have missed him. His family was gone.

But then he'd thought of Leah and making that call to her had saved him. Making that call to his dead brother's fiancée, his best friend, had brought him to Vermont.

To Dena.

Dena let out a moan that made him increase his thrusts. She moved with him and soon they were both flying to the finish line.

"Carter…" she breathed into his ear.

"I've got you," Carter said. "I've got you."

He took a moment to gaze down at her beneath him. Her brown hair fanned out around her head in shiny waves, the dim glow of the lamp on the bedside table picking up some golden highlights. Her lips were parted as she let out staccato breaths, a moan mixing in now and then that plucked Carter like a guitar string. Her nipples were rosy and taut and each time she arched her back, they grazed his chest, sending more vibrations through him.

Dena had admitted to loving his touch, but her touch did things just as wild to him. Never had a woman stirred up such desire in him. It was as if he'd been waiting for her and her alone to unlock the gates he'd put up around his heart.

He was just glad he didn't have to wait any more.

Chapter Fifteen

Saturday morning was clear and crisp. The perfect day for snowshoeing through the woods. Dena had gotten up extra early, mainly because she hadn't been able to sleep. It seemed the only way she could get a full night's sleep was in Carter's bed. Sleeping nestled against his strong, warm body gave her a peace she desperately needed right now.

She'd spent Wednesday and Thursday night at his cottage, but insisted on coming home to her house on Friday night. "I've got some work to catch up on," she'd told Carter Friday morning. "Spending most of Thursday with my intern, Nikolas, set me back on a few things."

"Boo to work stuff," Carter had said, the pout on his lips almost convincing her to say screw it to the work stuff.

"I'll spend all day Saturday with you," she'd told him. "Besides, you need a little time to miss me."

"It only takes thirty seconds apart for me to miss you," he'd said.

God, she could eat him up when he said things like that. Carter somehow managed to be a geeky gamer, a poetic compliment giver, an adorable bunny daddy, *and* a smoking hot lover all at the same time. The man shouldn't exist outside of a romance novel.

276

But somehow he did. And he was hers. She wasn't sure how she'd gotten so damn lucky, but she wasn't going to question it. She was merely going to enjoy this thing with Carter. She was going to accept his help if the Gary thing crept up on her again, and she'd give him her help if he felt the need to drink a problem away. They'd be there for each other.

She looked forward to seeing Rohen again too. While her intern was a good kid, he didn't need her. He came from a great Maplehaven family, got excellent grades, had the perfect girlfriend, and knew what he wanted out of life. Being an intern to Dena was merely another step toward a golden future that was pretty much a guarantee for Nikolas.

Rohen didn't have that guarantee. His life had been shattered by rogue shots, intent on throwing him off course. He was making his best effort to overcome his circumstances, but Dena could tell it wore him down. On Thursday night, she and Carter had gone for dinner at Mountain View Pizza and though Rohen had worked his butt off busing tables, there was a defeated hunch to his back as he moved about the restaurant. If someone wasn't looking out for him, life might swallow him.

Fortunately, Carter *was* looking out for the boy and Dena was ready to assist however she could. She actually felt called to do so. Odd, because she mostly avoided teenagers, not having loved her own teen years all that much. It was different with Rohen though. He had an old soul trapped in that teenage body of his and Dena wanted him to succeed.

She sat on the bench in her mudroom now, pulling on her snow boots as she prepared to go to

Carter's. Dakota had promised her an exceptional adventure and she knew her brother wouldn't disappoint. He may be a pain in her ass sometimes, but he never let her down. Never. When she'd explained about Rohen, he'd gone all soft as only Dakota could.

"Poor kid," he'd said. "Sometimes I forget that not everyone was as lucky as we were growing up with Mom and Dad."

"I know," she'd said. "They were phenomenal parents. Still are."

"When Leah and I returned home from Fiji, our refrigerator was full of food Mom made for us. We should seriously consider renting our parents out to people in need of care."

"We'd make a killing. Too bad they make a habit of being nice to everyone for free."

"Damn," Dakota had said. "They're always destroying our money-making schemes."

Dena's phone vibrated on the bench beside her now. She picked it up and warmed all over at Carter's handsome face popping up on the screen.

"Hey, sexy," she said.

"Right back at ya." Just his voice got her all hot. "Tell me you're getting your sweet ass over here. I missed you last night."

"Are you whining, Carter Bennett?"

"Yes. I'm not afraid to admit it. I slept like shit last night and it had everything to do with your absence."

"I slept like shit too."

"You did?"

"Tossed and turned. It's as if I can't sleep unless you're cuddled up behind me now."

"I love everything about that sentence," Carter said.

"I thought you might."

The line went quiet for a minute then Carter said, "Here's a crazy thought. What if you slept here tonight and then did the same thing for all the nights that followed?"

Dena pulled her phone away from her ear and stared at it for a long moment until she heard Carter calling her name.

"Umm, are you asking me to... move in with you?" Her heart thumped like the beat in a nineties hip-hop song.

"Yeah. I guess I am. Yes." Carter sounded a little bewildered that he'd asked this question and that they were actually discussing it. He cleared his throat. "Listen, I love you. I love having you here with me. I hate when you have to go back to your house."

"But your cottage is also your place of work. Won't having me and my stuff around interrupt you?"

"Yes, but in the best possible way." He chuckled. "Besides, you do have a job to physically go to during the day. So you won't be around *all* the time."

"But you don't work normal hours. I'd hate to mess you up."

"Dena, I think about you nearly every second of every hour," Carter said. "I'm beyond messed up. In fact, having you here more might alleviate my symptoms."

"Your symptoms?"

279

"Yeah, constant thinking about you. Relentless wishing you were here. Chronic picturing you naked. Terminal waiting eagerly for you to come over. If I knew you'd begin and end every day in my arms, I might be cured."

"Okay." The word escaped from her lips before she'd let her logical brain analyze the proposal from all angles. It was as if her heart had answered for her.

"Okay?" Carter's hopeful voice solidified that she'd given him the correct response.

"Yes, I will move in with you because beginning and ending every day in your arms sounds marvelous."

Carter let out a whoop that made Dena have to pull the phone away from her ear again. "I can't wait to move you in here! Right after snowshoeing. Today. Promise me."

"I promise." His eagerness was contagious. She should be incredibly nervous about this change in her regularly scheduled programming, but she wasn't. Not at all. She wanted to box up all her stuff right now and beam it over to his cottage.

"Okay, get your ass over here. Let's get this snowshoeing out of the way."

They hung up and Dena immediately called Jacy. "I did something crazy."

"Do tell, sister," Jacy said. "I'm all ears for something crazy. Especially coming from you."

"Carter asked me to move in with him like a minute ago and I said yes."

Jacy screamed and Dena winced at the sound.

"This is so great! I'm so happy for you, Dena. You guys are perfect together and I knew it would all work out." Jacy let out another squeal. "Who else knows?"

"Just you. I hung up with Carter and called you first."

"Twin sister priority. Nice. When is this happening?"

"Dakota is taking Carter, Rohen, and me snowshoeing this morning, so after that." God, in a few short hours, she'd be *living* with Carter. That notion made her want to dance around.

"I can help you. Give me a call when you're ready. We'll have you packed up and on your way in no time. I can recruit a few others too."

"Thanks. Sounds good to me." Actually it sounded wonderful.

"You'd better tell Mom and Dad first before they hear it through the ever busy Maplehaven grapevine."

"This is true. Okay, gotta go. See you later."

"So happy for you, Dena. So happy."

She hung up and walked to the garage. Once inside her SUV, she opened the garage door and used the hands-free option to call her father.

"Yes, my darling daughter," William said when he answered.

"Hi, Dad. I've got some news."

"Is everything all right?"

"Yeah. In fact, everything is more than all right," Dena said. "I'm moving in with Carter. Today."

"Hi, honey." Her mother picked up the phone. "What did you just say?"

"She said she's moving in with Carter," her father explained. "You're sure that's what you want?" Just like William to make sure she knew what she was doing. He'd never forbid her to do anything, but her analytical side did come from him. He'd want to ensure she wasn't being rash.

Was she? She had surprised herself a little with her quick answer to Carter. It wasn't like her not to weigh the pros and cons. She rarely made snap decisions.

"Oh, William," Chennie said. "Now she's questioning her choice."

"It's my job as her father to make sure she questions her choices," William said. "Dena, I'm not saying moving in with Carter is a bad idea. He's a great guy and I've seen the way he looks at you, the way he treats you. It's a spot-on match, but I want you to consider everything you'd be giving up by moving into his cottage."

Cooking for one.

Sleeping alone.

Waking up alone.

Being lonely.

Being bored.

Missing Carter.

She could definitely stand to give up all of those things, but she knew what her father meant. Her independence. Her home. Her privacy.

"Do you love him?" Chennie asked.

"Yes," Dena said. "So much."

282

"That's all that matters, honey," Chennie said. "If you have love, everything else will fall into place."

"Your mother is right," William said. "We have love and look at us. Still going strong after all these many, many, many, *many* years." Her father puffed out a breath.

"Mom hit you, didn't she?" Dena asked, chuckling.

"She did."

"Love is good to have," Chennie said, "but sometimes you need to keep your man in line."

"Also good advice," Dena said. "I'll admit to not thinking this through all the way, but for once, I think acting on emotion is the right way to go. I do everything with my head and it usually turns out all right. I'm trying using my heart this time and hoping for the best."

"That's all we ever hope for you too, Dena," William said. "You're too amazing not to have the best."

"Carter makes you smile," Chennie said. "That's a wonderful place to start."

"Yeah. I think this is going to be one of those times where I look back and say, *Good thing I said yes.*" The Gary thing was behind her now. She was all about moving forward. Living with Carter was a giant step forward and it felt right.

"We're here for you no matter what happens," Chennie said.

"We're here for you to pack up boxes and move stuff," William added.

"Good, I was hoping you'd say that. I'm going snowshoeing this morning, but I'll give you a call when I get back. Jacy is doing some recruiting too."

"Okay, talk soon," William said. "Congratulations, Dena."

"We love you," Chennie said.

"Love you guys too."

Dena ended the call and smiled all the way to Carter's cottage. *Our cottage* by the end of the day. That made goosebumps rise on her skin. She'd never lived with anyone before. What if Carter found out things about her that he simply couldn't tolerate? Maybe he would hate all her cow figurines mixing in with his stuff. Perhaps he wouldn't understand her need to have a pitcher of water in the fridge at all times. She only liked to drink cold water. Room temperature water irritated her.

Maybe her fussing over what outfit to wear to work would aggravate Carter. Although... he'd actually helped her pick one out before, so maybe that wasn't something she had to worry about. Besides, since Rhode Island, she'd taken her whole style obsession down a notch. Carter's casualness was rubbing off on her.

What else would rub off on her? What if she was no longer herself? What if she and Carter became some weird hybrid combination of themselves?

She took a minute to inhale deeply and squeezed her hands on the steering wheel. Why was she letting all these silly thoughts bounce around inside her head? She loved Carter. He loved her. They never fought. Even when she'd pushed him away, he hadn't lashed out at her. He'd been understanding and patient and amazing.

They'd figure this thing out. And hopefully have a damn good time. Together.

****

Carter heard Dena's SUV pull up in his driveway and his palms instantly got sweaty. Had he actually asked her to move in with him? Aside from his family when he was growing up, he'd never truly lived with anyone else. He'd spent a few weeks with Leah when he'd first moved to Maplehaven, but that was different. It wasn't technically *living* with someone. It was more like *staying* with someone. Did he have what it took to coexist full time with another human?

A female human?

He enjoyed his bachelor lifestyle. Or he had anyway, but he hadn't been lying to Dena when he said he missed her when she wasn't around. He did think about her all the time. He did want to go to bed with her and wake up with her every day.

He wanted to live with her. Hell, he wanted more than that, but this was a good start. And she'd said yes so she must have wanted the same thing as him.

This was going work. He wouldn't allow it not to.

His doorbell rang and when he opened the door to find Dena in a pair of black leggings, black snow boots, and a white ski jacket with a fur-lined collar, he knew he'd made the right decision about living with her. Long brown braids stuck out from under her bright purple knit hat and the cold outside had pinked her cheeks. She was adorable and sexy at the same time and he didn't care if they made it to snowshoeing or not.

"Hi." She raised a purple gloved hand and wiggled her fingers.

"Get in here." He grabbed her hand and tugged her inside until her body was up against his. "Is your answer still yes to moving in?"

"Do you still want me to move in?" She looked up at him, her eyes twinkling and letting him know his invitation had delighted her.

"I do. Now I'll have someone to do my laundry, cook for me, clean the house..."

"Carter Bennett, you listed all the reasons I agreed to move in. Because *you* will do *my* laundry, cook for *me,* and clean the house." She brushed a kiss to his lips. "And I expect back rubs on demand."

"Oh, boy. What have I gotten myself into?" He pulled her hat off and held it out of reach, laughing when she jumped up and down trying to get it.

"Hey, you can kick me out at any time if it doesn't work out," she said, suddenly serious.

He lowered his hand and gave back her hat. "And why won't it work out? Do you think I'm going to be difficult?"

"No, I... I don't know. I'm kind of nervous," Dena said. "Excited, but nervous."

Carter stepped up to her and wrapped his arms around her. "I'm excited but nervous too. Holding you like this, though, in *our* cottage, makes me confident we're doing the right thing."

She rested her head against his chest and inhaled. "This does feel incredibly right, doesn't it?"

"The rightest."

"Are you two done being all mushy?" Rohen asked from the open front door. "Because I don't think I should witness any more of this."

"Sorry, man." Carter released Dena and nudged her away a bit. "There'll be no more of that."

"No more?" Dena made a frowny face.

"Not for the next few hours. After that…"

"La, la, la, la, la," Rohen sang as he put his fingers in his ears.

"Okay, okay," Carter said. "Let's go snowshoeing."

"Are you sure you guys want to do this?" Rohen didn't step into the house, as if he believed he might be asked to leave.

"Of course we do," Dena said. "We're just a little crazy this morning."

"Or a lot crazy," Carter said. "I asked Dena to move in."

"And she didn't laugh in your face?" Rohen asked. "Sweet."

Carter put his hands on his hips. "No, wiseass, she didn't. She accepted and now can think of nothing else besides sharing space with me."

Dena rolled her eyes. "Will these delusions be an everyday thing?"

"Hey, I create worlds for my games out of thin air. My whole existence is a delusion. You're the one real thing in it." Carter glanced back to Rohen. "She is real, isn't she? Tell me we didn't accidentally create a holographic image of a hot babe."

"Dude, we're good," Rohen said, "but not that good."

"C'mon, you two clowns." Dena walked to the door, shaking her head. "The trails are waiting as is Dakota." She wiggled her keys. "I'll drive. Last one to the SUV is bear bait."

"Shit." Carter scrambled for his jacket, but Rohen and Dena were already bounding down the walkway and hopping into her vehicle.

"I hear bears like dorks!" Dena called as Rohen laughed in the back seat.

Carter shook a fist at her then wrestled into his jacket and locked the front door. He pulled on a gray knit hat and got into the passenger seat. "As leader of the Ergon army, it will be up to you," he poked Dena in the bicep, "to save us puny humans from bears."

"We'll see." Dena started the SUV.

"Hey, what did I do?" Rohen asked. "I've done nothing to get on your bad side, Dena the Destroyer. I'm here to serve you."

Dena raised her eyebrows at Carter. "See, the kid gets it. You should take a lesson from him."

Carter turned around and scowled at Rohen. "Ass kisser."

Rohen raised his hands. "Hey, she's the reason I'm going snowshoeing instead of staring at the walls of the group home until I have to go to work. She's saved my Saturday."

"Fine," Carter said. "I guess she's awesome."

"Hence why you want to live with me," Dena said. "To bask in my awesomeness."

They continued busting each other's balls until Dena pulled into the Birch Peak Adventures parking lot. Dakota was leaning against the building, but he raised a hand in a wave.

Dena gave her brother a hug once they all got out of the car then stepped back. "Dakota, this is Rohen. He's Carter's intern."

"Nice to meet you." Dakota shook the boy's hand.

"You too, sir."

"Oh, you can call him Dakota... or dumbass," Dena said. "He'll respond to either."

"I wouldn't insult the guy who's going to lead us into the wild," Rohen said.

Dakota grinned. "I like this kid. I should have gotten an intern."

"You already have one," Carter said. "Doesn't Krista's son want to be you when he grows up?"

"True. Luke's interest in adventuring has not waned in the least. I thought maybe because Noah will be Krista's husband that Luke would switch to wanting to work at the sawmill or to woodworking, but he still wants to take over this place." Dakota motioned to the building behind him.

"What if you have your own kids?" Carter asked. "Won't you want to hand this place down to one of them?"

Dakota shook his head. "I'd never assume that one of my own kids would want to be handed the place. I didn't want to work at the sawmill when my dad asked me."

"Which worked out great for Jacy and me," Dena said. "I could crunch numbers for any business, but I love doing it for the sawmill."

"And that's why you're Dad's favorite child." Dakota picked up a set of snowshoes he had leaning against the building and held them out to Dena.

"I really am the favorite."

"Let's see how long you're Carter's favorite," Dakota said, passing snowshoes to Carter. "I heard you asked her to move in with you."

"You heard correctly. Any tips?" Carter asked.

"Yeah, don't let her outlaw man night. The guys and I need a place to get our video game fill."

"Man night can continue," Dena said as she gave Rohen his snowshoes. "As long as I can have girl night where we watch romantic comedies and eat chocolate."

Carter held out his gloved hand. "Deal."

"See, this is going to work out fine." Dena shook his hand and beamed a smile up at him.

They spent the rest of the morning wandering around the woods. Snow crunched softly under their snowshoes as Dakota pointed out various tree species and wildlife to Rohen who appeared to eat those facts as if he'd been starving for such information. The boy had his own information about California wildlife to share as well and Carter may have learned a thing or two himself.

Everywhere they explored, Rohen took pictures with Carter's phone. "I like to use photos as inspiration for drawings," he explained.

Carter promised to upload the pictures and loan Rohen a spare laptop he had back home. "It's gathering dust. You're welcome to it."

"You're too nice to me," Rohen said.

"No such thing." Carter clapped the kid on the back and Rohen's smile made him want to do as much as he could for the boy. What would it take to get him out of that group home? What were the requirements? Did he have what it took to oversee the upbringing of a teenager?

Would Dena be on board?

Carter made a mental note to research this tonight and talk it over with Dena. He'd never felt so compelled to take action for someone as he did for Rohen. It was almost as if he'd known the kid in a previous life or something.

"That was a blast," Rohen said when they returned to Carter's house. Well, his *and* Dena's house by the end of the day hopefully. "Though I miss California, Vermont is kind of beautiful."

"That's how I felt when I came here too," Carter said. "I thought I was strictly a city guy, but the tranquility of the woods can't be beat."

"Do you ever miss the city?" Dena asked.

"Not really, no," Carter said. "So maybe I was never a city guy."

Dena slid her arms around Carter's waist. "Maybe you're right where you're supposed to be now." She glanced over her shoulder at Rohen. "You too."

"Maybe," Rohen said. "There had to be an easier way to get here though." He jiggled his car keys. "Okay, I have to go so I'm ready for work. Thanks again, people."

"No problem," Dena said. "We should chat about what other stuff you might like to do. Dakota's got a million adventures we can go on."

"That would be cool." Rohen gave them both a wave and turned to go to his car. Halfway there, he swiveled back to face them again and pointed to Dena. "Good luck with your moving."

"Thanks. He's the one that will need the luck." She arrowed a thumb to Carter. "I don't think he's remembering how much stuff I have."

"Only the essentials come here," Carter said. "The rest we torch."

Dena swatted his chest. "We're not torching any of my stuff!"

Carter shrugged. "I tried."

Rohen's laugh wafted up to them as he got into his piece of shit car. Again, the engine made all manner of sickly noises as he started it and thundered down the street.

"Good God," Dena said. "That car has to go."

"Far, far away." Carter pushed his key into the knob at his front door. "I have a feeling, however, that astronauts on the International Space Station can hear that car." He tugged Dena into the house. "Now, first order of business is to make room for you."

"Fortunately, you don't have a ton of stuff," Dena said after turning in a circle in the living room.

"Most of my stuff is in my office. That's the junk I really need."

Dena put her hands up. "And I have no intention of spilling into that space at all. That's yours. You've got to have a place to work undisturbed."

"My, aren't you considerate?" Carter pulled her into a hug.

"I really am." She slid her arms under his jacket, her hands rubbing his back. "I do intend, however, to invade every other available space in this cottage. My cows are going to love it here."

"Have at it, my lady. My cottage is now your cottage." He squeezed her and got excited all over again that she'd be moving in permanently. That he'd be able to see her every day.

Which made him think about Rohen.

He arched back a little so he could Dena's face. "Can I ask you something?"

"Always." She rested her hands on his chest and focused that forest gaze on his face.

"Rohen. What do you think about him?"

Dena sifted out a breath. "I think he's great. Talented. Smart. Funny, despite everything that's happened to him. I enjoyed spending time with him today."

"Yeah, me too." Carter shed his jacket and hat. "I hate that he has to go back to the group home after work tonight though."

"He deserves better."

"That's what I was thinking."

Dena smiled a little. "This cottage does have *two* bedrooms."

"You noticed that too, huh?" Carter rested his hands on Dena's shoulders. "Would it be totally crazy if I went to that group home and… you know… made some inquiries?"

"It'd be crazier if you didn't." Dena put her hands atop his. "Spending time with him is as natural as breathing. And he's a good kid. I'm likely to be more trouble for you than he is."

Carter laughed. "But I like your kind of trouble." He brushed his lips against hers. "Let's start getting you set up in here, then maybe we could both make a visit to the group home."

"I'd like that."

The question was, would Rohen?

Chapter Sixteen

"You can pitch that, but save that," Dena said to Jacy as she buzzed around her house, trying to pack in an organized fashion. She never imagined moving out of her house. Sure, she'd wanted to find someone, but she hadn't ever allowed herself to picture what would happen *after* she'd met that someone. She loved her house and it had been a real find. Within walking distance of Dakota's and Jacy's houses, she'd liked knowing her family was close by.

And they still would be. Carter's cottage wasn't far from Birch Peak Adventures or her parents' house. Actually, nothing was all that far in Maplehaven. A person could walk from one end of the small town to the other in about an hour and pretty much see all there was to see of the area.

Now she'd be sharing space with the man she loved and possibly a teenage boy who fit right in with everybody. Dakota had taken an immediate liking to the kid as she and Carter had. Dena was curious about visiting the group home later today to find out what options there were for... freeing Rohen.

"Tape! Where's the tape?" Leah called as she folded flaps of the box in front of her.

Jacy hadn't been kidding about enlisting some moving help. Currently, Jacy, Dakota, Leah, William, Chennie, Kyle's wife and Leah's fourth grade colleague Heidi, Noah, Krista, and Krista's son Luke were all furiously loading boxes. At this rate, Dena would have everything packed in no time.

"Here's the tape!" Luke ran over to Leah and helped her seal the box.

Noah stepped over to the box and hoisted it onto his hip. "I'll take it out to my truck. I think I've got room for a few more things then I'm full."

"I still have room in my truck," Dakota said.

"Thank God for all these men and their trucks," Heidi said. "What would we do without them?"

"Make too many trips. That's what you'd do," William said as he took a box Chennie handed him. "Okay, who's riding with me to help unload at Carter's?"

"I will," Jacy said. "I'll make sure Carter's giving you prime space in the closets, Dena."

"Excellent." Dena nodded at her sister. "And if he's struggling over which nerdy T-shirts to throw out to make room for me, tell him anything with The Three Stooges on it can go."

"Roger that." Jacy saluted Dena and followed their father out to his truck.

Everyone worked together and in a few hours, the only thing that remained in Dena's house was her furniture.

"What's happening with this stuff?" Dakota asked.

"It won't all fit in Carter's cottage." Dena angled her head at the couch. "Besides, maybe I want to rent this place out. Seems a shame to get rid of it completely. I could rent it furnished."

"There's my practical, financially-minded sister." Dakota slung an arm around her shoulders. "I knew you wouldn't be completely consumed by all the romance of moving in with someone."

"Renting is good business. I'm all about the numbers. Always." She pointed to the rocking chair in the corner of the living room. "I want that though. Dad made it."

"Got it." Dakota grabbed the chair then paused by the front door. "Anything else?"

Dena scanned the kitchen, living room, and dining room of the place she'd lived for the past seven years. While she loved the house, she couldn't say she'd made a ton of memories inside it. Carter's cottage would be different.

"Nope. That's it." She followed him out and hopped into her SUV which was stuffed with some of the smaller boxes. The rest of her family was at Carter's and hopefully she could convince them to unpack everything too. She'd bribe them with pizza and booze.

After a short drive—one that would have been shorter if Dakota hadn't gone like ten miles per hour in front of her to bust her chops—she parked in front of Carter's cottage.

Which I'll have to stop calling Carter's cottage. This was her address now. Well, once she filed all the paperwork to make it official.

She got out of the vehicle and her family and friends were indeed helping unpack. Bless them. Popping the trunk, Dena walked to the back of her SUV as her phone rang. She dug it out of her pocket, but didn't recognize the number so she stuffed it back into her pocket and proceeded to grab a box from the trunk.

Her phone rang again. She set the box on the little wall by the garage and checked the phone. Same number.

"What the hell?" She swiped the screen. "Hello?"

"Is this Dena Brenton?" an unfamiliar female voice asked.

"Yes. Who is this?"

"This is Shepherd Memorial Hospital. Do you know Rohen Sears?"

Dena immediately sat on the wall, her legs wobbly. "Yes. Is he okay?"

"He's been brought in due to a car accident. The police think his brakes quit on him. He's in surgery right now."

"Surgery!"

"What? Who's in surgery?" Jacy had suddenly appeared beside her, but Dena held up her finger in a wait-a-minute gesture.

"A logging truck hit him from the side when he didn't stop at a red light. We're doing what we can for him. Your business card was found in the pocket of his pants. We didn't see any other contact information. Are you a relative?"

"No. Rohen lives at the group home in town, but I'll be right there."

She hung up before she could be told that only family would be permitted to see him. Between her and her sister, Dena had enough friends at the hospital. She'd get herself in there. She'd be there for Rohen when he woke up.

298

Because he would wake up. Wouldn't he?

"Oh, God…"

"What happened to Rohen?" Jacy asked.

"Something happened to Rohen?" Carter nudged Dena around to face him and the rest of her family and friends who had gathered near the driveway. "What's going on, Dena?"

"We never should have let him leave in that stupid car." Dena's hands shook. "What's wrong with us?"

"Back up," Carter said, taking her hands in his. "Tell me what happened?"

"He had a car accident. His brakes quit. A logging truck…" She had trouble swallowing. "A logging truck hit him. He's in surgery."

Carter marched into the opened garage straight to his car, not uttering a word.

"We'll finish bringing in the boxes," William said. "Then we're right behind you."

Dena didn't even have the ability to say thank you to her father. She had no words right now as she got into Carter's car. Rohen had to be all right. He had to be.

"This feels fucking familiar," Carter said. "Why do good people always get screwed?" He stepped on the gas and his car bolted out of the garage. "And I keep letting people in here." He pounded on his chest. "I've got to stop doing that. The Universe doesn't want me to have anyone."

"You have me." Dena reached for his arm, but he jerked it away.

"Yeah, for how long?"

Carter's tone made Dena wince. Though she knew he felt genuine concern for Rohen, anger crackled around him too. His hands strangled the steering wheel and he drove well above the speed limit.

"Let's keep clear heads here." She clamped a hand onto the door handle as Carter took a turn.

"My head is clear," Carter bit back. "Crystal fucking clear. I finally understand how this world works. Good people die and I'm not allowed to love anyone. I need to remember this basic truth. Get it through my goddamn skull."

"Rohen's not dead." Not yet, and if there was any fairness in the cosmos, he would make it out of this alive. He'd already had enough shit in his life. Only good things should be on his path now. "And you're allowed to love. Me, Rohen, Leah. Anyone you want."

Carter shook his head. "Not without Fate saying, *Sorry, I'm about to kill this person that you love.*"

The car's speed increased and Dena put her hands on the dashboard. "Carter, slow down! You're not going to have to worry about Fate killing anyone. You're going to be responsible for it yourself."

He gave her a wild-eyed look, and for a second she was reminded of how Gary looked right before he sliced her stomach with that knife. If she couldn't see the hospital a little farther down the street, she would have demanded Carter pull over and let her out of the car.

Instead, she shut up and let him swerve into the hospital parking lot, tires screeching. He took the first spot he found and was out of the car almost before he'd shut off the engine.

"Carter!" Dena jogged to catch up to him. She grabbed his arm and he spun around so fast she squeaked.

"Look, I'm not going to stop you from coming inside. Rohen likes you and he should have someone in his life who isn't going to bring him bad luck." Carter slapped his chest with his hands. "I'm bad luck. For him. For you. For everyone. All those boxes you dropped off at the cottage should go back to your house. If you move in with me, how long before something happens to you too? You have to get out of my Circle of Doom."

He turned back toward the hospital and started walking before Dena could string words together to form an intelligent sentence. Clearly, she wasn't going to be able to talk any sense into him right now. Not when they didn't know how Rohen was. Not when he was so upset. Not when he thought all the world's unfortunate situations were his fault.

She followed him into the hospital. At the front desk, he said Rohen's name and the receptionist started in on the family-only speech.

"Hey, Marissa," Dena said, stepping up next to Carter. The nurse standing behind the receptionist turned around and gave Dena a smile.

"Hey, Dena." Marissa's smile faded. "Is someone in your family here?"

Dena shook her head. "No, all the Brentons are accounted for, but we know Rohen Sears."

Marissa tapped the receptionist on the shoulder. "It's cool. She's the only contact we have for the kid. He's from the group home."

The receptionist nodded. "I see. What about him?" She pointed to Carter.

"This is Carter Bennett. Rohen is his intern from the high school." *And he's the man I was going to move in with because we are in love.* At least that had been the plan. Dena wasn't sure what was happening anymore.

"How is he?" Carter appeared to have calmed down some since coming in, but the way he gripped the counter between them and the receptionist told Dena he wasn't ready to be totally rational yet.

"Follow me," Marissa said as she rounded the front desk and started down a hallway.

Dena walked behind Marissa and let out a breath when Carter fell into step beside her. They turned into a small office to the right and Marissa motioned for them to have seats across from a metal desk. The wall was adorned with diplomas belonging to a Doctor Ethan Bukowski.

"Doctor Bukowski is our best surgeon on staff," Marissa began, leaning on the edge of the desk and facing Dena and Carter. "Initial assessments showed that Rohen's left side was damaged from the impact of the logging truck to his vehicle. He was unresponsive at the time of ambulance arrival, was revived on-scene, and brought directly here. The doctor wasn't sure of the extent of Rohen's injuries, but suspected internal bleeding so they rushed him right into surgery. We haven't heard any updates yet, but you will be the first we tell when we know more."

"Is he…" Carter cleared his throat when his voice came out raspy. "Is he going to be okay?"

"Not enough information to make that call right now, I'm afraid, but be assured Doctor Bukowski will do everything he can for Rohen." Marissa pushed off the desk. "Can I walk you back to the waiting room?"

Dena stood, but when Carter didn't immediately join her, she turned to Marissa. "Could we maybe have a moment in here? Then I'll make sure we get ourselves to the waiting room."

"Sure thing." Marissa squeezed her shoulder. "Take your time."

After she left, Dena lowered back to the chair beside Carter's. He'd slid his glasses to the top of his head, his dark hair pulled away from his cheeks. His face was in his hands as his elbows leaned against his knees.

"You have no idea how bad I want a drink right now," he said.

"A drink won't make you feel any better," Dena rested her hand on his back, encouraged when he didn't shrug her off this time, "but I can. This situation is awful. I get it. But we have each other now, Carter, and that makes us stronger. Stronger than our fears. Stronger than our weaknesses. Rohen needs us to be strong."

He nodded, slowly raising his head to look at her. "What I said? Before? About you going back to your house?" He pulled his glasses back down to rest on his nose and raked his hand through this hair. "I didn't mean that. I was… I was mad and frustrated and a prick. I'm sorry."

"You're scared to lose Rohen," Dena said, her voice cracking on the kid's name. "I am too. He's come to mean something to both of us though we haven't known him that long. Not in this lifetime anyway. And you've had enough loss in your life."

"But that's no reason for me to lash out at you. Especially knowing about your experience with Gary. The last thing you need is some dude you thought was a good guy going all psycho on you. You mean so much to me."

"You mean so much to me as well, Carter. I love you and if someone told me I only had another hour to live, I'd want to spend that hour loving you. We have to play this game of life for however long we're granted. The true tragedy would be if we wasted time being apart when we could be together. I've already wasted our time with my fears. Twice." She held up two fingers. "Let's not let that happen anymore. For any reason."

Carter cupped her cheek, his thumb running along the seam of her lips. "Wise advice from the leader of the Ergon army."

"Not advice," Dena said. "An order. One you have to follow."

"I'll do my best." He kissed her gently then tugged her to her feet. "C'mon. Let's get to the waiting room."

They walked hand in hand back to the waiting room where all the Brentons plus Noah, Krista, and Heidi were already camped out. The next few hours were going to be rough, but at least they weren't alone.

****

Save the kid, save the kid, save the kid. The words looped over and over again in Carter's mind as he sat beside Dena in the hospital waiting room. The scent of sterility and stale coffee turned his stomach and he wanted out of there, but there had been no word about Rohen yet.

What's taking so long?

Was this Doctor Bukowski not as good as the nurse had said? Had she been trying to put their minds at ease, offer them false comfort? If someone came out and told them Rohen was gone, Carter wasn't sure he could keep his shit together.

He was barely keeping it together now. Only Dena's hand in his brought him any relief as they sat there, and he didn't deserve her consoling. He'd been a complete dick on the drive over. The way he'd talked to her… what the hell was wrong with him?

A light squeeze on his hand made him look over at her. Her hair was hooked behind her right ear, most of it gathered on her left shoulder. Even with worry etched into her features, her face was a masterpiece. Long eyelashes fanned around her hazel eyes and her pink lips were glossy with the lip balm she had applied a few minutes ago. Strawberry if he wasn't mistaken.

God, he wanted to take her home—to *their* home—and forget everything else. That he'd been a douche. That he could lose her at any moment. That Rohen might not make it.

"You want a water or some coffee?" Dena asked quietly.

Carter shook his head. "I don't think my stomach is equipped to handle anything in it right now."

She squeezed his hand again and pulled his arm a little closer to wrap her other hand around it. "I'm sure we'll hear something soon."

William leaned forward from his seat on the other side of Dena. "This is a top notch hospital. Rohen is getting the best care."

"They saved my Luke," Krista added. She and Noah sat together across from Carter and Dena.

Carter recalled hearing about Luke falling into Brenton Lake and Noah rushing in to pull the boy out. If only Carter could have been there to save Rohen from that truck hitting him, but he was never in the right place at the right time. He always ended up getting bad news after it was too late to do anything about it.

And why had he let Rohen drive that car? He'd heard how bad the engine sounded. The kid had *told* him it was a piece of shit. He could have loaned Rohen his own car for Christ's sake. This entire scenario could have been avoided if the damn brakes had worked. If Rohen made it, Carter would buy the boy a brand new car. Anything he wanted.

"Excuse me?"

Carter looked up to see a woman in a long wool dress coat standing in the doorway of the waiting room.

"I'm looking for Dena Brenton," she said, her brown eyes searching the room which was filled with Brentons.

Dena gave the woman a wave. "Over here."

306

The woman approached. "Hi. I'm Anne Heywood, social worker at the group home where Rohen Sears currently resides." She stuck her hand out.

Dena shook it then gestured to Carter. "This is Carter Bennett. Rohen is his intern."

A small smile appeared on Anne's lips. "Ah, yes. I had lengthy discussion with Rohen about you when he returned to the group home late one night this week, Mr. Bennett. I couldn't reprimand him though. He's over the moon to be interning with you. His excitement was too wonderful for me to bark at him. He's been… solemn since coming to us."

Carter's throat stung. "Rohen is quite talented and a great kid."

"Agreed," Anne said. "He's got a good head on his shoulders too." Her brows furrowed. "The news of his accident is difficult to wrap one's head around. No one deserves such a thing, but him least of all." She shook her head. "Anyway, I've been sent to wait for news on his condition so if you folks need to lea—"

"We're not going anywhere." Carter's voice came out meaner than he'd intended, but there was no way he was leaving without seeing for himself that Rohen was all right.

William got up as did Chennie. "We're going to get something to drink. Be back in a few." To Anne, he said, "Here, take my seat."

"Thank you." She lowered to sit next to Dena. "We appreciate you investing your time in Rohen."

"I believe we've invested more than that," Dena said.

Carter nodded and looked at Anne. "We were planning to pay the group home a visit today."

"Oh? Did you have a problem?" Anne asked.

"Just with Rohen having to live at the group home," Carter said. "We wanted to give him another option."

"You want to adopt him?" Anne's lips turned up in a small smile. "No one ever wants the older kids."

"We do," Dena said. "We want Rohen. How can we make that happen?"

Carter squeezed her hand now, loving that she wanted Rohen as much as he did. Loving absolutely everything about her. It might be selfish of him to love her, to want her, but as she'd said, whatever time they had left on this blue marble he wanted to spend together.

"I can come out to your house and do a home study," Anne said. "Rohen is almost of legal age to be on his own so a lot of this decision is up to him. If he feels comfortable with the two of you, then we can make this official fairly quickly."

Assuming Rohen makes it. Carter shook that thought from his head. He felt deep down in his bones that he and Dena were meant to have Rohen in their lives. The Universe owed them this for all the shit it'd given all three of them.

"Great," Dena said. "Let's schedule that home study then."

Anne pulled out her phone and with a few taps, they had an appointment on the calendar for early next week.

William and Chennie returned with bottled waters for everybody and Chennie sat beside Carter while Dena got up to talk to Jacy. He'd always liked Dena's mother. The woman had the kindest eyes. Solid mom eyes that had the unusual capacity to both comfort and berate. Right now they were tuned to full comfort.

"I'm glad my daughter and Rohen have you, Carter," she said. "I know you make Dena happy and you've been so patient in waiting for her to sort out what happened in Rhode Island. You're a good man."

She wouldn't think so if she'd been on the car ride to the hospital.

"Thank you," he said instead of ratting himself out. "I'm a lucky man. That Dena would even consider being with me is something to be thankful for."

Chennie's lips twitched up. "She's changed with you." She waved a hand toward her daughter. "Look at her. Not that long ago, she'd never be caught dead wearing leggings and an oversized sweatshirt, and I've never known her to take an interest in the wellbeing of teenagers. Love has loosened her up some. That's your doing, honey." She patted his forearm then got up to sit beside William again.

Carter got up to stretch his legs and Leah came over to hug him.

"How are you?" she asked.

"I'll be better once a doctor comes out and tells us something," he said. "How do you go to work every day and worry about all those kids you teach? I meet one and I'm a wreck over him."

Leah hugged him again. "Oh, I want to take half of them home with me," she said into his shoulder. "But then I remember how much kids eat and I'm good with letting them go back to their own homes."

Carter kissed the top of Leah's head for making him laugh. "At least Rohen is old enough to make some of his own money."

"This is true." Leah backed out of the hug. "I hear he's working over at Mountain View Pizza."

"Yeah, Kyle was cool about giving him a job."

"And I'm sure Rohen will be back at it in no time," Leah said.

He was about to say he hoped she was right when the double doors at the opposite side of the waiting room finally opened. A tall doctor with a thick crop of red hair scanned the area while everyone froze like statues.

"Doctor Bukowski?" Carter propelled his way toward the man. No one besides the people for Rohen sat in the waiting room so he could only be the bearer of news about the kid.

"Yes," the doctor said. "I'm specifically looking for Anne Heywood."

Anne stepped forward. "These people have been here all this time for Rohen too. They can hear whatever you're about to say."

Nodding once, the doctor put his hands in the pockets of his scrubs. "Let me start by saying Rohen is one tough kid. His left arm was shattered by the impact of the truck. I imagine his car door crumpled like paper against a logging truck of that size. We

310

operated and had to give him a couple manufactured parts in that arm. The degree of mobility he'll have is hard to determine yet."

Carter's heartbeat thundered so loudly in his ears he could barely hear what the doctor was saying. Dena came to stand beside him, her small hand slipping into his, and he calmed enough to focus on the words. Words that sounded horrible.

Manufactured parts? What the hell?

"A few ribs were broken, one of which punctured his lung. We stopped the internal bleeding, but he's having trouble breathing on his own right now. He's hooked up to a ventilator at the moment. We'll monitor him, but he might need additional surgery."

Dena's hand tightened around his and Carter managed to keep himself from totally falling apart.

"Several facial contusions have been stitched and bruises are showing," the doctor continued. "He doesn't appear to have any head injuries. From the damage to his arm and ribs, I have a feeling he put his arm up to shield his head." The doctor raised his own arm in a protective stance in demonstration. "When he wakes, we can further investigate."

"You expect him to wake?" Carter asked.

"I do. Not sure of the timetable on that, but other than difficulty breathing on his own, all his other vitals are good."

"Can we see him?" Dena asked.

The doctor looked to Anne. "That's up to Ms. Heywood here. We let the group home representative handle that when the patient doesn't have family."

Anne turned to Carter. "Let me go see him first, okay? I have to file reports in cases like this, but you can visit as soon as I'm done. I'll be as quick as possible. I know you both are eager to be with him."

Carter nodded, still ruminating over the extent of the injuries the doctor had described. The kid wasn't breathing on his own. *Jesus.* A shattered arm. Broken ribs. Punctured lung. He hated every one of those phrases. How he wished this was a video game he could shut off or reprogram.

But this was real life.

Anne followed the doctor through the double doors, and Carter stared as the doors swung back into position.

"He's strong and going to pull through," Dena said softly. "We have to believe that."

Carter pulled her up against him, burying his nose in her hair, grounding himself through her warmth. "Yeah," was all he could muster.

A strong hand gripped his shoulder. He looked up to meet William's gaze. "We're all praying for him, son."

The word *son* and the kind touch made Carter's eyes prick at the corners, but he took a deep inhale, the scent of Dena's hair giving him something else to focus on.

Dena navigated him to some seats closer to the double doors. She spoke to her father and mother for a few minutes and it was decided they would leave for now with the rest of her family and Noah, Krista, and Heidi. Only Dena and Carter would be permitted to see Rohen anyway. No sense in all of them hanging around.

312

"You call us after you see him or if there is more news," Jacy said, giving her sister a hug then Carter.

Dakota wiggled his phone. "Got a call asking for help cleaning up the logs that spilled out of the truck. Newbury Street is closed because of the accident."

"I can bring my excavator," Noah said.

"I'll get a truck over there to assist," William said. "I imagine the original truck was from out of the area as we didn't have any big deliveries scheduled for our sawmill today."

Dakota nodded. "See you there."

In a matter of minutes, just Dena and Carter occupied the waiting room. Dena sat beside him, her arm sliding along his shoulders. "A day can get all turned around, can't it?"

Carter puffed out a breath. "You got that right."

"But I believe in happy endings," she said. "This doctor gives off a competent vibe. Rohen is getting the best care."

"I just want to see him." Although, would it be too much to see the kid all beaten up? He remembered being called to identify Chase's body with Leah. Images of the condition of his brother and Leah's parents and sister had plagued him long afterward.

But Rohen was alive. His brother hadn't been. That was a major checkmark in the positive column. And he had Dena by his side now.

"I'm glad we met him before this," Dena said. "The thought of him having no one but a social worker here for him makes me sick."

Carter shifted to put his arm around her now. "We'll make it so he always has us."

He'd make sure that kid—and Dena—had everything they ever wanted in the world. If he accomplished nothing else in his life, Carter would bring only happiness to these two people who had come to mean family to him. He might not have his parents or his brother, but if he stepped out of the gloom of that, he could see the Universe was trying to make it up to him by sending Dena and Rohen his way. He hadn't expected them, but now that they were in his life, he'd do whatever it took to keep them there.

Chapter Seventeen

Dena almost couldn't look at Rohen. She and Carter stood by the boy's bedside, and though she was relieved to be near him, the stitches on his cheek and at his temple, the purple bruising around his left eye and on his jaw, the bracing and bandages on his left arm, the machines beeping and hissing as they helped him breathe… God, it was too much to take in.

The strangled noise that came from Carter's throat when they'd entered had nearly ripped her apart too.

"No one should have this happen to them," Carter said. "No one."

"He's young," the doctor said. "His body was in top form before the accident which is a good thing. That makes it more likely healing will be smooth and complete."

While that sounded like good news, Dena had a hard time letting go of the words *he was in top form before the accident.* Why hadn't she picked Rohen up on her way to Carter's for the snowshoeing? She had to pass right by the group home to get to the cottage. It would have been so simple for her to stop and get him, but she figured teenagers liked to come and go as they pleased. They liked having their own wheels.

But the goddamn wheels should stop when you stepped on the brakes.

"I'll leave you guys alone for a little while. Talk to him. Let him hear your voices. I've witnessed that go a long way in improving patients' conditions." The doctor made an adjustment on one of the machines hooked to Rohen then left the room.

Carter had remained frozen to a spot beside the boy's bed, not getting any closer, not stepping back. Finally he looked at Dena. "Do you think he is in a ton of pain?"

"Not right now." Dena hooked her arm around Carter's waist and leaned into his side when he moved his arm and made room for her. "Right now, I'm imagining that he's still thinking of the fun he had snowshoeing with us." She could almost hear the boy's laughter as they'd trekked through the woods with Dakota telling them tales of some of the crazy customers he'd had over the years.

God, had that only been this morning?

"That's how I'm trying to picture him. Hiking ahead of us. On his own two feet. Not the slightest bit winded by the physical activity."

Now a machine breathed for him. Dena buried her face in Carter's shirt, needing to look away for a moment to keep her composure. Sniffing back her emotions, she said, "He'll be hiking with us again as soon as he's ready."

Carter pulled her into a full hug and the two of them held each other for a few long, quiet moments. Then Carter released her and took steps closer to the bed. Closer to Rohen. He reached out a hand and placed it on the boy's right shoulder.

"We're here, buddy," he said softly. "You focus on what you need to do to walk out of here.

We'll focus on what we need to do to give you a home."

Dena took Rohen's right hand and slid her palm beneath it. An IV was stuck in the top of that hand, but she was careful. Lowering into the chair beside the bed, she said, "Carter needs help bringing Dena the Destroyer to life. You have to wake up and see that he doesn't try to make me a set of boobs with fighting skills. I've seen some of the comic books he owns. I do not want to be one of those chicks."

Carter let out a small laugh. "I wouldn't dare." He rested his hands on her shoulders from behind the chair. "Thank God you're here with me." He pressed a kiss to the back of her neck.

She reached back and put her hand atop his on her right shoulder. "I'll always be here with you. No matter where *here* is. You're stuck with me now."

"More like you're stuck with me. You? You're a prize. Me? Not so much."

Dena swiveled around to see Carter. "You're just what I wanted."

"Even if I act like a jerk sometimes?"

"Even if you act like a jerk sometimes." She patted his hand. "You didn't turn away from me when I was the jerk who pushed you aside. I won't turn away from you now. Never again."

"Good, because we have to convince Anne that we can take this kid in and provide for him."

"Sounds as if we'll have to convince him too. Anne said it would be mostly his decision."

Rohen just had to wake up and *make* that decision.

They spent the next three hours by his bedside, but there was no change in his status. The doctor convinced them to go home, promising to call the moment something changed. When they got back to the cottage, Dena wasn't surprised to see that all her boxes had been unpacked with a note from her parents explaining they'd helped Jacy and Leah organize her stuff as best as they could.

The postscript read that if anything was missing, Jacy probably had commandeered it because she kept finding things she wanted to borrow.

"Your family should go into the moving business," Carter said as he took in all her clothes hanging in his bedroom closet.

Dena opened a drawer of the dresser to find her underwear had been folded. "They are rather amazing, aren't they?" She turned to face him. "You realize you get all of them in this deal, right?" She motioned between the two of them.

"Sweet."

"You say that now, but will you still feel that way when they are talking about you to everyone in town." She held up a hand. "And trust me, Dad knows everyone in town and he's not afraid to brag to all of them."

"Guess I'll have to give him shit to brag about then."

"You will. I don't move in with losers." She rose to her tiptoes and captured his mouth with hers, the contact doing much to leach away some of this rollercoaster of a day. "Let's have a bite to eat and snuggle."

"Sounds good."

Dena felt even more at home in the cottage with her stuff there now. By the time they got to the couch and turned on the television, they'd discussed getting a few essentials for what would become Rohen's bedroom if he chose to live with them, what time they planned to go see Rohen tomorrow, assuming they didn't get a call about him before then, and the first vacation they wanted to take him on once he was healed.

"It's got to be Disney World," Dena said firmly. "Everyone loves Disney World."

"True, however, gamers love their comics and Universal Studios has more comics-based attractions," Carter countered.

"Okay. We'll do both then." Somehow talking about these plans made Dena believe Rohen had to be all right.

They spent the next week working and visiting Rohen. Sometimes Dena went with Carter. Sometimes she went alone and took her work with her. Numbers could be crunched whether she was in her office at the sawmill or by Rohen's bedside at the hospital. Carter often brought his work too when he came without Dena. At night when they sat at their dinner table, Carter would tell her all about the progress he was making on his game.

"Sometimes when I get stuck on something," he'd said one night, "I just look at Rohen and a solution comes to me. I think he's sending me stuff telepathically."

"I wouldn't be surprised if he was," she'd said. "Think about how quickly he made himself a necessary presence in our lives. Extra-sensory mind games could be a logical explanation for how he achieved that."

Carter had gotten up from his chair across the table that night, rounded to her side, gotten to his knees, and placed a kiss on her cheek.

"What was that for?" she'd asked.

"You just said extra-sensory mind games were logical." He'd grinned. "You've been hanging around with me enough for the craziness to infect you."

She'd turned in her seat, making room for Carter between her knees. Hugging him so his head rested against her chest, she'd said, "If extra-sensory stuff is logical, then so is Rohen waking up."

Because the more days that went by, the less likely it was for him to awaken. They both knew that, but mostly they tried to think positively. Dena's mother, who was part Native American and a former nurse, had even performed a healing rite over Rohen two nights ago.

Anne from the group home had come and done the home study. She'd seen no reason that Rohen wouldn't have a good home with Dena and Carter because they both had great jobs and could provide a roof over his head, food, and healthcare. Anne had dug up a few arrests in New York on Carter, but she'd also done enough research to find articles about Chase's death. Carter had launched into an explanation, but Anne had simply put her hand on his forearm to stop him.

"You've made some mistakes born out of trauma." She'd waved a hand toward Dena and the cottage surrounding them as they sat at the dining room table. "Your life is on track now. If you are in charge of Rohen, I know you'll both be focused on what's best for him and all your decisions from this point on will be to benefit him."

They were ready make those decisions. Now. Today.

But so far, all they could do was wait.

On Sunday, Chennie and William had invited everyone over for dinner at their house. Carter and Dena had gone to visit Rohen in the morning, but the only good news was that the cuts and bruises on his face were healing nicely.

"I keep thinking he's going to open his eyes when I'm visiting him," Dena told her mother as she grabbed a big bowl of salad and took it to the dining room table. "I stare so hard at him, willing him to wake up."

Chennie rubbed her hand over Dena's back as she placed two bottles of salad dressing next to the bowl. "And that's what you have to keep doing, honey. Visiting, willing, praying. Whatever it takes, right?"

"I wish I had a magic wand or something." She gripped the back of one of the chairs. "I want the three of us to be together."

"Things between you and Carter are all right though?" Chennie asked.

"As all right as they can be," she said, "but we're on pause until Rohen wakes up." It was hard to celebrate her feelings for Carter when Rohen's condition was still a big unknown. "I want to fast forward so all this is behind us."

"Well, you know we're all sending Rohen, Carter, and you all the good vibes we can." Chennie gave Dena a hug—one of those healing mom hugs that no one else can quite master. "I know it will be a major victory when Rohen wakes up."

Victory...

Rohen was fighting a battle, wasn't he?

After dinner and some solid family time that did much to lift Dena's spirits, she convinced Carter to grab some of his drawings. They stopped at the group home and asked Anne for a few of Rohen's pictures—ones that had been spared destruction by other kids.

At the hospital, Dena hung Carter's and Rohen's artwork around Rohen's room.

"This is a great idea, Dena," Carter said as he helped.

"My mother said Rohen waking up would be a victory and that made me think of games and winning battles. I thought if he was surrounded by images he liked and ones he created, it might bring him back."

Carter folded her into an embrace. "I'm overcome by how much I love you right now." He hooked her hair behind her ear and met her gaze. "I know we've been on autopilot lately. Working, coming here, hoping. I haven't given *you* enough attention."

She put her fingers to his lips to stop him then cupped his cheek. "Rohen needs our focus right now. There will be time for us."

After a kiss that made her want to take back those words and demand Carter's *attention*, she stepped back and looked at their efforts. "It looks nice in here. You both are so talented."

"There's room for one more picture though. Right here." Carter tapped a blank section of wall directly across from Rohen's bed.

"Do we have any more pictures?" Dena asked. "I hung all the ones I had."

Carter nodded and went to the big portfolio he had used to bring in the artwork. "This one." He slid it out and showed it to Dena.

It was of her and it made her look like a goddess. Her hair was nearly touchable in the picture, perfect waves of brown cascading down a shoulder. The green used for her eyes was luminescent and flecked with brown. Her skin was pale and flawless and her lips were turned up in a slight smile.

"When did you do this?" she asked.

Carter shook his head. "I didn't." He pointed to the bed. "He did."

"Rohen made this?" She traced a finger along the edge of the picture, her eyes watering and her throat stinging.

"Yup. Before he even met you," Carter said. "I had a picture of you on one of my computers in my office. He saw it on the first day of his internship. I remember watching his hands move as if he hardly had to look at the real photo of you to get it right. As if he already knew you."

She felt the same way about the kid.

"I feel weird saying this because it's of me," she said, "but it's... lovely."

Carter pressed a kiss to her temple. "Newsflash, Dena: You *are* lovely." He grabbed the tape and hung the picture on the wall. "Now you're watching over him." He put the tape back in the portfolio. "C'mon, let's go home."

Giving her picture one more look then studying Rohen for a minute as his chest rose and fell due to the ventilator he was still hooked to, she blew a kiss to him and sent up yet another prayer that he'd open his eyes soon.

Carter took her hand in the hallway and they were almost to the elevators when Marissa yelled, "Guys, guys! He's awake!"

****

"Did she just say he's awake?" Carter asked in a low voice.

Dena turned to see behind them. "My friend Marissa is indeed waving us to come back to Rohen's room."

Carter yanked on her hand and the two of them ran down the hallway to meet the nurse who was at the door of Rohen's room.

"I paged Doctor Bukowski and he'll want to examine Rohen, but I knew you guys had just left. Glad I caught you." Marissa beamed a smile at them and opened the door. "Go on in. When the doctor comes, you'll have to get out of the way though."

Carter didn't waste a second. He pulled Dena into the room with him and nearly cried like a fucking baby when Rohen blinked sleepy blue eyes up at him.

"Hey, buddy." He rubbed the kid's shoulder. "The doctor is coming. Don't move too much."

Rohen couldn't speak due to the ventilator tube down his throat, but he raised his right hand and reached for Carter.

Immediately taking his hand, Carter was greatly encouraged by the strength of the boy's grip. "Squeeze my hand if you remember being in an accident."

One squeeze and a roll of a single tear from the corner of Rohen's right eye.

Dena grabbed a tissue and wiped at the tear. "Are you in pain?"

Another squeeze. "Shit, he is."

Marissa stepped around Carter and adjusted one of the IVs. "That will help, but the doctor should be here in a few minutes and we'll assess everything." She offered Rohen a smile then pointed to a drawing to the left of the bed. "And that picture of the fairy with those beautiful wings... I want to buy it. My daughter's birthday is next week and her life will be complete with that picture hanging in her room. I'll pay anything for it."

Only Rohen's gaze moved, first to the fairy picture Marissa had indicated then around the room. Another few tears escaped from his eyes and Dena dabbed at them.

"I don't know if you can afford a Rohen Sears original, Marissa," Dena said. "These are all one-of-a-kind originals."

"I'll refinance my home. Whatever. We *need* that picture."

Another squeeze. "I think he's willing to negotiate a fair price as soon as he's able," Carter said.

The doctor bustled in. "Welcome back, my friend," he said as he glanced at the monitors by the bed." He turned to Dena and Carter. "I need to check him out. Can I have Marissa escort you to the waiting room?"

"Of course." Carter gave Rohen's hand a squeeze. "We're so happy you're awake, man. So happy. We'll see you in a bit."

Rohen didn't let go of his hand and Carter had trouble swallowing around the lump in his throat.

"Listen, they won't leave without seeing you again, Rohen," Doctor Bukowski said. "I promise. They've been here every day since you were brought in. Trust me, they want to see you awake and well as do I."

Slowly, Rohen's grip loosened and Carter slid his hand free, though it killed him to do so. He wanted nothing more than to stay by the kid's side, to talk to him, to make sure he was going to be all right. Letting the doctor examine him, however, was the only way to do that.

Dena leaned over and brushed Rohen's blond hair off his forehead. After pressing a kiss there, she said, "We missed you." She swiped at another tear from the boy's eye then tugged Carter out of the room behind Marissa.

In the waiting room, Carter held Dena's hand as they sat huddled together. He was most likely crushing it, but she didn't complain and he didn't think he could stop himself anyway.

"He was pretty alert," he said. "That has to be good."

"I was thinking the same thing," Dena said. "He could answer your questions."

"Yeah, but I have a billion more."

"I know. Me too." Dena leaned her head on his shoulder. "Can I call my family?"

"Absolutely."

"I'll call Dad," she said as she pulled out her phone. "He'll get the word to everyone else."

Carter tapped his foot as he listened to Dena talk to her father. While he loved hearing phrases like *He's awake* and *He looks good,* he was keenly aware that Rohen's road to recovery would not be an easy one. A shattered arm would require physical therapy, and there was no guarantee he'd gain full mobility. Broken ribs were painful. He'd broken one during a bar fight after Chase died. Rohen had *multiple* broken ribs. Not to mention, the whole punctured lung business. Being awake was good news, but what other news would come their way now?

He didn't have to wait too long to answer that question. Doctor Bukowski came into the waiting room about an hour later.

Carter and Dena immediately stood at the sight of the doctor.

"That kid has a strong will to live," Doctor Bukowski said as he walked them back toward Rohen's room. "We removed the ventilator tube and he's successfully breathing on his own. All his levels look great. I think the surgery we did when he first came to us helped and that's been healing all the time he's been under, like the cuts and bruises on his face. His arm seems to be doing well also. He shouldn't be up and about just yet and he is still in quite a bit of pain, so we'll keep him here and manage and monitor all that for a few more days." The doctor smiled as they stood just outside the room. "He's eager to see you two. I talked to the social worker from the group home this week, and she mentioned you want to adopt him. He doesn't know, does he?"

Carter shook his head. "No. We didn't get a chance to discuss it with him before the accident."

"In fact, we'd only made the decision to inquire about it the day of the accident," Dena added. "I'm so thankful we'll get the opportunity to actually do it now."

"I think this is just the news he needs to catapult his recovery into the miraculous level. You can go see him." The doctor shook both of their hands and started to leave, but then turned around and pointed into the room. "That drawing of the battle-ready unicorn right above the bed. Is that for sale?"

Carter laughed. "I'm sure I could part with it. It's one of mine."

"Who knew a hospital room would be such a great gallery for the two of you crazy artists?" Dena asked.

"With talent like that, you could hang that stuff anywhere and attract attention," Doctor Bukowski said. "My wife has an obsession with unicorns. She insists on unicorns in every room of the house. That battle one is one I could stomach hanging in my man cave."

Carter put a hand to his heart. "Ah, my goal has been achieved. To bring unicorns to the male masses."

The doctor laughed. "Have one of the nurses page me after you've seen Rohen and we'll discuss the sale."

Carter saluted the doctor then turned to Dena. "C'mon. Let's go see Rohen."

The boy looked much improved simply because the ventilator had been removed. When he noticed the two of them in the doorway, a smile stretched across his face though his eyes looked tired.

"Hi." His voice was scratchy, no doubt from the tube that had been in his throat for days.

"Hey," Carter said as he stepped into the room. A room that did, in fact, look like an art gallery now. "You have no idea how good it is to see you awake."

"Yeah," Dena said as she sat on the end of the bed, giving Carter the chair. "How do you feel?"

"As if a logging truck plowed into me." Rohen squeezed his eyes shut for a moment. "My fucking brakes were gone." He shook his head against the pillow beneath him. "I was cruising down Newbury Street and I saw the red light. I stepped on the brakes and nothing happened. I had a second to think, *Oh, shit*, and then that logging truck was suddenly in my face. Literally." The kid's body did a quick shake and his facial features contorted in pain. "I can't grasp the fact that I'm actually alive."

"My brother was part of the cleanup on Newbury Street," Dena said. "He described the scene as gruesome. Your car was obliterated. The logging truck wasn't badly damaged, but those things are built like tanks."

"What about the driver of the truck?" Rohen asked, his concern giving Carter another reason to love the kid.

"Totally fine," Carter said. "Except that he's traumatized, knowing he flattened you. He's called the hospital several times to ask about your status. I'm sure someone will notify him that you're going to be okay."

"If not, he'll hear it when we shout it from the rooftops of Maplehaven," Dena said, grabbing onto Rohen's ankle then rubbing his leg.

"Don't go climbing any rooftops on my account," Rohen said. "I don't want to have to visit either of you in the hospital."

"Good point," Carter said. "Let's all try our best to stay out of the hospital."

"Deal," Rohen said. "How much time have you guys wasted coming here to watch me sleep?"

"No wasted time," Dena was quick to say. "We wanted to be here for you."

"In fact," Carter shot a glance to Dena who simply nodded, "we want to discuss something with you. Something important."

"Yeah, go ahead. Get another intern," Rohen said. "I understand. Someone else should get my spot. I'm going to be so behind anyway and you have so much to teach a worthy apprentice."

Carter held up a hand to stop the boy. "No, no. Not about your internship, which is still yours, by the way." He arced his arm around the room to indicate the artwork. "If you think I'm letting anyone take your spot when together we have this much talent, we need to get the doctor back in here to re-examine your head."

Rohen's blond brows furrowed over blue eyes. "Then what do you want to discuss with me?"

330

"Well, we've been talking to Anne Heywood, the social worker at the group home," Carter said.

"Yeah, Anne. She's nice." Rohen shifted in the bed and winced at the pain the movement must have caused. "She actually listened when I told her about my drawings getting destroyed. There was nothing she could do because it had already happened, but it was cool of her to actually hear me."

"She heard us too," Dena said.

"Heard us when we said we wanted to adopt you," Carter said slowly. "You know, only if you were interested in that of course."

Rohen's wide-eyed gaze traveled from Carter's face to Dena's then back to Carter, his mouth slightly agape. "Adopt me? You want to adopt me? Seriously?"

"If you're not cool with that," Carter said, "we get it. No problem." Though it felt like a gigantic problem to Carter. He'd set his heart on taking the kid in. There'd be a hole in his life if Rohen didn't accept. "We understand if you'd rather wait out the year until you're eighteen and then be off on your own."

"It's just that we feel called to take care of you," Dena said. "You fit with us. I don't know how else to describe it."

Carter held his breath as Rohen blinked at each of them. When the boy's lips slowly turned up into a broad smile, an official surge of delight washed over Carter.

"I feel as if I fit with you guys too," Rohen said. "When I'm with you both, I miss my parents less. I miss California less. Things don't suck as much when you two are around."

"Does that mean you want us to adopt you?" Dena asked.

Rohen reached out his right hand to Carter who took it without hesitation. "Adopt away."

Dena clapped and threw her arms around Carter who never let go of Rohen's hand.

"You know if your ribs weren't broken, she'd be crushing you right now," Carter said in a voice strained with absolute elation.

"She owes me a hug then, when I'm intact again." Rohen accepted the kiss Dena gave him on the cheek though. "But I want my own room," he added.

"You got it, kid." Carter felt as if his parents and Chase were present in that room right then, giving him their blessing, approving of this family he was starting. "We'll even spring for a car with functional brakes for you."

"Amen to that." Rohen high-fived Carter then his face grew serious. One of the stitched up slices on his cheek gave him a badass look, but Carter could see the kid still inside who wanted a place to belong.

He was more than happy to provide that place.

"You go to one internship fair and your entire life can change," Rohen said. "When I woke up today, I thought that if I hadn't awakened—if I'd died—no one would have cared because my family was gone already." He rubbed his eyes and sniffed. "But I guess that was crazy thinking because I scored another family."

"And we would have mourned the loss of you, Rohen," Carter said. "More than you can imagine."

"Life is full of bonus points, isn't it?" Rohen grinned.

Carter smiled back. "All you have to do is be willing to play the game."

"You guys are in the art selling game too. Marissa really wants to purchase your fairy picture, Rohen." Dena pointed to the drawing.

"I didn't dream that?"

"Nope, and the doctor wants Carter's military unicorn," she added.

"Shit, I'm glad I woke up." Rohen turned his head to see all the pictures. "You guys hung these?"

They both nodded.

"Thanks."

Dena went to stand by the drawing of her. "No, honey. Thank you. I mean, look at how gorgeous you made me. Dena the Destroyer better look this good."

"We'll make sure she does," Rohen said.

Carter loved how the kid was already referring to them as a *we*.

"You know…" Dena tapped a finger to her chin. "If you guys are going to sell your creations, you're going to need someone to manage the financial end of it."

"You have someone in mind?" Carter winked at her.

"I do."

"Is she good with numbers?" He walked over to her and played with the ends of her hair.

"She's an ace with numbers and loves to support the arts." She lifted a hand and hooked his hair behind his ear.

"I'll close my eyes if you guys want to make out," Rohen called from the bed.

"Advantages to adopting an older kid," Carter said. "He understands the importance of making out."

"I'm sure we can refrain until we leave," Dena said as she wiggled out of Carter's reach.

Carter snapped his fingers in defeat.

"Sorry, man," Rohen said. "I tried."

"No worries. I'll catch her later."

They visited with Rohen until Marissa came in and said he should get some rest. With promises to come see him first thing in the morning, Carter led Dena out of the room. He surprised her by picking her up and twirling her right there in the hallway until she squealed.

"Put me down, you nut!" She squirmed in his hold, but her laughter filled the hallway.

He stopped and planted a kiss on her lips. One that turned heated in no time. He couldn't wait to touch her again now that he wasn't so worried about Rohen. It had been too long and touching her was what fueled him.

"Let's take this home," Dena whispered against his mouth.

Maplehaven really did feel like home now.

Epilogue

One month later...

Dena rearranged the thumbnail pictures of Rohen's and Carter's artwork on the website, *Level Up Designs*, she and Carter had set up to sell their work. They had made many sales both locally and nationally so far, and as word got out, the business would grow. Carter spent his days developing games while Rohen was at school, but in the evenings, the two of them could be found somewhere in the cottage, furiously creating. Dena loved to watch them work. It was like witnessing magic appear on a blank page. The way they each used color, light, and shadow to make their pictures seem almost three-dimensional was genius. She was working on branching out to other products like T-shirts, hats, and laptop and cell phone skins featuring their work. The possibilities were endless.

Internships were officially over, but Carter was still teaching Rohen stuff about video game design and the kid was a sponge, soaking up every word, tip, and technique. Dena had seen some of the simple games Rohen had coded, and while she still sucked at playing them, she could appreciate the talent of both Rohen and Carter.

Mostly, she just loved seeing them be together.

They'd finalized the adoption while Rohen was still in the hospital, so when he was released Dena and Carter already had a bedroom set up for him. By the end of that first day at the cottage, it had seemed as if Rohen had always been a part of their lives. The three of them found an easy rhythm to living together and not a day went by where they didn't laugh together. Dena finally understood the joy her parents had felt in having children and she'd begun thinking more and more about actually giving birth to one.

Someday.

Maybe not that far into the future.

She hadn't discussed that with Carter yet, but every now and then, when she was with him, her mind conjured up this image of a cute little boy with unruly black hair, big brown eyes, and glasses. She fell more in love with that vision the more times she had it.

Her intern at that sawmill, Nikolas, had performed extremely well as had his girlfriend, Savannah, who had worked under Noah. Both Dena and Noah had given them high ratings and glowing recommendations, and Dena looked forward to the next opportunity to mentor one of Maplehaven's high school students. Of course, Rohen would always be her favorite intern even though he hadn't been her intern at all.

Maybe that's not true. Perhaps he'd been interning with her *and* Carter for the job of son.

"Can you scan this one for the website?" Rohen asked her as he slid an amazing drawing of a salivating wolf in a misty forest onto the dining room table. The black wolf's eyes glowed bright green and appeared to be looking right into Dena's soul.

"How do you get the eyes like that?" She picked up the picture and angled her head at it. No matter how she moved, that wolf had her in its sights, as if she were its prey.

Rohen shook his head. "Top secret artist trick."

She swatted at him, but he shuffled out of reach. "Punk."

Laughing, he wandered into the kitchen and opened the refrigerator. He was always opening the refrigerator. For a tall skinny kid, Rohen ate more than Carter and Dena combined. She had no idea where he put it all.

His arm was still in a cast with a sling bound to his torso to keep it immobile, but fortunately that was not his drawing arm. Healing was going to be lengthy because of the degree of damage to that arm, but Doctor Bukowski was optimistic about a full recovery. If Dena knew anything about Rohen, it was that the kid wouldn't accept anything less than a full recovery.

"He's got a warrior's spirit," Carter often said about Rohen and Dena agreed. Rohen never complained about the pain, the inconvenience of being reduced to one arm, the fussing Dena did over him.

He was just happy. Happy to be out of the group home. Happy to be with Dena and Carter as he told them almost on a daily basis. Seeing him happy made Dena happy too.

"Did I hear the refrigerator open?" Carter appeared in the kitchen. "Again?"

"Breakfast was hours ago," Rohen said as he pulled out some fruit salad.

Carter pretended to look at his wristwatch—one he wasn't actually wearing—and raised his eyebrows. "Like two hours ago, kid."

Rohen set the bowl on the island counter and went to the cupboard for a smaller bowl. "I need fuel to heal this." He gestured to his arm.

"He's got a point," Dena called from the dining room table.

"Okay, but maybe he could leave some food for the rest of us." Carter may have been ribbing the boy, but he immediately grabbed a big spoon from the drawer and scooped fruit into the bowl for Rohen.

"Are you going to tell me that you didn't eat a ton when you were my age?" Rohen sat on a stool at the kitchen island to dig in to the fruit.

"He can't remember that far back," Dena teased.

"Hey," Carter said. "Whose side are you on, woman?"

"Right now, Rohen's because look at his latest drawing." She held it up and Carter applauded then squeezed Rohen's shoulder. "But I could be on your side if you make me some tea," she added.

"One tea, coming up, beautiful." Carter bustled into action.

Dena watched her two males in the kitchen and a deep contentment enveloped her. What had happened to her in Rhode Island was a distant memory. The slice in her stomach had healed and only a faint scar remained. The anxiety that someone else might hurt her was gone. She was safe. With Carter and Rohen. With her family. With the small town of Maplehaven. The kind people who only gave kind touches made her brave and filled her with love.

As she basked in this happiness, something vibrated on the table. Dena moved aside several drawings she'd been scanning to the website. "Rohen, your phone is requesting your attention."

Rohen slid off the stool and picked up the phone as Carter carried over a mug of tea. When the boy's cheeks pinked a little after he swiped and read the screen, Dena grinned.

"Uh-oh, is it a girl?" she teased.

Pink cheeks got pinker.

"I think I'll finish this fruit in my room." Rohen jammed the phone into the back pocket of his jeans then grabbed the bowl of fruit, but Carter stepped in front of him.

"Hold on there, Slick," he said. "You didn't answer Dena's question. I find that interesting."

"Very interesting," Dena echoed.

"Okay, yeah, it's a girl."

"A nice girl?" Dena asked.

"A pretty girl?" Carter asked at the same time.

"Nice and pretty," Rohen said, trying to skirt around Carter, but not having any success. He finally huffed out a breath, knowing he wasn't getting out of there until he gave them more details. "Her name is Kara and she's in all my classes and she's been carrying my books because I'm an invalid."

"Ah, from page 81 of the book ***Ways to Get a Chick to Notice You***: Appear vulnerable with an injury." Carter gave Rohen's shoulder a little shake. "Good plan to take advantage of a disadvantage."

"I really should have a little fun with this." Rohen gestured to his bound arm with his chin.

"But you'll be a gentleman to this nice and pretty Kara, right?" Dena got up and stood beside Carter.

"Always." Rohen looked beyond them to the hallway. "Can I go to my room now?"

"Of course." Carter stepped aside. "Don't keep Kara waiting."

Dena giggled as Rohen rolled his eyes at them then disappeared into his room. "Having a teenager to tease is great fun."

"Agreed." Carter put his hands on her hips and pulled her up against him. "You know what else is fun?"

"I have a few ideas." She reached up on her toes and captured Carter's mouth in a kiss that could have set the hallway on fire.

"I like your ideas, beautiful." Carter's voice was low as he pressed his arousal against her. "In fact, I *love* your ideas."

Rohen appeared back in the hallway and Carter cleared his throat as he walked into the kitchen. Dena had to bite back her laugh at the stiff way Carter moved. *Poor guy.* All revved up and nowhere to go. She'd make it up to him later.

"Umm, is it all right if Kara comes over to watch TV?" Rohen asked.

"Sure," Dena said, encouraged that Rohen didn't think it would be uncool to have Kara meet them.

"Fine by me," Carter called from the kitchen.

"Thanks."

"We'll try not to embarrass you," Dena whispered as Rohen made his way to the living room.

"Try hard." Rohen sat on the couch as he texted. "Really hard."

"While we wait for Miss Kara to arrive," Carter said, apparently ready to stop hiding behind the kitchen island, "why don't we give this new game I've been working on a try?"

"While I love the artwork and everything," Dena said, "you know how terrible I am at these games."

"You'll like this one," Carter said, sitting on the couch. A look passed between him and Rohen that Dena couldn't decipher. "At least I'm pretty sure."

"Fine." Dena sat between them. "But don't make fun of me when I fail."

Carter pressed a kiss to her temple. "Never, my love."

Dena picked up a controller and held it out to Rohen. "Do you want to try it out first?"

"No, you go." He waved the controller away as Theo hopped up into his lap.

They'd released the bunny, but it didn't want to leave. Each time Carter set it out on the back patio, the white rabbit didn't make a run for the woods. When Carter opened the sliding door to the cottage, however, Theo hopped right back inside.

"Guess he wants to be adopted too," Rohen had said. And so Theo had become a permanent part of the family. It was always good luck to have a sacred bunny around, wasn't it?

Dena waited for Carter to load the game. When a graphic of Dena the Destroyer came up on the TV screen, she laughed. "Damn, I look good."

"As promised," Carter said.

"Do I get to play her?" Dena wiggled the controller.

"Yes, you be her," Carter said. "And I'll be…" A second later, a character named Carter the Conqueror stood beside Dena the Destroyer.

"Oh," Dena got the edge of the couch cushion, "he's hot."

"And apparently has better eyesight than the real Carter," Rohen said.

"What kind of conqueror wears glasses?" Carter picked up the other controller. "That's the beauty of video games. You can be a better version of yourself."

Dena leaned over to bump her shoulder against Carter's. She dropped a light kiss on his cheek. "I happen to love this version right here."

"Thanks, beautiful." Carter gave her a quick one-armed hug.

"Do you want to make out?" Rohen asked. "I can close my eyes."

Carter looked around Dena to see Rohen. "You know one of these times I'm going to answer yes to that, so you'd better be prepared."

Rohen gave him a thumbs up then went back to petting Theo's soft, white fur.

"How do we play this game?" Dena asked.

"First of all, we get our shoulders out of our ears." Carter pressed his hand on her left shoulder.

"I'm sorry," she said. "I get nervous playing video games."

"No reason to get nervous. This is about fun." Carter hit start.

"Wait!" Dena shouted. "You didn't explain how to play yet."

"It's pretty intuitive," Carter said. "You'll get the hang of it."

A path through a wooded scene opened up in front of the two characters on the screen and Dena hit *up* on the controller to make Dena the Destroyer walk beside Carter the Conqueror.

"Are things going to jump out of the woods at us?" Dena chewed on her bottom lip as her eyes scanned the trees on either side of the path.

"Relax, Dena," Carter said. "Keep walking for right now."

"I want to be ready to kick some ass." She bounced a little on the couch cushion. "Are we playing against each other or together?"

"Together," Carter said. "Always together."

"Okay, what's our objective?"

"So many questions," Rohen said.

Dena elbowed him lightly. "I have no idea what I'm doing."

The path led to a clearing in the woods. Orange-gold light filtered into the space as it appeared to be almost sunset. A gazebo made of tree limbs stood in the center of the clearing. Gorgeous white flowers on a vine garland wound around the entire structure.

"Oh, that's so pretty," Dena said.

Carter the Conqueror took Dena the Destroyer's hand.

"Hey, how did you do that?" Dena looked down at the controller. "What did you press?"

"Hang on a minute," Carter said, putting his hand over hers so she couldn't press anything. "Just watch."

Dena focused her gaze on the TV screen. Both characters walked to the gazebo without either she or Carter doing anything on their controllers. Once in the gazebo, the orange-gold glow gave way to pink, then purple, and finally a shadowy black. Fireflies flickered greenish-yellow around the dark silhouettes of trees then tiny white bulbs illuminated the gazebo.

Where Carter the Conqueror was now on one knee before Dena the Destroyer.

Suddenly Dena realized they weren't playing a game at all.

Carter hit his controller once and text appeared next to his character, which he read aloud to her. "I love you so much, Dena the Destroyer. You've destroyed the loneliness I felt and filled my world with more happiness than I thought possible. I want you by my side for all our quests. Will you marry me?"

More text popped up at the bottom of the screen that said, *Press A for Yes, B for Yes.*

"I didn't make a No option," Carter whispered in her ear.

"Oh, Carter, I don't need a No option." She hit A then launched herself at him.

He fell against the back of the couch and wrapped his arms around her.

"You should definitely make out now," Rohen said, laughing. "Theo and I will both close our eyes."

Carter didn't waste a moment. He pressed his mouth to hers and they shared their first kiss as an engaged couple.

"I love you, Carter," Dena said when they had to come up for air. "Consider me conquered."

"Conquering will come later," Carter whispered. He hit a button on his controller and used his finger to turn Dena's head toward the TV screen.

Dena the Destroyer scooped up Carter the Conqueror in her arms, making them all laugh as they watched from the couch. She carried Carter the Conqueror down the path as the moon shined above them and stars twinkled in the sky.

The text beneath the characters read, *A new quest awaits.*

"I think I won my first video game," Dena said.

And it was one she was so glad she'd played.

If you enjoyed *One Kind Touch*,
please consider leaving a review
and recommend my books to your friends.
Thank you!

If you have a book group, I'd love to interact with you!
Email me at cdepetrillo@yahoo.com
or message me through Facebook for options.

Author Contact:

Website and Newsletter Sign-up:
www.christinedepetrillo.weebly.com

Facebook:
www.facebook.com/christinedepetrilloauthor

Find our cozy Reader Group, SMALL TOWN HEARTS, on
Facebook and join!

Books in the One Kind Deed Series
Contemporary Romance

One Kind Heart (Book One)
One Kind Kiss (Book Two)
One Kind Touch (Book Three)

*Check www.christinedepetrillo.weebly.com for
release dateson books in this series.*

Read on for a sneak peek at *One Kind Ride!*

Sneak Peak at *One Kind Ride*

Chapter One

"But there has to be another flight besides the one I booked and missed." Jacy Brenton took a deep breath and gripped the edge of the counter separating her from the airport personnel. If she didn't get back to Maplehaven, Vermont for her parents' fortieth wedding anniversary party, she was going to get kicked out of the Brenton family.

Sure, her trip to New Orleans to hang with her old college friend, Claire, had been fantastic—that was why she'd extended her stay for two more days—but now she regretted leaving Maplehaven when she had. She should have waited until *after* the party.

"There is another flight. This one." The airport worker pointed to the gate across from the counter. "But this flight is sold out. Everything to Vermont for today is sold out as I've told you."

"But it wasn't my fault my first flight out of New Orleans to Baltimore was delayed due to thunderstorms." Jacy slumped her body against the counter, knowing full well she was whining. As the youngest in her family—even if it was only by being born a minute after her twin sister, Dena—she excelled at wearing the brat persona when necessary.

347

Not being able to get home seemed like a brat-worthy application.

"I understand that, Miss Brenton," the airport worker said, "but I literally don't have a free seat on anything heading north right now." She typed for a second on her keyboard, squinted at her monitor, then shook her head. "The earliest flight I have headed to Burlington is tomorrow at 10:15 a.m. Can I book that for you?"

Jacy straightened to her full height though what she really wanted to do was throw herself to the floor and pitch a fit. "Yeah, go ahead." She'd miss the party tonight, but she still needed to get home so Dena could choke her.

"We're sorry for the inconvenience," the worker said. "Can I upgrade you to first class on that 10:15 flight for free?"

"Sure. Thanks." She could appreciate the airline's attempt to keep her happy.

Even if she wasn't happy. At all.

Dena and her brother, Dakota, were going to kill her when they found out she wasn't going to make it home in time for the party. If any of the three of them were going to screw up though, it was her. Dena was far too organized to make a blunder like this one, and Dakota was Maplehaven's Golden Boy who did no wrong. Only Jacy would have tossed caution aside and stayed in New Orleans to party as if she were back in college.

But damn, it's been so much fun.

Making the phone call to Dena, however, would not be fun.

She accepted the ticket from the airport worker for tomorrow and found a seat among the passengers waiting to board the flight. *Her* flight. The only one that would rescue her from this mess. Man, her parents would be so disappointed. Family was the number one thing with them. How would she make this up to them?

Sighing, she pulled out her cell phone and hit Dena's contact. While it rang, she glanced around at the waiting passengers. A wide variety of people took up the space and dozens of different conversations combined into a dull hum. A hum she wouldn't be traveling with because these people were all leaving in about fifteen minutes while she had to wait until tomorrow morning. She'd have to get a room at the hotel across the street from the airport. She'd have to find somewhere to eat. She'd have to spend a night where guilt was her only company.

"Shouldn't you be in the air?" Dena asked when she answered.

"Umm... yeah. About that." Jacy pinched the bridge of her nose. "My flight out of New Orleans was delayed due to thunderstorms which made me miss my flight out of Baltimore to Burlington. I can't get a flight to Vermont until tomorrow morning."

"Tomorrow morning!" Dena's voice screeched in Jacy's ear. "We've had this party planned since December! It's May now. You knew it was coming!"

Well, this is going as expected.

"I know, I know," Jacy said.

"Why didn't you come home two days ago *as planned*?" Dena's voice had all the tone of the older, more mature sister. The tone that—on occasion—got right under Jacy's skin. Not often. Generally speaking she got along famously with her twin and Dakota, but every once in a while, Jacy reached her limit.

Right now was one of those times. Add in that nothing exciting ever happened in Maplehaven, not to Jacy anyway, and a fortieth wedding anniversary party was a huge deal. God, she hated feeling so powerless. Why hadn't teleportation been invented yet?

"Look, Dena, I was having some fun away from home. Some fun I deserved. I work just as hard as you do and earned that vacation time."

"Easy, Jacy. No one is saying you didn't deserve a vacation. You absolutely did, but it could have been timed better is all. Mom and Dad will miss you at their big party. We'll all miss you."

Shit. Why did Dena have to say stuff that made it impossible to stay mad at her?

"I know. I feel like scum about all this." Jacy ran her hand through her long, brown hair, wanting to yank it out in frustration. "You can video conference me in and I'll say hello to everyone."

"Or you could take my seat," a deep, gravelly voice from her right said.

Jacy turned to face the man seated beside her. Had he been there this entire time? Had he been listening to her conversation?

Had he offered her his seat?

"Excuse me?" She gave him a quick once-over, her gaze immediately zooming in on muscled arms full of tattoos. That was hot. His reddish-blond hair was buzz cut military short to his skull and a trimmed beard surrounded his mouth and jaw. A pair of dark sunglasses hung on the collar of his army-green T-shirt, which left his eyes uncovered for Jacy to see.

Bright and blue and stony.

Nonetheless, he'd offered her his seat, right?

"If you need to get on this flight," he began, "you can have my ticket. I'm not in any rush, but it appears you are." He gestured to her phone with his big hand. A really big hand. But something wasn't right with the skin on his palm. It was puckered and scarred.

And the moment he noticed that she noticed, he dropped his hand to rest on his denim-covered thigh. Palm down.

"I can't take your ticket," she said, but she could hear the hope in her voice.

A low rumble came from his throat as if he were losing his patience. Already? They'd only conversed for mere moments. "Look, lady. I'm offering you my seat on that plane." He pointed to the airplane clearly visible attached to the gate now. "If you want it, take it. If you don't, enjoy your night in Baltimore."

He reached between his knees and grabbed a camouflage-print duffel bag. Standing, he hoisted the bag to his shoulder and glanced down to her.

"I can walk to the gate or to the ticket counter," he said. "Choice is yours."

Dena's voice finally registered in her ear. "JACY! What is happening?"

Right. She was still on the phone. With a look up to this... this savior, Jacy said, "I'm coming home

351

today. Don't tell Mom and Dad I almost didn't make it. Or Dakota." She tapped the screen before Dena could say more and stood. "I'll take your ticket, Mister…"

But he was already walking toward the ticket counter so Jacy grabbed her suitcase and chased after him. His big, black combat boots brought his long legs to the counter in record time. When Jacy came to stand beside him, she found he was taller than her five-foot-eight-inch height. He was probably nearer to six-foot-three, using Dakota and his best friend, Noah, as reference heights. He appeared to be well in control of all that toned body and he smelled good too. Like soap and… hero.

Within a matter of minutes, he wiggled a ticket at her. "Well, go on. Take it."

Shit. How long had he been waving it at her as she checked him out?

"Thanks." She let one of the straps of her purse fall off her shoulder and pulled out her wallet. "Let me pay you for this."

He shook his head. "No need. I swapped it for your ticket out tomorrow. It all evens out."

"It absolutely does not even out," Jacy said quickly. "You're giving up your seat for today and you'll be stuck here for an extra night. You are saving my ass, dude. Big time." She pulled out some money. "At least let me pay for your hotel stay."

She held the money out to him, but he pushed her hand away. His rough palm surprised her. It appeared her smooth knuckles had caught him off guard too because they both jolted and took a step back from each other.

"Keep your money." He stepped around her and walked away without another word.

Jacy turned and followed him with her gaze until he was no longer visible. She glanced back at the airport worker at the counter. "That was weird, right?"

"You didn't know him?" the worker asked.

Jacy shook her head.

"Then it was a little weird, but hey, you got your ride home, right? Call it a kind deed and enjoy your flight." The worker offered her a bright smile.

Jacy rapped her knuckles on the counter. "Right. Will do. Thanks." She wheeled her suitcase toward the gate and checked the ticket. First boarding group.

Sweet. She couldn't believe her good fortune, but even more, she couldn't believe a random stranger had given up his ticket. Who did that? Luckily for her, that guy did. And she'd never know his name.

Chuckling to herself, she handed the ticket to the worker at the gate then nearly skipped down the gangway. She found her seat in the last row by the window. After stowing her luggage in the overhead bin, she settled in her seat. If Dena kept her mouth shut about all this, Jacy's parents would never know how close she'd come to missing their shindig. Fortunately, the twin bond was strong and Jacy was certain Dena wouldn't rat her out.

By tonight she'd be schmoozing with Maplehaven's finest, having slipped right back into her role as Jacy Brenton, Brenton Sawmill's marketing/human relations executive and member of

Maplehaven's founding family. She'd be hearing all the same stories from all the same people while eating all the same foods.

Not at all like her time in New Orleans with Claire. The past week had been amazingly stimulating. Full of interesting people, flavorful foods, energizing music, and limitless chances to party, Jacy had nearly lost herself. In the best possible way. She'd felt renewed, refreshed, reinvented. Claire had taken her to all the hot spots and the culture, the art, the energy had filled Jacy with such creativity. She was ready to use some of what she'd gained in the sawmill's marketing to help it branch out even farther.

Assuming Maplehaven didn't suck her soul dry again.

She loved Vermont. She really did. No disputing that the state was gorgeous and the people wonderful. She adored her house two streets over from Dakota and his wife, Leah. She enjoyed the convenience of everything being so close by in the small town. She was challenged in her job at the family's sawmill, but it was all the hours she *wasn't* at work that bored her. She had her family and her friends, but everything was so… predictable.

New Orleans had been anything but predictable. Everything was different from one moment to the next. She never knew what would happen around the next corner. She'd danced until her legs ached and drank far too much, but it had been a wild ride. One she'd needed.

One she'd promised Claire they'd enjoy again sometime soon.

Looking out the window and watching the bin of checked luggage roll toward the plane, Jacy's thoughts turned back to the mysterious stranger who had given up his seat. What was his story? Was no one waiting for his return to Vermont? Or perhaps he wasn't returning, but visiting instead from somewhere else. She tried picturing where a guy who looked like he did called home, but only an Army barracks came to mind. He definitely gave off a military vibe and not just because he'd swooped in and saved her day. Standing next to him at that ticket counter had felt... protected. As if he'd actually go to battle for someone who was important to him.

Which made her wonder if he had someone who was important to him. Someone female.

And what was with that palm of his? It looked as if he'd flattened it out on a frying pan on high heat. Whatever had happened to him had to have hurt like hell. Jacy remembered burning her wrist when she'd fumbled with her flat iron one morning while she rushed to get ready for work. She'd attempted to catch it by shooting her arm out to pin the runaway iron to the wall. Unfortunately the heated plates seared her flesh pretty damn quick. She rubbed at the slight scar that still remained. Judging by the scarring on that man's palm, whatever had burned him had either been molten or against his skin for more than mere seconds.

She'd never know his story though. He'd made himself scarce after pushing her money away. He didn't have to leave so rudely. She had just been trying to thank him.

Huffing, Jacy looked toward the front of the plane. It certainly was full. Except for the seat beside her. She hoped her seatmate would be interesting. After her New Orleans experience, she was in the mood to meet more people, to learn about them, to exchange new stories. A whole world existed outside Maplehaven with all kinds of different and exciting people in it. She wanted to collect as many as she could.

Wiggling to a comfortable position in her seat, Jacy went back to watching out the window. The checked luggage bin was almost empty. The flight would be taking off soon and she'd be toasting and hugging her parents in congratulations before she knew it.

"Wonderful."

Jacy's head snapped to the aisle at the low, raspy voice. Mr. Take-My-Ticket stood there, his body looking too big to be contained by the confines of the plane. A broody gaze studied her then roamed to the empty seat beside her.

"What are you doing here?" The question came out harsher than she'd meant.

He rubbed his forehead. "Sitting next to *you* apparently."

She didn't like the way he said *you*, as if she smelled bad or something. She didn't. She sniffed quickly anyway. Just to be sure.

"I mean, how did you get a seat? They told me—repeatedly—this flight was sold out."

"They had a last minute cancellation."

"And you took it?"

He held his arms out to his sides, those tattoos wonderfully on display. "I'm here, aren't I?"

She'd been hoping for someone interesting to entertain her on the flight home. This dude definitely qualified. "Well, sit then."

He hesitated for a moment then maneuvered his body into the seat. In the tight quarters of the row, his shoulder brushed against hers. She didn't move away, but he leaned on the opposite arm rest, clearly looking for space between them.

"I bet we'll be great friends by the end of this flight," she said cheerfully.

That cold blue gaze slowly rose to meet her hazel one. "I've had two people die in the seats next to me on flights."

Jacy froze for a moment. *Die?* "I gotta get off this plane."

**Check www.christinedepetrillo.weebly.com
for release dates
on books in this series.**

Books in the Warrior Wolves Series

Paranormal Romance
Wolf Kiss (Book One)
Wolf Fire (Book Two)
Wolf Vow (Book Three)
Wolf Angel (Book Four)
Wolf Sun (Book Five)

Check www.christinedepetrillo.weebly.com for release dates and other books.

Books in the Shielded Series

Sci-Fi Romance
SAFE (Book One)
PROTECTED (Book Two)
SECURE (Book Three)

Books in the Maple Leaf Series

Contemporary Romance
More Than Pancakes (Book One)
More Than Cookies (Book Two)
More Than Rum (Book Three)
More Than Pizza (Book Four)
More Than Candy Corn (A Halloween Novella)
More Than Cocoa (Book Five)
More Than Biscotti (A FREE Christmas Novella
available on my website only)
More Than Peaches (Book Six)

Check www.christinedepetrillo.weebly.com
for more information.

Other Available Titles
by Christine DePetrillo

Alaska Heart

Firefly Mountain

Kisses to Remember

Abra Cadaver

Lazuli Moon

Young Adult Romance
writing as Christy Major

Run With Me

Sail With Me

Co-writing as Goodwin Reed

A Less Perfect Union

About the Author

Christine DePetrillo can often be found hugging trees, conversing with dragonflies, and walking barefoot through sun-warmed soil. She finds joy in listening to the wind, bathing in moonlight, and breathing in the fragrances of things that bloom. If she had her way, the sky would be the only roof over her head.

Her love of nature seeps into every story she tells. As does her obsession with bearded mountain men who build, often smell like sawdust, and know how to cherish the women they love. Today she writes tales meant to make you laugh, maybe make you sweat, and definitely make you believe in the power of love.

She lives in Rhode Island and occasionally Vermont with her pack—a husband, a cat, and a big, black German Shepherd who defends her fiercely from all evils.

Find Christine's other titles at
www.christinedepetrillo.weebly.com.
Connect on Facebook at
www.facebook.com/christinedepetrilloauthor,
on Twitter at @cdepetrillo,
in **Small Town Hearts Facebook Group**,
and on Instagram @christinedepetrillo.

Made in the USA
Middletown, DE
24 December 2019